To Judy & Earl,
   Best of Friends

Ingrid

THE FABUWEATHER FORECAST

INGRID BLANCO

*The characters and events portrayed in this book are fictitious.
Any resemblance to persons, living or dead, is coincidental and
not intended by the author.*

For My Family
Through all Kinds of Weather

THE FABUWEATHER FORECAST

If you stand at the end of the line long enough,
eventually someone says, "about face."

Author Unknown

CHAPTER ONE

The words *FabuWeather Forecast* were written above a television image that was anything but fabulous. Rippling arrows superimposed on storm clouds indicated approaching cold fronts and rain, and a shot of a car abandoned to the weather, water as high as the driver's window, was followed by footage of furniture floating around someone's living room.

"Winds of up to 81 miles an hour are knocking down everything in their path," Claire said, looking directly into the camera, "and outlying areas of the Florida coast are showing signs of flooding. At this point, it's a little too soon to say just how much of that hurricane is actually going to hit us," she continued in a voice that gave no indication of anti-climax, "and if we're lucky, westerly winds will push the storm back out to sea, but we're keeping a close eye on things and a storm watch is in effect."

It didn't happen often, but occasionally Claire gave a totally straight report, so when one minute and fifty-two seconds had passed, leaving only enough time for her forecast, it became clear that this was going to be one of those days. Whatever else, Claire always ended with the five-day forecast. The traditional grid with highs at the top and lows at the bottom was her way of letting the public know that she was dependable, and that no matter how unorthodox the rest of her report might be, she and WJTF were solid and mainstream and could be counted on.

The five-day forecast was so familiar, in fact, that no one at the desk really paid much attention to it. Even though their profiles were aligned like ancient Egyptian hieroglyphics as they looked at the weather map in apparent concentration, it still took a minute before anyone noticed that on this particular day in August, 2005, the image that usually completed the weather had been replaced by a…pill dispenser box. It was the same shape as the weather grid and, like the grid, had the days of the week on it, but it was nonetheless a pill dispenser. A hand opened the first box, and the camera zoomed inside to a man in striped pajamas peering through a venetian blind. Between the slats were clouds pierced by animated zigzags of lightning. The man groaned, turned from the window, and went back to bed, closing the lid of the pillbox behind him. The lid on Tuesday opened into a movie theater. Inside the theater, the same man who had been looking through the blinds was now watching a movie and eating a big tub of popcorn, thunder and lightning cracking outside. Wednesday was a repeat of Monday except, this time, it was a woman peering through the slats. She looked out to see a bright yellow sun wearing big black sunglasses. Thursday featured the same woman now at the beach in a lounge chair where she was rubbing suntan lotion on her legs, and Friday and Saturday, the woman at the beach was surrounded by throngs of people. Sunday was a return to rain, clouds, and the man in pajamas. The week ended with the man closing Sunday's lid behind him to the accompaniment of the news team's laughter, especially the laughter of Katie, who excelled at gaiety.

The camera panned the news desk's cheerful banter before it focused in on the two anchors, who tripped over words interjected with laughter as they signed off for the evening, Reed and Katie, a merry duo.

"Hey I thought the report had to have the same ending every time, no matter what," Fletcher said, once the camera was off them and their daily postmortem had begun. Except for Claire, the team was still at the desk, a large S-shaped slab of charcoal granite, which the station had invested in to make JTF look more like network and less like local. A row of television monitors all tuned to JTF was behind the desk, and taped pulsating sounds of newsroom activity preceded and followed each broadcast. After the news was over, the team stayed in their seats so they would still be in broadcasting mode when they made their comments. "You can tinker with the content," quoted JTF's burly sportscaster, "so long as the structure is firm, fixed, and immutable. I mean, don't get me wrong, I liked your ending, but I was surprised."

"That was the idea," said Claire, returning to her chair at the desk. "Your surprise…and," she added, lowering her eyes modestly to neutralize the presumption in the rest of her statement, "delight…was supposed to mimic our viewers'. Your reinforcement would make the audience reaction that much stronger."

"Suppose we didn't like it?" Fletcher asked, squinting under the glare of the overhead light.

"You're too professional not to like it," Claire smiled, and it was the sweetness of her smile, more than her answer, that made sense to him.

Fletcher still looked confused and skeptical. "Yeah, but a consistent structure…" he said, trying to remember exactly what it was Claire always said.

"Screw consistent structures," said Katie, who was much more interested in the storm watch, which had cut into her time, than in the pill dispenser segment. "How come we gave up good air time for a goddamned watch?" Her face was bright and garish under the glare of the lights.

"Relax, Katie. A hurricane in Florida can do a whole lot of damage…anyway, I checked with Dan. I knew you didn't have anything."

"That's not true. I had my hit-and-run," said Katie, neglecting to mention that her hit-and-run involved no fatalities.

Fletcher didn't like these debates and began to shake his foot in nervous agitation, ready to leave. He had only gone into broadcasting after a knee injury had cut short a promising career in football, and his body, which was big, brawny, and alert, still hadn't adjusted to the requirements of a sedentary career. Sitting was not part of his repertoire, and more often than not his comments were in the nature of winding things up so that his restless body, which was like a car parked in neutral while his foot pumped on the gas, could spring into action.

Katie dabbed her glistening forehead with a tissue. "A hit-and-run is better than a watch," she continued. "There's real human misery there, not possible disaster. I had good footage, too. Three kids, sitting by the side of the road, crying. I mean, you could at least have gone for a warning."

"Hey, I'm already stretching it with a watch. The winds are a mile under definition as it is," Claire countered, tucking an obstinate strand of hair behind her ear.

"Women, so technical and petty," said Katie, stacking her papers into a neat pile in front of her to let everyone know that the conversation was over and that she was ready to leave.

"Girls, girls, knock it off, you two," Reed's voice cut in. As senior anchor, Reed was the last word in their ongoing battle for air time, at least when their news director, Dan Liebowitz, wasn't there. "Fact is, neither of you had squat, and we stretched a thin day to thirty minutes."

"My concern, Reed, is that we stretched it to transparency and that viewers will see through it. Dire warnings of bad weather are pretty ridiculous when the sun is shining." Katie looked at Reed earnestly. "The pill dispenser was cute, very imaginative, but it has nothing to do," she said, turning back to Claire, her auburn hair swinging behind her, "with the way you *pilfered* my time."

"There is a hurricane in Florida, Katie. And even though it looks like it may ultimately be a dud, for now it's news," Reed rebutted. The newsroom had no windows, and the absence of natural light placed additional emphasis on what he said. "Whether it ultimately affects us or not, there is still a human disaster down there, and a lot of people are being impacted by it. The hurricane may not be local, but in this instance, I have to agree with Claire that it is the weightier of the stories."

Katie hated giving in to Reed, or to anyone for the matter. She especially hated the last word quality of his pronouncements, as if his authority were pre-ordained. Even so, as long as she had to take orders from someone, she preferred that it be Reed and not someone who might actually have a legitimate claim to authority, like Claire. A merit system could blow everything for Katie. It could expose the lies in her resume—the fact that her degree was from Penn State and not the University of Pennsylvania, and that her previous newspaper experience had been a lot less than the four and a half years she'd claimed. It could even mean that she might lose her job to someone with actual news credentials, someone who wrote her own reports. All of them were lucky to have their jobs, but she and Reed were especially lucky because they were the highest paid and the least talented among them; and Katie was shrewd enough to know that deference to Reed established the precedent of deference to the anchor's chair.

Reed was only too willing to cooperate in Katie's self-serving view of newsroom reality. Why would he object? It gave him added authority, and he knew he could use the boost from her apparent respect. Even though he hadn't deceived anyone to get his job, he was sure he didn't deserve it, and if his predecessor hadn't dropped dead of a heart attack, there was no doubt in his mind that he would still be a field reporter. That was several thousand broadcasts ago and should have been enough, he frequently told himself, to overcome his anxieties; but time and experience hadn't been able to eliminate the permanent catch in his throat that had developed immediately after his promotion to anchor. The catch had been audible from the moment his voice stepped over the body that had fallen on the floor seven years ago, and even though considerable coaching had helped create an approximation of self-assurance, the catch wouldn't go away. He tried psychotherapy, speech therapy, and yoga, and when none of those worked, he tried drinking two fingers of double malt before each broadcast. After a while, he had one drink before each broadcast and two or three after, but that didn't work either, and in the end only added a bulbous, pitted nose and a slight tremor in his eye, a quiver of the kind produced by a small hovering insect, to the catch in his voice.

CHAPTER TWO

Claire had none of the insecurities that afflicted her co-workers. She had gotten her job at JTF after four years as an assistant professor of meteorology at Columbia University, and within days she had mastered the skills it had taken the others years to develop. Never before had the advantages of a superior education seemed so obvious. Work that everyone else thought of as involving a long, slow learning curve had come to her as quickly and easily if she had been doing it all her life.

And, in a way, she had. Standing in front of a camera was not so different from standing in front of a classroom, and the only real difference, according to her former colleagues, was that one job was worth doing and the other wasn't. Years of education—in which each successive degree ratified the successful completion of the last and was an endorsement to teach at a celebrated university—were, from their narrow if lofty vantage point, wasted on a place like JTF. It was as if Claire had chosen minor league ball over the majors. Why would anyone do such a thing?

The presumed explanation was fame and fortune. Why else would she leave a profession that allowed, no encouraged, her to pursue her own interests and that gave her a three-day, nine-hour workweek into the bargain? What else could possibly attract her to a job that involved saying and doing pretty much the same thing day after hazy, hot, and humid day for what had to be a fairly meager salary?

Even Geoff, who could usually be counted on to back Claire up, thought she was making a big mistake. "What can possibly be going through your mind?" he asked, his British accent growing opportunistically stronger with each passing year in New York. "The denial of tenure is no reason to make a career change. I mean, you had to know that you couldn't get tenure without a published book. Not at a place like Columbia anyway."

They were sitting in her car eating take-out. There was nothing but a paper bag between them, and, for a moment, he was tempted to take matters in hand—*be the man*—remove the food and draw Claire to him. He decided against it. They had always been comfortably collegial, and approaching Claire now, when she was feeling more and more estranged from her old life, seemed risky, so he decided to hold off until he had a better sense of how she would react.

"I'm not exactly empty-handed. I have four articles and a book contract," she said petulantly. "A book contract from a major publisher," she added when there was no reaction. "And I have great teaching evaluations."

He looked at her sympathetically. "Close, my dear, but no cigar."

It was the wrong choice of words. Close but no cigar: a four-word dismissal of years of achievement. As early as the fifth grade, when Mrs. Golub asked for volunteers to teach ten minutes of class, Claire had known that she wanted to be a teacher. She wanted to stand in the front of the room, and facing everyone else, she wanted to inform, entertain, evaluate, and take charge. Only two other kids had raised their hands that day, Rory Chiang and Josh Finkel, and to determine who would go first, Mrs. Golub let them pick from folded pieces of paper with the numbers 1, 2, and 3 on them. Claire got 3. It was exactly what she had wanted. Going last gave her a chance to size up and outdo the competition. Winning was pure pleasure, as innocent as beating her parents at gin rummy during summer nights on Lake Kennebago when Claire would slap her tenth and winning card down or say "so sorry" with feigned and exaggerated politesse, as, taking her mallet, she would whack one of her parents' balls off into the shrubbery in a game of croquet. Their pleasure at her spirit and skill seemed so genuine that Claire—who had no brothers or sisters to protest her victories—came to associate winning with everyone else's pleasure, and when, on the day that she taught Mrs. Golub's class, she gave a little quiz, she was completely unaware that her classmates were not charmed by her precocious mischief-making. Those early school days had been the beginning of the unremitting academic success that had led Claire to eventually transfer her performance from one side of the desk to the other; and those same early days, and all the days that followed, were the experience Geoff had so casually dismissed with the phrase close but no cigar. They were also the years of experience that Columbia would have brought to a conclusion with a single vote of the tenure committee if Claire had given them the satisfaction of sticking around for their decision.

"Think about it," Geoff had said as they sat in her parked car watching the traffic on Broadway. He was wearing a cotton sweater-vest over an Oxford shirt, and his pants, baggy cords, hung loosely around legs that were prissily pressed together. "Weathermen aren't scientists. For them, a stellar performance takes place in the movies. They're personalities, whatever that means. Is that what you want, do you want to be a personality? Of course," he paused and looked at her with an intensity that suggested he might have preferred to express his appreciation nonverbally, "you've got the looks for it, but a mind," he laughed, "is a terrible thing to waste."

"You laugh," she had said, absently looking at the colorless hairs on his spongy, boneless hands, "because you are quoting a TV commercial, because you have fallen prey to popular culture. But Geoffrey, it's really snobbery and not popular culture that you're the victim of." Geoff cocked his head. Was it really possible that Claire, who had always impressed him with her insight, could have so little self-understanding? Could it be she had no idea of her own elitism? "I mean," she continued, very pleased with her new conception of things, "the weather is the greatest show on earth—doesn't it deserve something more than the hackneyed, trite, and monotonous television reporting we've become accustomed to?"

Criticized and no longer feeling the least bit amorous, he went on the offensive, his little battalion of small white teeth a row of shields raised against attack. "Okay, okay, but trading New York City for a pit stop? Chucking it all in favor of…Katie and Reed?" He pronounced their names with such obvious scorn that Claire felt in momentary sympathy with them. "An assistant professorship at Columbia University, an advanced degree from MIT, and a number, albeit modest, of published papers would certainly get you something somewhere."

"'Something somewhere?'" Claire repeated the words slowly and thoughtfully, impressed that two words whose meaning was so vague could have such specific implications. Her car was on the incline facing the Broadway entrance to Columbia, whose stately wrought iron gates, open in permanent invitation, were an ironic distortion of the fact that the university's standards prevented the vast majority of applicants from attending and the vast majority of scholars from teaching there. "Look," she said, fed up with the attack on her newfound profession, "I know you have a very low opinion of television. I know you think that no one pursues anything in depth, but don't you see? That is precisely why I want to do this. I think it's wrong that television should have so little to recommend it, and even if I can't change the medium, I can at least make the weather segment into something worthwhile." She looked out the window where the sun, momentarily exposed by a break in a large cloud, looked as plump, bright, and optimistic as an egg yolk.

"And you really think they will let you do that? You really believe they will let you make changes in the way they go about things?"

"Geoff, one sentence a day is all that I'll need. One sentence about the beauty or horror or serenity or excitement of that day's weather, and everyone will listen. I'll quote the poets; I'll do a rain dance. When I report the weather, the air will tremble with the season. One sentence a day, and we'll all pay rent to our universal landlord: the weather."

Geoff contemplated Claire for a minute. He had always considered her wonderfully sensible, but here she was, naïve, quixotic, and proud. It was almost as if she imagined that by finding a larger audience, she could make Columbia regret their decision and wish she was still among them. Claire's other colleagues from the meteorology department had thought her departure was about the pursuit of fame and fortune, but they were wrong; celebrity was far too mundane to interest Claire, whose goal was nothing less than to educate the masses and become the Socrates of weather forecasting.

• • •

Russo and Goodwin had no idea of Claire's ambitions. They had been so dazzled by her resume that every other consideration had been obscured, and they never stopped to ask her why she was interested in working for them. If they had treated her the same as other applicants, if they had not been so busy trying to sell her on JTF, then they might have discovered that she had grandiose ideas about the role she would fill and no intention of conforming to their conception of what a reporter should be. But their satisfaction over MIT coming to JTF and their excitement over being in the company of someone so…so advanced had a profoundly disorganizing effect on their thinking, and neither Goodwin nor Russo was inclined to say anything—and that included a job description—which might have discouraged Claire's interest in working for them.

Claire took their laissez-faire approach as a tremendous vote of confidence. She couldn't get over it. They had devoted her entire interview to a description of JTF's history and role in the community, and without asking a single question about how she envisioned the job, they offered it to her. She didn't even have a demo tape, but still they wanted her. She had no inkling, of course, that their high opinion was equally rooted in their own self-doubt and that her mere presence gave JTF a credibility it otherwise lacked. All she knew was that things seemed to be working out, and that in contrast to the disaster her academic friends had predicted, television might be the best thing that ever happened to her.

CHAPTER THREE

"We had calm clouds in a slow sky today," she said on the evening news only her second week into the job. It had been a beautiful day, and that was what Goodwin and Russo thought Claire was probably trying to say, but a slow sky? That was not the way reporters were supposed to talk. If she had flubbed her lines or looked away from the camera that would have been something they could deal with, but Claire had no problem with the technical aspects of reporting. It was her language that was a problem, and no one, not even Dan Liebowitz, knew how to respond to her odd choice of words. They decided to let the incident pass without comment. Maybe, with a little more exposure to television, she would catch on to what was expected of her.

Claire took their silence as further proof of the station's willingness to innovate and continued on the course she had started. If all JTF had needed was someone who could read the data from the service, they would have given the job to a communications school graduate; but since they had hired her instead, she thought it must be because they wanted to make some fundamental changes in the way they went about things. She couldn't have been more mistaken, but it wasn't until she ended a report with a quote from William Wordsworth that their disquietude gave way to outright alarm. Who spoke that way on TV? Was she nuts? Was she on some kind of mission? Who did she think she was? University degrees or no university degrees, professorship or no professorship, this was a television station not a university classroom, and Claire had to conform to it.

"It's just that she's really smart and knows a lot," Liebowitz had told Russo after the Wordsworth quote. "You're not used to it, that's all." Dan was sitting in Russo's office where they were playing catch with a Day-Glo tennis ball.

"It's not her intelligence I object to," Russo prickled and lobbed the ball sideways over Dan's head, practically breaking a lamp. "I mean, give me a little credit. It's just that it's sort of arrogant, don't you think, quoting poetry? And using words that people don't understand? I mean, why tenebrous? What's wrong with overcast?"

"Why don't you ask her?" Dan suggested, wryly amused by the problem of having someone too good for them.

Claire's work space was part of a complex of cubicles that always reminded Russo of low-income housing, at least until he stepped inside her gray particleboard enclosure, which, with all of its machinery and charts, resembled the cockpit of an airplane. She had been running a crawl about a thunderstorm when he entered, and a procession of constantly changing numbers flanked the bottom of her Doppler radar screen. Seeing her examine the data so closely, the tip of her forefinger on a chart next to her computer, her slip slightly visible under the thin material of her blouse, it all had a funny effect on him, and he didn't know whether it was envy for her passion or simply passion for her that he was feeling. Already, he was beginning to weaken and he hadn't even said a word.

"It was overcast last night and this morning," Claire said, anchoring a curl behind her ear.

"Yeah? So?"

"So if I say it's overcast now, too, then it's as if the weather never changes when, in fact, that is the one thing the weather is always doing. It never stays exactly the same. Look at the radar."

"That's true," Russo said pensively, "but viewers are used to the word 'overcast.' They like it."

"How do you know they like it?"

"Ratings."

"How about if we do this," Claire said, and Russo suspected that she was being patient with him, humoring him like his wife humored their six-year-old. "Let me try doing things differently for a little while. If ratings go down, I'll do it your way."

"If ratings go down, we'll be out of a job. This is not a laboratory, Claire. Experiments are very pricey on television."

Claire didn't argue, even though she was convinced that with time she could win the public over. Russo was equally persuaded that more time would be a mistake, but luckily for Claire, he found that he was having a hard time saying no to her. She had such highly articulated features, such a lovely, full mouth. For a moment he pretended to do mental arithmetic, all the while knowing he was going to give in, until finally, after more apparent calculation, he said, "Okay. Two weeks. We'll give you two weeks. But that's all."

The numbers eventually developed, but not in the two weeks he gave her and not before ratings fell. Claire panicked. The idea that people might switch to another channel had seemed no more likely than that students—who had lined up to take her classes—would transfer to another section. Claire had been so confident the public would like her that she hadn't given any thought to what she would do if she wasn't a success, but when finally she forced herself to think about it, she realized her choices were limited.

She could copy her competition at WFYI, the relatively popular Louis Martin, but that was unthinkable. As someone who'd staked her success on being authentic and original, the idea of imitation was worse than failure. Not only that, she would have been imitating a fraud, a former model who, to counteract the obvious perception that he'd been hired for his looks, filled his reports with so much unnecessary technical information that, paradoxically, it only reinforced the impression that he was more interested in presentation than precipitation. Standing next to the weather map in a smartly tailored suit, which delineated his triangular physique, and sporting a deep December suntan, which enhanced his blond hair, he would smile irrelevantly into the camera as he referred to radiosondes, radiometers, the Beaufort scale, and the general circulation model, never mind whether anyone knew what he was talking about.

Another alternative would have been to adopt the style of her predecessor, Norwood Fossil; but if that was the only way to succeed, Claire would never have left academe. Fossil was an ex-military man who had studied meteorology in the navy and his clipped, terse style only worked when the weather was like an army of advancing clouds and approaching storm fronts. "Storm clouds are heading this way," he would say, chin up, barrel chest out, and well-padded shoulders back, as if he was leading troops of clouds across a field of sky. Unlike Martin, whose eyes would occasionally twinkle with irrepressible joy—how had he learned to do that?—Fossil's martial delivery was characterized by the grim-faced determination of the battlefield. It was only when he signed off for the evening that he allowed himself a momentary reprise from the harsh realities he had presumably once witnessed, and smiling matter-of-factly into the camera, his mouth one more crevice in the rough terrain of his face, he would end his reports with an upbeat statement about the silver lining of clouds. "And remember," he would say, reluctantly acknowledging life's brighter side, "every cloud has a silver lining."

• • •

"You don't have to be exactly like the others," Russo said, when it became obvious that their two week experiment had failed; and if they had not been alone in his office—if she had not been *called in* to his office—the statement might actually have helped. "Look at Al Roker, he's entirely his own man, and he's got a huge following." Claire waited patiently, wondering how far the boom was going to be lowered.

"It's just," he said, standing in front of his desk, his arms thrust back like a lever to prop up his considerable bulk, "now I want to say this right," he paused, "I don't want you to misunderstand me, but the people who watch our station, well we're not PBS, and if they don't understand you, it makes them think there's something wrong with them. They might think you're putting them down. I mean, any imbecile is supposed to understand the weather, right?"

"Well, Don, it took me a long time to understand the weather too, and I still don't understand it fully."

"Claire…"

"I know, I know, and I'm not trying to be cute. It's just that clouds don't have silver linings, and what I'm trying to show, Don, is just the opposite. I'm trying to illustrate that, far from being a product of philosophy, nature is a force beyond man's control."

"I gave you the extra time you asked for—I gave you two weeks," he said, seeing that she was not quite ready to accept defeat. His wife and three children—two big, one small—backed him up from a photograph on his large executive desk. "I have no problem with your doing something different so long as ratings are high," he continued when Claire, who was looking at the blue and white Matisse poster on his wall, the same one she'd had in college, didn't say anything, "but time is money, and, incidentally, weather is money too. Did you know that Fossil computed the comparative financial value of a storm, a hurricane, a drought, and sunshine?" he said, absolutely deadpan.

"Which makes the most?" Claire laughed, a hollow feeling in the pit of her stomach. "Cyclones? Should I report a tornado a week? Maybe throw in the occasional blizzard just to make sure there's a surplus in the budget?"

"Nooo, that's not what I'm saying," Russo backed off, "all I'm saying is get rid of the adjectives, at least until the public gets used to you," he said, relieved to be laying down the law. "And cool it with the poetry too. You don't want to scare the public off."

"I didn't know poetry was scary," she answered.

"No, no, that's not what I mean. You know what I mean," he said, looking at her very intently, not really sure whether she did. "But if you're gonna quote poetry, make sure that a fifth grader can understand it."

"Seriously?"

Russo shrugged.

CHAPTER FOUR

Inenubilable, a. rare {f. ln-2 + L.} e nu bil-ar to make clear (see enubilate v.) That cannot be cleared of clouds of mist or (fig.) of obscurity; indistinct; inexplicable

Mrs. Garafollo was an English teacher at Bridge Haven High School who listened to the weather every evening while she did the dishes. She would wait for the five-day forecast, generally ignoring everything leading up to it, until she knew what weather to expect the following day; but, as she explained to public relations when she called JTF, she couldn't help hearing the station's new reporter refer to inenubilable skies. She could hardly believe her ears. "I had never heard the word before and went straight to my Webster's Unabridged. It wasn't there," she exclaimed, "and I had to refer to two other dictionaries before I finally found it in my supplement to the Oxford English Dictionary!" She was really happy now. "To be perfectly honest, if one of your other reporters had used the word, I might have thought they were making a mistake, but this young woman strikes me as rather literate and I just couldn't imagine that she'd gotten it wrong. That's why I'm calling. I think Claire Day is a great addition to the news team, and I want to congratulate you on hiring her. She's so good, in fact, that I've decided to assign the weather to my English classes."

• • •

Mrs. Garafollo's call to the station several months earlier had been the result of Judy Strongman's suggestion that Claire use an impossibly long, hard to pronounce word on television. They were at their usual posts in Judy's Park Avenue kitchen, where Claire, completely frustrated by her conversation with Russo, had gone to complain, and it was there the linguistic plot was hatched.

Claire was seated on a stool, her hands cupped around a mug of tea, her elbows on a granite island in the middle of a room lined with shores of counters; Judy was waiting for her English muffin, a knife with a wad of butter poised for attack. "Buoyant little things, aren't they?" Judy said as her muffin popped three inches into the air. "You should follow their example, show some spirit."

"What do you mean?" Claire leaned forward, interested.

"I mean go for it. Instead of getting rid of the adjectives and poetry, use some really dazzling language in your next report, language that requires your bosses to look outside their caves. What do you have to lose? Your ratings are in the toilet anyway. The worst they can do is fire you, and if that happens, what difference does it make? You haven't worked there long enough for it to count yet anyway. Just make sure that you don't list JTF on your resume when you apply for your next job," she laughed.

Claire was fascinated. She had never been let go (as getting fired was euphemistically described, like someone had simply loosened their grip instead of flinging you away) and had always thought it would be a shameful experience; but in the spirit of her newfound professional adventurism and in the context of a romantically aggrandizing imagination, she was willing to consider the possibility that getting fired was like a rite of passage into a world where personal safety and security were less important than commitment to principle, something like going to jail for participating in a demonstration.

"There's a list of words TV won't allow," Judy had continued enthusiastically, "but they're mostly curse words and body parts. So long as you don't use one of them, I don't see what's to prevent you from using any word you like. If I were you, I'd hit 'em with the longest, most obscure word you can think of." Judy's eyelids snapped open and shut like the blinking light on her microwave. She was wearing a vintage dress from Second Hand Rose, the thrift shop she owned and managed—shocking pink with a pattern of interlocking green and blue triangles—and her appearance, as flamboyant as her suggestion, made it clear that she was not easily intimidated.

"Ju...dy," a male voice boomed out. The voice preceded the body by several rooms.

"In here," she yelled back, "we're in the kitchen, Murray." After Murray had pushed open the swinging door and given Claire a hug, Judy said, "Give me an adjective that describes some aspect of the weather, an obscure adjective, a long one." He looked healthy and robust from golf, crossed clubs on the collar of his white knit shirt.

"Oh," said Claire, "I don't know if I want to go that far."

"How far?" Rachel, Judy and Murray's seven-year-old daughter, asked from behind the door of their Sub-Zero. "What are you talking about?"

"Where are your manners?" Judy pulled her away from the fridge by the shoulder of her T-shirt. "Aren't you going to say 'hello'?"

"Hello. Mom, what is there to eat?" She stomped her foot impatiently.

The gesture did not go over. "Later Rachel," Judy said in a sharp voice. "Don't you have homework to do?"

"I did it."

"Then check for errors."

Rachel made a face, which bunched her features together in a dark little knot, but that was all the challenge she was prepared to mount.

"How many letters?" Murray asked.

"It's not for a crossword puzzle," Judy said, pacing the floor, deep in thought, distracted. Murray started to say something, but Judy shushed him with an outward palm.

"It's coming, it's coming, wait, don't talk." She was in a state of high mental alert. Then, suddenly, like the English muffin that burst on the scene, it broke from her. "Inenubilable!" she shrieked. "That's the word I've been trying to think of! Inenubilable. Remember?" She stared at Claire and waited for her to burst out laughing.

The word was a relic from their college days. In her freshman year, Claire had decided to read the entire Oxford English Dictionary, A to Z, in preparation for a major in English. She had wanted to have an exhaustive vocabulary, and she did, up through the letter H. But halfway through I—at the word inenubilable to be precise—she gave up. No one, including her extraordinarily literate roommate, Judy, knew the meaning of the word, and its obscurity seemed to represent both the futility of her project and the pointlessness of majoring in English. Her objectives, like the word itself, were unclear and indistinct, and after briefly casting about for something else to focus on, she decided to do what had been obvious from the start and switched her major to science.

"I can't," Claire had said, both horrified and tantalized at the prospect of doing something so outrageous. If Russo had trouble with tenebrous, she could just about imagine his reaction to inenubilable.

"Why not?" Judy asked, in love with the idea. "If you're going down anyway, it may as well be with a splash."

The argument was persuasive, especially since, fundamentally, Claire agreed with it. She knew that it jeopardized her job, but it looked like she might lose her job whether she used the word or not. And even if she didn't get fired, there was the possibility she might quit. After leaving Columbia and getting the first job she applied for—a job for which she had no working experience!—she suddenly realized that her stellar credentials counted for a whole lot more *outside* the university, where they impressed, than inside, where they were common. She was not ungrateful to JTF and really appreciated their willingness to hire her, but she hadn't traded the high, elusive, politically modulated standards of the university simply to navigate the low, elusive, shifting tides of television ratings, and if JTF didn't like what she had to offer, then she was quite sure there was some place else that would.

• • •

She dressed conservatively when she gave the report. Standing beside the chroma-key in a demure beige suit intended to downplay her little rebellion, she stuck the word into a phrase, half swallowing it rather than articulating it clearly, and, with pounding heart and sweating palms, predicted inenubilable skies. A shock wave went through her entire system. Six syllables; the word had six syllables! No one used six-syllable words on television. No one used six-syllable words whether they were on television or not! Stunned by her own daring, she tried to persuade herself that what she had done was not so outrageous—after all, how could one word (one word!) be such a big deal? But in her heart she knew that long, obscure words were as unacceptable as cursing; they were unpatriotic, possible grounds for getting fired, tantamount to insurrection…almost like using French.

When the broadcast was over, she had fully expected to be summoned into Russo's office right away, but before Russo even had a chance to get angry, calls started coming in to the station, and, instead of calls of complaint, they were from viewers who wanted to know what inenubilable meant and why it wasn't in their dictionaries. Literally within minutes of the broadcast, before the news team had even finished meeting, the switchboard had become a firmament of lights illuminated by a curious public. One person had wanted to know if George W. had coined it. Someone else thought it was an accounting term. The public was caught, dangling from the hook of its own ignorance, thrashing about to free itself from personal limitation at the same time that it was inextricably and irresistibly connected to the woman who had baited the hook. Who was she; where did she come from; where did she get her clothes; was she married? In one day, the station received more telephone calls than it had in the several months preceding, and all of them had to do with Claire. Curiosity abounded and the woman who had triggered it was, in the tradition of instant celebrity, becoming a source of public fascination from one day to the next.

The truth was that even before the inenubilable report had aired, if he had listened to his wife, Russo could have known that Claire was beginning to attract a following. Days earlier, Barbara had told him the buzz was teenage girls were deciding it was cool to watch the weather lady and that their daughter, Jennifer, who never watched anything but sitcoms and hated shows with information in them, had started watching the weather. She liked the poetry part. The poetry! That should have caught his attention, but nothing really registered until the calls started coming in to the station. Then, he woke up and his mind started racing. He could see it all before him, Claire becoming another Oprah, a role model for the young. Instead of book clubs, there could be a poetry club—Claire's monthly selections. Why not? His own daughter referred to Shakespeare, Yeats, and Frost as Claire's poets. It was wild! Russo saw it all before him: the zoo, the botanical garden, and the Audubon society would be asking her to speak at their events; Greenpeace would request her endorsement; John Deere would want her to promote lawn mowers; anything having to do with nature, conservation, or ecology would be hers—*theirs*—for the asking.

"When you get a few minutes…" he had said to Claire the day following her report. He was in a tough spot because he knew he should reprimand her, say something stern—after all, she had flagrantly ignored his instructions—but he was going to have to talk out of both sides of his mouth because he now wanted her to keep on doing exactly what he had told her to avoid when he said to keep it simple.

Russo's tone was respectful. "Twenty-five, thirty students," he had said, referring to the English teacher, Mrs. Garafollo's phone call and looking out his office window, "assuming they all do their homework, is not the kind of response we're looking for." Claire stood patiently in front of his desk, waiting for him to turn around.

"I have to admit," he said, after a weighty pause, "that you had me going there," his choice of words intended to imply that his melodramatic posture had been something of a joke they could enjoy together. He was facing her now, his head less attractive than his back, which, at least, was large at the top and nicely tapered at the waist, unlike his face, which was at inverse proportion to his back and built down from a small forehead to a large jaw, a physiognomy more designed to chew than to contemplate. His large jaw encompassed a large mouth, which appeared to Claire, who saw things with the detailed observation of someone who had spent years looking through a microscope, to conceal a grin beneath its grimace—it was something about the way his mouth muscles were twitching and the way he hastily concluded their meeting without ever really reprimanding her.

When Claire left Russo's office, she realized that she wasn't terribly surprised that her gamble had paid off. Things were *supposed* to work out for her. Why wouldn't they? Her pedigree consisted of the best attributes from all of life's major categories, including genes, which had produced health, height, and green eyes; an education, which had produced entrée and overwhelmingly positive assumptions on her behalf; religions, which, on her mother's side, had produced Protestant independence of mind and, on her father's, Jewish respect for learning and laughter;

and altogether, they had produced the self-confidence that goes with the aforementioned. Things were meant to work out for her, and when, after the inenubilable report aired, they did, there was nothing terribly unexpected about it.

More surprisingly, after Claire left Russo's office, he also came to believe that her success could have been predicted. In fact, the more he thought about it, the more it seemed to him that he *had* predicted it and that Claire's success was proof of management's eye for talent. Sure, they'd had some misgivings about her, but wasn't that natural considering her unorthodox approach? And yes, they'd been uptight when she first began introducing the adjectives into her reports, but who wouldn't have been? She was doing something different and change was always unnerving. The point was that *even though* they'd been apprehensive, and *even though* they had wanted to rein in her unorthodox style, they had been willing—television pioneers that they were—to take a chance on her.

CHAPTER FIVE

Despite Claire's self-confidence and Russo's self-deception, it was only Katie who had actually foreseen Claire's success. From the moment Claire had walked into the station wearing French penny loafers—which meant they had three inch heels and were more tapered than their American progenitors—Katie had perceived a rival who could blow them all out of the water. And it wasn't because Katie had an eye for talent either. To the contrary, she had no idea why anyone would read poetry or be intrigued by an adjective. Her fear was based solely on her conception of the world those adjectives came from—which, as she imagined it, was educated, confident, independent, and daring—and based on her dread of the world they implied—which was Ivy League, privileged, and enlightened: a world that would expose the inferiority of her own background.

In the environment of Katie's childhood, self-improvement was a luxury reserved for the rich and entitled, and getting ahead essentially meant getting out of the house. As the sixth of seven children, Katie's course had been defined by the needs and desires of others, and it had been an obstacle course designed by human frailty and navigated by thwarting, feigning, avoiding, and seducing—all methods she had used to claw her way to the top. There she had settled into the anchor's chair as if it were her throne, and from it she had looked down on the rest of the news court with a condescension based on the assumption that success and superiority were pretty much the same thing. That was, at least, until Claire came on the scene and transformed their hierarchy into a meritocracy. Up until that point, Katie and Reed had been the king and queen of the news court, and everyone else, as Katie saw it, was a mere courtier at their flanks. Within a few short months, however, Claire had changed all that, and according to her conception of things, the only royalty were the sun, the moon, and the stars, and the only court was in the kingdom of nature.

Katie's fear of Claire exploded into full-blown panic when the inenubilable report aired. Up to that point, thanks to Claire's low ratings, Katie had been able to tolerate her presence on the news team, but as soon as the inenubilable report was broadcast—even before the phone calls started coming in to the station—Katie's anxiety radar zoomed way up. It would not have been the first time, after all, that this kind of thing had happened; there were precedents for unpredictable success. Who, for instance, would ever have thought that Sister Wendy—a bucktoothed nun, for God's sake—would be such a hit? And who would have imagined that the rumpled, disorganized Andy Rooney would have a following? It was the fear that Claire would achieve that kind of oddball recognition and that inenubilable would be the watershed word to catapult Claire to stardom that catapulted Katie into Russo's office where, livid with anger, as if the word had been a phrase and the phrase an attack personally directed at her, she found herself strenuously objecting to its use.

She had known she was overreacting when she burst in on him, high heels clicking like castanets, like demanding fingers snapping imperiously; but she was afraid something beyond her control was taking place, and she wanted to oppose it.

"It's only a word," Russo, the advocate of fifth grade poetry, found himself saying.

"Give me a break Don," she seethed, her fair skin blotchy with anger. "I've never even heard the word before," and then, not giving him the chance to point out that her ignorance did not strengthen her position, she added shrilly "What is this, a TV station or an English class?"

"Take it easy, take it easy. I don't know why it bothers you so much," Russo said, thinking that maybe what really bothered Katie was another woman on the set, a woman who, among her other attributes, had a vocabulary. "Cut her a little slack, why don't you? I mean, she's only just begun."

"Christ, I hate to think how she'll finish if this is how she's starting. Don't you get it? She wants to change everything around."

Ordinarily, before Claire joined the team, Russo would have found a way to placate Katie, who had effectively used her ratings as leverage to get preferred parking, a wardrobe, and a raise out of the station's meager resources. But although he wanted to keep her happy, her complaints and requests had begun to feel like blackmail, like they had a tacit "or else" tacked on; and Katie's anger, which was suspiciously out of proportion to the provocation, had gotten him to thinking that maybe he could use Claire to keep Katie in check.

"Don't worry, she's not going to change anything," he said flatly, looking at his watch in a gesture of dismissal. But that wasn't really true because he had begun to feel a little of the same thing Katie was feeling, only in his case, it wasn't anxiety but more like a hum inside him, like a motor kicking in.

• • •

His statement, of course, turned out to be entirely inaccurate. By the end of Claire's first few months, she had changed everything, and Katie, the former queen of the news court, had come to look like a pretender to a throne that didn't exist, while Claire, who delivered her report from way off to the side, was getting central billing. And to make matters worse, Katie couldn't even complain. How could she complain about a situation that benefited the entire station?

It was only when Claire went into overtime—like the day she extended her report by thirty seconds simply to keep a promise to some third graders in Peekskill—that Katie could legitimately protest. Claire frequently took liberties with the content of her reports and no one challenged her; but overtime was another matter, and when Claire's report cut into Katie's, she felt that she had a legitimate right to complain, ratings or no ratings.

The promise had come about as the result of a nationwide science project that Claire had helped set up, and to do her part, she had visited an inner-city school in Peekskill. While she was there, she promised some third graders who knew absolutely nothing at all about nature that she would explain morning dew to them on television, and that, *that,* was the reason she cut into everyone's time! If anyone else had pulled a stunt like that there would have been all hell to pay, but Claire was JTF's darling, their Renaissance woman, a ratings bonanza, and no one was the least bit inclined to stand in her way.

Her morning dew report—many of her reports were given names—was shot on the lawn of an estate where, as if she were a mermaid on a lily pad, Claire crouched in a sea of grass. The camera zeroed in and then moved right past her to focus on a single blade of grass, a bead of dew like an inverted pendant dangling from its head, as a voice-over said, "As forth she went with early dawn to taste the dew-bespeckled lawn." Then, with the loyalty of a faithful dog, the camera followed Claire to a large old oak where she sat on the single wood slat of a low-hanging swing surrounded by yellow and white jonquils. "Does the flower outgrow the seed?" she asked ten thousand viewers. "Or does it simply blossom?" she queried, her lips as red as currants, her curls as brown as bark. "We often talk of things that we outgrow, such as habits, childhood, friends, and relationships. But, we might ask, does the spring outgrow the winter or does it simply grow out of winter? Isn't spring just an example of nature's inexorable forward march as, year after year, with unerring timeliness, it brings us this?" she asked, gesturing to the flowers surrounding her while the camera moved back to pan the entire scene. A small crowd of onlookers applauded.

The cameramen looked at each other and grinned. Cu...ut.

"God bless that woman," Russo said to Goodwin, back at the station, "and God bless her lead-ins." They were all gathered backstage around one of the station's television sets: Don Russo, Phil Goodwin, Dan Liebowitz, Katie, Reed, and Fletcher, a blur of support staff in the background. JTF occupied two floors of a former theater, and broadcasting was shot on what had been the stage with viewing and discussion reserved for the area behind it. "The way she uses vocabulary," Russo continued, shaking his head in admiration but lacking the words to say just how she used it.

"Language," Goodwin corrected, "the way she uses language, not the way she uses vocabulary." Russo didn't like being corrected in front of the others, but he kept quiet, reminding himself instead that he had more shares in the station than Goodwin, just in case it ever came to that.

A commercial break followed Claire's woodland scene before she was back on camera holding a bouquet of daffodils. Leaning in to smell the flowers, she took a long, deep inhalation before she began her forecast.

Toooo much, tooo fucking much, Goodwin and Russo roared with delight, fully persuaded that everything Claire did was further proof of her magic. That woman is too much. Russo was punching the air with a clenched fist in an emphatic show of victory. They had done it; they were on route to major recognition. If things continued the way they were going, they could leave obscurity behind and maybe get a job with one of the networks. Money, power, it could happen!

Then, as if there were something wrong with taking such obvious delight in their ace reporter, Goodwin grew serious. "She's Ronald Reagan after Jimmy Carter," he said, leaning forward thoughtfully, elbows on knees, chin in palms. "She's what the people want. She's relief from the oppressively technical predictions we'd gotten used to, relief from Louis Martin's moronic solemnity," he said, quoting Dan, even though Dan had pulled up a chair and was sitting right next to him.

"She could be wrong," Katie commented, "and," she added somewhat hesitantly, "her report cut into my time." She had gotten up, ostensibly to do something, but mostly to display herself full body. More and more, she was thinking that she had better capitalize on what she had.

"Wrong about what?" Russo asked, hardly seeming to see her, a sharp note of irritation in his voice. He was getting tired of Katie, of the envy he had begun to detect in everything she said. He turned away from her and toward Goodwin so that all she could see of him was his protruding paunch.

"About her predictions. Dramatization is an exaggeration of facts. By dramatizing the weather, she could misrepresent it," Katie said, grasping at straws.

"So what?" they exclaimed in unison.

That's a good question, Katie thought, as she retreated from the group and went to get her things together. So what? So what? she asked herself repeatedly as she drove over to City Hall, the answer to the question seeming to lie in its repetition. What if Claire were really wrong? What if there were some kind of disaster while she was spouting poetry? Would it make any difference? Would it be bad for Claire?

• • •

Katie's trip to Freddy's office was unannounced, and she knew he wouldn't like it. He never liked it when she popped in. He would probably keep her waiting just to show who was boss and to prove that he treated her the same as everyone else. Katie absolutely hated that. It wasn't the waiting that drove her nuts so much as the idea that she should be on an equal footing with the rest of the public and that Francine—Francine!—would be the one to decide when she would be admitted. Francine would be seated at her desk in the outer office, apparently absorbed in her work, apparently indifferent to Katie's presence, while Katie would be seated in the reception area immediately outside but in view of the outer office, apparently engrossed in a magazine, apparently indifferent to Francine's presence, each of them vying for greater indifference to the other, until, with a smug smile and a slight nod of the head, Francine would say, "The mayor will see you now."

On the occasion of her present visit, Katie was less impatient than usual. She was feeling insecure and wanted the reassurance of Freddy's support even if it meant spending ten minutes reading *Newsweek*. While she was waiting, her mind wandered back to the first time she had gotten protection. She had been working in a canning factory to pay her way through college when a position opened up on the factory floor. Another girl was in line for it, but Katie had been able to persuade the foreman of a different division of the factory to offer the girl a better job than the one in contention. The girl accepted, much to her later regret because, after the paperwork had been completed and she'd transferred to the other branch, it turned out that the job had been dependent on funding that hadn't come through. That experience taught Katie that it never hurt to have the big guns on your side. It certainly hadn't done her any harm at JTF. Not that Freddy had specifically said or done anything on her behalf, but everyone had noticed that when there was a pack of reporters thrusting mikes into his face, it was Katie's he spoke into. The favoritism worked for both of them. It gave Freddy the reassurance that, unlike the others, Katie wouldn't ask questions he couldn't answer, and it gave Katie a competitive edge. The edge had eventually become a springboard, and from it, she had risen to the anchor's job.

Predictably, Freddy was irritated that Katie had shown up unannounced and decided to add an extra seven minutes to the ten he usually made her wait. It looked better, and, as if minutes were stature, it helped counteract the feeling that he was diminished by her visits, as if he had nothing better to do than wait on her whenever she felt like dropping by. They were in his office on the second floor of Bridge Haven's city hall, a busy municipal building that had recently been constructed to replace the old one. Presumably, this newer structure had advantages over its predecessor, but except for the modern and well-lit ladies' room where you could actually see yourself in the mirror, Katie couldn't imagine what they were. The building's architect and interior decorator, if it had had one, seemed to have gotten together and, in an inspired moment, agreed on…light gray: everything was light gray—carpeting, walls, upholstery, room dividers, all gray. Perhaps, Katie mused, they were the result of one of those theories about the effect of color on behavior, in which case, she had to wonder, what behavior gray was supposed to produce.

"Did you see the state of the season address last night?" she asked as soon as she walked in to his office, as if the question were pressing enough to justify an unannounced visit. She kicked off her spike heels, power pumps she called them, and sank into his leather sofa, the one he used to soften people up.

Freddy looked momentarily confused. "You mean the weather report? Yeah, I saw it. Is that what she calls it?" he asked, wondering about the political overtones of the phrase and whether Claire Day was thinking of running for office.

"No, of course not. It's just that she strikes me as, I don't know, maybe kind of ambitious," Katie said.

"Ambitious? How so, ambitious?" He scratched his head but quickly removed his hand, remembering that the doctor had told him not to. He'd had a slight growth on his forehead removed and the scab had begun to itch.

"I don't know, something about her."

"You think she's bucking for your job?" he asked, hoping she wasn't bucking for his, but thinking that if wrestlers could be governors then meteorologists could be mayors. "Not likely," he answered his own question. "She's a meteorologist, not a news reporter. Pretty damn good one too."

"You think she's good?" Katie asked, a note of insecurity in her voice. Freddy pretended not to notice.

"Yeah, why not? I mean, what's wrong with her?" he asked. "She's just a little ditsy, that's all."

Katie got up and, walking around him to the back of his chair, massaged his shoulders. Once again, Freddy completely failed to understand her, and she was relieved. She could not function effectively if she was clearly understood; yet, that was the one thing he really did understand about her. Not only that, he respected it.

"You're right, you're right. I don't know what it is that bothers me about her," she pouted, her insincerity regained. "There's just something, I don't know, kind of arrogant about her."

"When I was a kid," he said, "and I would get into a fight, my mother always told me to give candy to the guy I was fighting with. 'Win him over,' she would say. My mother was a good politician. If she was alive today, God bless her," he crossed himself, "she could run for office." Freddy loved to reminisce about Mama and his boyhood in the Bronx, and Katie considered it part of her job to listen with polite interest. But this time her interest was genuine. Maybe Mama Coniglia was right: maybe she should try to befriend Claire.

"I just don't think she pays enough attention to the weather, what with all her poetry and everything. Suppose," she said, moving from behind his chair to the space between him and his large executive desk and rubbing her stockinged foot under the cuff of his trouser, "there was some really bad weather coming—I don't know, a drought or something—and she was busy reciting Shakespeare?"

"Dream on," said Freddy, eager to get off the subject of Claire and to talk about his campaign. He had been to the barber and looked younger to Katie. For some reason, men always reminded her of boys after they'd been to the barber. "First of all, we don't have that kind of weather in Bridge Haven. Second of all, that's not the real reason people watch her. She's not about the forecast." He was wearing a very dark navy blue suit, a very white, very starched shirt, and a red tie; he looked highly respectable, almost handsome. He was getting ready to make his next political commercial and he wasn't thinking about Claire Day. The only woman on his mind at the moment was Phyllis Boxer-Stanton, his opponent for the Republican nomination.

"Wait a minute," he said, and sat behind his desk, which had been cleared of everything except a blotter and a family photograph. "Tell me what you think of this," he said, leaning slightly forward and looking extremely earnest. "Hi. You know me. I'm Freddy Coniglia, and I've been Bridge Haven's Mayor for the past three years. Some of you may know me from the new gym at the high school, and others may know about me because of the new senior citizen center…"

"Aren't you going to mention Boxer-Stanton?" Katie asked when he had finished. He wagged his index finger in a negative gesture. "There's another ad for that. The incumbent only talks about his own record, never about his opponent's. Unless, of course, the opponent takes the lead. For now, I'm leaving her to the spinmeisters. Listen," he said as he opened a drawer and took out a tape recorder. A woman's voice—Freddy said it was important that it be a woman's voice—said, "Phyllis Boxer-Stanton blows hot and cold. Hot, she's for better schools; cold, she's doesn't know where she's gonna get the money to pay for them. Hot, she's for beefing up the police force; cold…"

Katie listened patiently. Image consulting was one of the two important services she performed for Freddy, and she wanted to do a good job so that he would continue to rely on her. But her heart wasn't really in it, and as soon as she'd made a couple of comments, just enough to let him know that she'd been paying attention, she exclaimed "Do you know what Goodwin said before? He said, and I quote, 'She's Ronald Reagan after Jimmy Carter. She's what the people want.'"

Freddy looked confused. He thought she was talking about his opponent. "It's much too early to make that kind of prediction," he said with obvious irritation. "The guy doesn't know what he's talking about."

"Not Boxer-Stanton," Katie said. *"Claire.* He was talking about *Claire.* He said 'she's what the people want,' Freddy. Think about that. 'What the people want.'"

"He said that?" Freddy asked, not knowing what to think. "Well, she's not what I want," he said, eyeing Katie lasciviously and moving in on her. "Too stuck up."

Fifteen minutes later, Katie tucked her blouse back in to her skirt, straightened it, and, pointing three fingers outward from her lips, blew him a kiss from his office door. Freddy hated that because the door was ajar and he was afraid Francine would see. Francine had eyes in the back of her head. She didn't miss a trick, and when you got right down to it, he thought chuckling inwardly at his mental pun, he was Katie's trick. But why was she being so flagrant? He crooked his index finger like a caterpillar and motioned her back inside his office, and then, with a forward gesture of his hand, indicated that she should close the door behind her.

"Jesus Katie, are you trying to ruin my reputation?"

"I have a reputation too, you know," she said, her color rising. Did he think his was the only reputation that could be damaged? But, the truth was that her indignation was reflexive, and she wasn't so sure about her reputation anymore. In fact, it was almost as if her reckless behavior, standing as she had with her body half out the door, was intended to prove that her reputation could withstand recklessness and that she still had enough power to take risks.

"Yeah, but your reputation, I mean…you have the reputation of…"

"Of what? Of what?" her voice had grown shrill, and Freddy, ever-vigilant and always conscious of Francine on the other side of the door, took hold of Katie's upper arm and walked her to the part of his office farthest from Francine, his grip pinching. Once they were standing by the window, he told her in a low voice that she had a reputation for being one terrific reporter and quite a looker besides. Others would be envious if they knew about the two of them, but, he added, looking toward the outer office—was that menace in his voice?—they couldn't know.

Freddy had come very close to calling Katie a slut, and she knew it. She hesitated. But not for long; she was in no position to end it with him, not yet. She might be needing his help pretty soon, and, in order of priority, she was more interested in finding a way to deal with Claire than in dumping Freddy. That was her first objective. Then, once Claire was discredited and she was on top again, she would see about him.

CHAPTER SIX

Claire was on the thruway. She had some of her best ideas while driving and sometimes got in the car specifically to plan her next report. She would make sure that she was thinking about the week ahead, turn on the radio, release the handbrake, step on the gas, and hope the juices would flow. At the moment, she was trying to think of a way to stretch her morning dew report into an entire series on humidity. She was also trying to find some good jazz. She was scanning the dial, up and down, but there was nothing but hip-hop and the tax cut. Suddenly she paused in her search for WBGO and listened more closely. Had she heard the reporter say Bridge Haven…or was she imagining things? She had been so preoccupied that she couldn't be sure. But yes, the radio reporter was talking about upcoming local elections in Bridge Haven.

Generally speaking, the voice was saying, few changes were expected, but with elections only a month away, Phyllis Boxer-Stanton was making unforeseen advances on the incumbent Freddy Coniglia. "Hey, that's my district," Claire said out loud, suddenly paying attention. According to Larry Johnson at 92.7, the all-that's-timely, all-the-time station, it was still an uphill battle for the Bridge Haven housewife who had never held public office and whose only real administrative experience was as president of the PTA. But she was effectively rebutting the criticism that she had no experience, and polls showed that she was making impressive gains, especially among women. Did her rival seriously believe—her campaign spokesman wanted to know—that raising five children and running a household was no experience? It was just that kind of experience, the deep sonorous voice of Larry Johnson quoted her as saying as Claire slowed down to listen more closely, that was important in a place like Bridge Haven, a bedroom community where people lived so that they could raise their children in a safe and secure environment with good schools.

"In the suburbs," it was Boxer-Stanton herself speaking now, her voice live, "real estate is about schools, and I'm talking about public schools. Perhaps my opponent does not recognize their importance as the basis for a strong community? If he does, I would like to know why he doesn't send his own children to them?" She paused. "Can it be that he doesn't think our schools are good enough?" Another pause. "If that's the case, why doesn't he do something to fix them?" Pregnant pause. "Who better than a mother," she went on, "who has been involved in the system as a parent, as a teacher, and as president of its PTA—who is better qualified than she"—a candidate with good grammar—"to determine what is really going on at the grassroots level and what is needed in the community as a whole?"

"Right on, Phyllis," Claire answered.

"In addition," the ambitious, articulate, and extremely self-assured housewife continued, "I have no debts to pay and no favors to return, and when I am elected," she was at her oratorical peak now, "I will act solely and exclusively in the interest of the community. My community.

The community I grew up in, and the community I raised my kids in."

"Okay," said Claire, "we get it."

But Boxer-Stanton wasn't finished—politicians never seemed to know when to stop talking—and went on to make the claim that it was a well known fact that her opponent was very much in the pocket of certain business interests in Bridge Haven. Claire gave a thrilled whoop, and Larry Johnson, who must have been even more delighted, saw his moment and pounced. Which business interests, Johnson wanted to know. By now, Claire had begun to lose her reception and had to raise the volume. Both the static and the voice of the intrepid Boxer-Stanton were extremely loud. The name DiMotta Contracting boomed into the car. "Could it be," the gutsy lady asked, "that Marie DiMotta Coniglia, wife to our Mayor Freddy Coniglia and sister to Artie and Vince DiMotta—co-owners and CEOs of DiMotta Contracting—had something to do with these awards?"

"Are you saying…" Larry Johnson's voice began and then disappeared into space.

CHAPTER SEVEN

The effect of Ms. Boxer-Stanton's accusations was not only felt in the car heading up the thruway, but also in the studios of JTF the following day, where word of the report was received with mixed response. Liebowitz was ecstatic because Freddy was a jackass and he hated guys like Freddy. He also hated Katie, who he saw as capable of hurting Claire, and he knew that an attack on Freddy was an attack on Katie. Russo's reaction could not be described as ecstatic, but he wouldn't have minded if Coniglia was replaced by someone with a little more class. He couldn't tell yet if Stanton-Boxer, or Boxer-Stanton (he really disliked names like that) was that person, but even though he and Coniglia got along, having someone like Freddy Coniglia as mayor made local news small-time, and Russo thought that, by association, it made him small-time too. Claire's celebrity had done a lot to change that, but as a man with a small Neanderthal forehead and a prognathic chin who had gotten low Cs at Boston College, Russo was afflicted with self-doubt, which his indirect but nonetheless important association with Freddy Coniglia had done little to discourage. Goodwin's reaction was more professional and less personal and was characterized by his usual sangfroid: basically, he didn't care what happened to Coniglia one way or the other so long as it was newsworthy. Since this little scandal had the potential of making news right up to and through the election, he was all for it.

Everybody had their own interest in what happened to the mayor, but it was Katie's reaction, at least as much as the fate of the mayor, that interested them most at the moment. That moment was not long in coming thanks to Michelle, the station's new makeup technician, who in all innocence, probably for the sake of making conversation, had already begun talking to Katie about the brewing scandal.

"I couldn't believe it, Ms. Connors. She was practically accusing him of being Mafia, or if not exactly Mafia, then of having ties. You know, his wife having a brother in contracting and all."

"What are you talking about, Michelle?" Katie asked absently, although the word "contracting" was grazing a neuron. Her mind was directed toward her upcoming report, and she wasn't paying much attention to Michelle, who had already impressed her as not worth listening to. Katie had somehow managed to talk the station into a thirty second promotional spot like CNN had done for Anderson Cooper, a kind of pastiche of her as conscientious reporter on the job, and it was in preparation for the final cut that she was getting her face dusted and her mind cleared.

"You know, yesterday, the radio interview with that woman, I can't remember her name, something with a dog in it," she said, adding more blush.

Dog…contracting…Boxer! "Are you talking about Boxer-Stanton? The woman running against the mayor?" Katie asked, violently grabbing the wrist of the hand brushing her face. "What did you hear?"

"Nothing," poor Michelle whimpered, suddenly afraid she had said something wrong. This was her first real job since graduating from Bridge Haven Community College, and she didn't want to lose it. Katie jumped up, pushed Michelle aside, and walked over to Dan, who was at his desk scanning the day's headlines. There were only two private offices at the station and they belonged to Goodwin and Russo. Everyone else, including Dan, had a cubbyhole.

"What's this about an interview with Boxer-Stanton?" she asked imperiously. She had just seen Freddy the day before and he hadn't said anything. This must have been breaking news.

Dan reluctantly raised his eyes from his papers, as if the question were interrupting his work. He looked at her slowly and appraisingly. "Have I told you how nice you look today? A little more sporty, less tailored perhaps, than usual. But I like it. You look like, I don't know, like a reporter."

"Dan!" she snapped his name like a military command.

Dan Liebowitz was considered genial and gentle by practically everyone who knew him, but he was as capable of malicious pleasure as the next man when provoked, and the ugly expression of outrage spreading across Katie's face, like an historical depiction of the pox moving across medieval Europe, was an awaited moment not to be dismissed as quickly as Katie had gotten rid of Michelle. He was taking aim, getting ready to fire his next salvo, but before he had the chance, she turned on her heel and stormed into Russo's office. Russo had just finished talking to his wife, Barbara, on the phone—they had been arguing about their phone bill (or almost arguing since he had decided to defer the brunt of his anger until he got home from work)—and was not at all receptive to an importunate female.

"Do you know anything about a radio interview with Boxer-Stanton?" the strident voice hurled itself from presumptuous Lancome lips into a hairy ear. Until a few months earlier, Russo had found Katie quite attractive and himself quite open to her flirtations; but for some time, ever since Claire had joined them actually, he had thought Katie looked different, less attractive, and he was much better able to resist her advances and withstand her assaults.

"Of course I know something. I'm in the news business. I get paid to know these things."

"Then how come I didn't know anything?" she asked, ignoring his sarcasm. He was in a bad mood, first his wife and now Katie; but, to his credit, he did not lose his temper and was able to achieve moderate self-restraint. "Hey, who's the reporter here? You or me?"

"Who's got the ratings, you or me?" she shot back, defending herself against imagined attack, her mind an exposed wire electrifying everything it came into contact with. She was terrified that Freddy might go down the tubes, and that she, in the wake of his downfall, would follow and sink into obscurity. The sudden, unforeseen possibility that her plans might founder or be dashed on the rocks of Bridge Haven's parochial shores was making her hysterical. She had been so focused on Claire, so intent on re-establishing her own importance and diminishing Claire's, that she hadn't even considered that something else might go wrong.

"What's the matter Katie?" Goodwin walked into the room and sat down. He was wearing a brightly colored tie with grinning cartoon characters on it, but although Mickey and Minnie Mouse looked happy enough, Goodwin himself was not in a good mood and, unlike Russo, was showing no inclination toward temperance. He had just come from a hair transplant session, and Katie's voice felt exactly like another needle stabbing at his brain. "Feeling a little bit threatened by a possible change in regime, are you?" he asked. Katie had no ready answer. She suddenly realized that her reaction to the interview with Boxer-Stanton was overstated and that she was on a very unsure footing. "Don't be silly," she stammered. "I just like to know what's going on," she added as flippantly as possible.

As soon as she had closed the door, Goodwin quoted her: "'I just like to know what's going on,' my ass. She's just afraid that her mike might lose its preferred spot by the mayor's mouth, or perhaps more to the point, that his mike might lose its preferred spot in her mouth."

Russo was surprised. He had always thought of Goodwin as having a kind of Lutheran reserve and a dry wit, which could occasionally become quite acerbic but was never even remotely sexual, and the comment added a whole new dimension to Goodwin's personality.

CHAPTER EIGHT

The mayor's office was in an uproar. Each of the lines on Freddy's telephone was lit up. Francine informed him that his wife was on one, his brother-in-law Artie was on two, the deputy mayor was on three, Katie was on four, his other brother-in-law Vince was on five, and his aunt was on six. And the phone was ringing. He pressed two.

"Yeah, Artie, of course I heard. No, there's nothing to worry about. What do you mean, how do I know? If she had anything…look, this is not something we should be talking about on the telephone. Come over later. Vince, too. After dinner."

That was all Francine heard, or thought she heard. It was hard to tell. Usually, she heard most of the mayor's conversations, even when his door was closed. It was rather annoying, actually, especially when she was trying to concentrate. His loud, boisterous voice, a voice constantly asserting more authority than she thought it had earned, would part the panels of her lace curtain mind and intrude like a gust of air disturbing her neatly ordered thoughts. The old city hall had heavy soundproofed doors, which the building's architects, in their infinite wisdom, decided to replace with particleboard when the building was renovated, and the new ones let every sound penetrate, except now, of course, that she wanted to hear what was being said.

Even if she couldn't actually make out every word, Francine could practically always hear the murmur of conversation, but this time there was complete silence. The reason was that the mayor was experiencing shortness of breath and had abruptly gotten off the phone. He didn't have asthma or emphysema; but every now and then, when he was under pressure, he would start hyperventilating, and whenever that happened, he would stop what he was doing, try to relax, and engage in deep, diaphragmatic breathing. He had an inhaler a pulmonary specialist had given him once, but since there wasn't really anything wrong with his lungs, those quick little inhalations just made his heart race. He had also tried yoga, which everyone said was good for tension, but he felt ridiculous sitting cross-legged on a pillow saying ommmmm, and, on top of that, he resented the intrusion of Eastern culture into American life. It was altogether too light, airy, and rice papery for his taste. Tofu and tai chi, too trendy, he thought; he was 100 percent Western male, hearty if not exactly hale, and fundamentally, he didn't believe in peace of mind. When he stopped being mayor, he was going to open a steak house, red meat for red-blooded Americans, he had already decided on that, and if it weren't for the possibility that he might become a restaurateur a lot sooner than he intended, he wouldn't even have been upset at the thought of leaving office. But this was not just about re-election anymore, he thought, taking a deep breath into his diaphragm, not his chest, so that his belly became extended and round: this was about the difference between a third term and a jail term.

He took a few more calls and smoothed ruffled feathers, but in the process of calming others, he got nervous again himself, especially since he wasn't sure what to tell people. He decided not to say anything else until he spoke to his lawyer, Joel Hirshenbaum, and gave Francine strict instructions to say that he was in conference. Francine was more than willing to conspire with the mayor because she felt empowered by collusion, especially when he gave her arm a little squeeze and told her to keep Katie waiting. But Joel had left on vacation the night before and wasn't likely to get back to him for a while, which left Freddy in the awkward position of pretending to be busy while the phone in the outer office rang off the hook. It was almost three hours before Joel finally called, and then all he had to say was not to talk to anybody until he came back. Three hours playing monopoly and that was all Hirsh had to say. It didn't matter; the point was appearances, business as usual. Freddy had to be careful not to communicate the wrong message. Looking nervous would communicate the wrong message and leaving early would too. So did his car, he suddenly realized, as he got to his parking place by the entrance to City Hall and looked at his shiny new Lexus through the eyes of someone who might think that a car like that cost too much for a local politician's salary. Now that he had come under attack, everything looked suspicious. He'd have to use his son's Taurus till this thing blew over, although that meant he would have to let Fred Jr. drive the Lexus, which was an idea that he hated. But his wife, Marie, didn't drive and their only other car was the Taurus, so what else could he do? Maybe he should lease.

He made a point of spending the entire day in his office, appearing too occupied with affairs of state to busy himself with petty politics, and in contrast to his usual practice of leaving the office a few minutes early, he left for home thirteen minutes after Francine had gone, mentally allowing her five minutes to stop and chat, another five to get to her car, and another three for good measure. He had originally planned to leave fifteen minutes after her but was too impatient to wait the extra two minutes. On his way out, just to show that he wasn't in any rush, he lingered at the water cooler and talked to various people before eventually heading to his car where, oh shit, a small group of reporters was waiting for him. He couldn't believe it. Just when he thought he had made a clean get away, the vultures appeared. He walked right through the little group, waved off the questions coming at him, hurriedly got into his car and pulled out of the lot, driving past Bridge Haven's courthouse, an extension of City Hall, to State Street. Then, even though he had waited all day to leave, he took a circuitous route home, dreading the moment of arrival and the grilling he was going to get. It wasn't that Marie was the kind of wife who nagged him the minute he walked in the door or questioned him about his job. Fact was she hardly took any interest in his work at all, assuming that, as mayor, he knew what he was doing and that, as brother-in-law, he would naturally favor family over strangers. That was so long as things went smoothly; but now that there were charges of impropriety, she would certainly want to know what was going on, and he didn't know what he should say. And even Hirshie couldn't help him with that, although maybe he should just follow Hirshie's usual advice and deny, deny, deny.

Freddy drove around his neighborhood—down Central, up Livingston, around Magnolia and Cornell Drive, and back to Central—running the whole thing through his mind. His neighborhood was in the nice part of town, and he stayed pretty much within its borders, making sure to avoid streets leading to the downtown section, which, despite some renewal, was still bleak and depressing. True, the areas near the mall and the Payless ShoeSource were looking slightly better thanks to a couple of new restaurants; but even if the appellation urban blight was no longer strictly speaking accurate, Bridge Haven was still a sad place without much history or current attraction. In the twenty years that Freddy had lived there, the demographics had shifted, and although there were still Blacks in the Flats, the Jews and Irish had moved out and a bunch of Dominicans and Bolivians—of all things—had moved in. The Dominicans lived near the southbound side of the train station, and the Bolivians, unmistakable in their bowler hats, had moved to its northbound side. But except for the gardeners, household help, and construction workers who'd gotten jobs at the plant by the thruway, the other people who lived downtown were unemployed malingerers. Freddy couldn't stand unemployment, and he resented these people who prevented him from representing a place with a good reputation. Still…he was the mayor of all the people.

 He leaned back, hung his left arm over the steering wheel so that he was driving with his wrist, while his right arm extended over the top of the passenger seat. But he couldn't pretend to be at ease, and after a couple of minutes of punk swagger, he stopped trying to relax and gripped the wheel with both hands. Accusations of dishonesty would devastate Marie if she believed them, or inspire her to action if she thought they were false, and both reactions were problematic. It would not, actually, be too bad for his image if his wife were up in arms about "politically motivated" charges and was seen as leading a counter-attack, but if it came out that he had allowed her to embarrass herself, knowing all the while that he was guilty of cronyism and racketeering, it wouldn't be too good for their marriage. On the other hand, if the truth came out, it wouldn't be too good for their marriage anyway, so…Freddy hadn't worked it all out in his mind yet, what he was going to say to her, but he was leaning heavily in the direction of flat out denial. If the whole thing blew over, there would have been no point in telling the truth, and if he was found out, he could always beg her forgiveness. Contrition had been very effective in the past, and even though it was only minor transgressions that he'd been forgiven, he might still be able to win her around if he worked at it long enough. And then again, in the event that Marie bolted, there was always Katie waiting in the wings, although she probably wouldn't be waiting if he wasn't mayor.

CHAPTER NINE

The problem of what to tell Marie was solved by the presence of two black Mercedes in his driveway, or to be more accurate, by the presence of two cars whose owners, Artie and Vince, must have been inside his house. Their cars were not parked on the sidewalk, as respect and courtesy would have dictated, nor were they parked front to back, which would have left one garage door accessible; but they were planted side by side where, like two highly developed forearms crossed over a chest striated with menacing ripples of muscle, they blocked the entrance to his garage.

It had been Freddy's own idea that Artie and Vince come over, but he'd forgotten that he had suggested it until he saw their cars in his driveway. Then, when he remembered, he also remembered that he'd said they should come after dinner. Typical, this was typical thug behavior. Knowing them, he had to assume that they'd gone to his house early for the express purpose of letting him know that their cars were like a dispossession notice, and that if he got them into trouble, his driveway would be permanently blocked. It seemed like everybody was trying to get rid of him.

He inhaled deeply. He was scared shitless that everything he had worked for, or rather everything he had been involved in, would go up in smoke and that he would end up poor and disgraced, although disgraced was more likely than poor thanks to a Caribbean bank account and Marie's money. Unless Marie decided to dump him—which could happen because she was very much under her brothers' influence and they could make her do what they wanted. Freddy was also under their thumb since DiMotta money had financed his first run, which had been very expensive and would take a lifetime to repay. It seemed a bit unfair since they had persuaded him to run in the first place. Not only that, they had persuaded him to mount an expensive campaign since a cheap campaign—given his lack of bona fides and considering the high cost of politics—would not be worth running. But, they had said, after a few years as mayor he could run for the next office up. Which office was that? Congressman? Big-time starts small-time, they had said, encouraging Freddy's ambition, which, thanks in large part to their flattery, had grown at inverse proportion to his accomplishment. Two years as alderman, they said, wasn't going to cut it. He was going to need money… a…lottta…money.

"Consider it a loan," they had said, and even though he had never actually agreed to run, they treated the matter as if it was settled and raised their glasses to his campaign. The gesture was somewhat intimidating because it took so much for granted. Doubt, debate, and suitability had all been swallowed in a mouthful of Asti Spumante. What was he supposed to do—tell them to lower their glasses while he thought things over? Not swallow until he gave the matter further consideration? Even on the level of bonhomie and celebration, they made Freddy cower inside, as if their largesse would hurt him.

After he became mayor, his self-image changed, and he began to think of himself as an exalted man of the world and them as despised men of the underworld who should surface as infrequently as possible. That was fine with them because they had no interest in being known anyway, and to the contrary, it had taken the appearance of their names in the papers to smoke them out of their garish Port Chester homes.

Freddy Jr., who, gangly, pimply, and sardonic, seemed to have become a full-blown teenager overnight, met his father in their driveway and said, "Uncle Artie and Uncle Vince are here."

"Could've fooled me. I thought those were your friends' Mercedes." What was the point of coming in two cars anyway? Their houses were less than three blocks apart. Maybe they preferred to travel like a funeral cortege, one car behind the other, he shuddered.

"Yeah, those guys are really mafia manqué, aren't they?" said Fred Jr. Freddy didn't answer because he wasn't sure he knew what that meant. At least his kid was getting a good education, a good parochial school education, he thought, slightly unsettled by the idea that his son might know more than he did.

Marie had not been expecting her brothers and looked at Freddy searchingly when he walked in the door. "I'll tell you later," he said without stopping, as he walked through the kitchen and into the living room. Neither Artie nor Vince acknowledged him. Vince was pacing and Artie was sitting, and both were frowning. Freddy decided to frown too, even though he always had a strong temptation to placate and humor them. Fuck it, he thought, there's no reason for them to get all bent out of shape when, so far, it's only me taking the heat.

It was Vince who started. "Looks like we got trouble."

"Could be," said Freddy, pouring himself a drink. He was hoping that they were expecting a different response from him and that he could throw them off course by agreeing, which, considering that the course they were on was designed to trammel him, seemed like a good idea.

"Do you think she knows anything? This Boozer-Stanton?"

"Boxer, not Boozer. I'm the boozer," Freddy laughed, holding up his drink and practically tripping over a basket of pine cones, an idea Marie had gotten from a Ralph Lauren catalogue.

"Whatever."

"I don't know what she knows," Freddy said, sitting in a recently re-upholstered hunter green armchair, also Ralph Lauren. Ralph Lauren was everywhere; he was even in bed with them: plaid sheets. A ménage à trois, Fred Jr., with his fricking French, had said.

"She's the opposition. She doesn't take me into her confidence. The only thing I know for certain is that she's smart enough to make unsubstantiated charges. If we don't respond to them—and I have no intention of responding—" Freddy paused, looking from one to the other, "and if they don't investigate," he paused again, "then there's nothing to worry about." Freddy was tired and wished they would go away. He hadn't even had time to get out of his work clothes, and his pants, which were unbuttoned beneath his loose shirt, were still too tight. His doctor had told him to lay off the pasta, that he was too short to carry so much weight, but just because he was short didn't mean he didn't like to eat. Life was beginning to seem very unfair.

"A lot of ifs, if you ask me," said Vince, the buttonholes of his tapered black shirt opening and closing like the mouths of fish every time he breathed.

"I don't think it's so iffy," said Artie, leaning forward in his chair. "I think it's almost certain that she'll investigate." His slacks were all bunched up in front of him, and Freddy wondered why his brothers-in-law always wore such tight-fitting shirts and such loose-fitting pants. "Look how far she's gotten with this stuff so far. A few days ago, nobody had ever heard of her. Now, she's in all the papers. If she dropped it now, she'd be the one looking bad instead of you. She has no choice; she's got to pursue it."

"You got a point there, Artie," Vince chimed in. "She's going to dig like a cat, and then she's going to find all kinds of shit."

Between the two, Artie was the smarter, and although Freddy always started by addressing both of them, he almost always ended by talking to Artie. "Yeah, I agree. She's got to pursue it a bit, but unless she has grounds for a criminal investigation—which I don't think she has—then she'll raise questions and raise eyebrows and leave it at that. That's all she really needs anyway to attract attention to herself, which is what this is all about." He looked from one to the other again, a technique he had learned in a training session on how to give effective presentations. Eye contact, the guy had said, try to remember everyone's name and make eye contact. But he couldn't make eye contact with Marie's brothers because they never looked back; so he looked at them without making eye contact, and when he did, he was always struck by how much they looked alike. All three of them, actually, Marie included, looked like their father: same hazel eyes, same crooked noses, same kinky hair, same everything. They could have been triplets.

"How do you know she doesn't have grounds for a criminal investigation?"

"Look, I issued an RFP and everyone had a chance to bid. Bids came in and bids were sealed. How was I supposed to know," Freddy asked, forearms out, palms upward, and shoulders hunched in feigned perplexity, "that yours would come in lowest?" They all smirked at each other.

"I'm not talking about construction," said Artie, crossing and uncrossing his legs. "I'm talking about collections."

"Yeah, collections." Freddy said, forming a bridge with his fingertips. "Like I said, it's a question of evidence. So long as there's no paper trail… did you leave a paper trail?"

"I write everything in here," Vince pointed to his temple.

"Well since your memory's for shit," Artie knocked Vince upside the head, "we're on pretty safe ground."

"No bookkeeping?" Freddy asked again.

"Not exactly what you'd call bookkeeping," Artie equivocated, his eyes averted. Freddy thought he was lying. "You know," Artie went on, "scraps—this person's address or that person's number. Maybe the occasional name and date, but nothing you could call evidence."

"Burn it," said Freddy. "Go home and build yourself a little bonfire. Get rid of it, all of it, all that stuff. All they have to do is call one of the numbers on those scraps, and…well, I don't have to tell you. "

"Yeah, well," said Vince, lamely trying to re-establish their advantage, "you better just hope it don't get that far."

Freddy didn't say that it wouldn't have gotten that far if it had never gotten started to begin with. In other words, if they hadn't lied to him from the start. If they hadn't told him that money was no object, he would never have agreed to run in the first place; if they hadn't led him to believe that they would finance his campaign, no strings attached, he would have stayed with the plumbing business. But they had lied, and after he had won the election, they explained that money was no object because it was *the* object. Hey, whatever happened to "money is no object," he had asked, and they had answered, nothing, nothing had happened to it because they had plenty of it, but that didn't mean it was free. Freddy didn't really think they were giving it away, did he, they laughed, slapping him on the back. Anyway, they had said, he shouldn't worry about it because they knew he didn't have cash, and they would find other ways for him to repay the "loan." The other ways were what was getting him in trouble with Boxer-Stanton and the reason they were in his living room.

• • •

And they were also what was getting Katie frustrated because she was dying to know the specifics of those other ways and needed to talk to Freddy. Instead, he was blowing her off, blowing her off after all the blow jobs, the little cocksucker. The DiMotta brothers might have planted Freddy in office, but she had done a lot of the gardening—a lot of the watering, tilling, and pruning of Freddy's performance—and it seemed to her only fair that she should have his ear now. Instead, it was several days before Freddy was willing to see her, and then it was only on condition that they meet in an out-of-the-way place where he wouldn't be recognized.

Katie was very eager for the meeting, although now that she might be in a position to get the scoop on the hottest story around, the one that would establish her as a solid reporter and not merely a scripted anchor, the story that would make her segment of the news more interesting than Claire's and silence all her detractors, she wasn't sure how to go about it. Maybe she should let JTF's new beat reporter, Jason Fremd, ask the tough questions while she provided the commentary. She certainly had no intention of becoming the Linda Tripp of journalism, the woman who ratted on her "friend," the mayor, she thought, as she zipped up Route 1 in her Volvo Sport. Above all, the important thing was to get the story. Once she knew the facts, she would figure out what to do with them. If they looked bad enough to bring Freddy down, she would ask him for an exclusive interview with the promise that they would work together on how to spin it. If, on the other hand, it looked like he might be able to squirm out of the mess he was in, then they could talk about strategies for keeping him in office. Either outcome could be made to work for her, if she handled it right.

Freddy was waiting in the rest area next to the Mobil station off Round Hill Road where it intersected with Route 1 near Fairfield. It took Katie a moment to spot him. His head was tucked inside a newspaper, which was all the space left him by the steering wheel of the Taurus he was driving, and he was wearing sunglasses and a baseball cap. All in all he looked like a parody of a criminal in disguise. Freddy couldn't do anything without being in a role, which was probably one of the reasons he had become a more successful mayor than anyone had expected: he had an idea about who and what a mayor was and he played the part. Authenticity in politics was hogwash, he believed, and anyone who thought it was any different hadn't had representation since Jimmy Carter equivocated his way through the presidency. Before Freddy got elected, he hadn't given any thought to what kind of mayor he wanted to be; but once in office, he discovered that his ideas about honesty were mostly sentimental and that his ideas about corruption were mostly practical, which meant that he practiced corruption and sentimentalized honesty and, all in all, was perfectly suited to office.

Getting in on the passenger side and feeling amused by his get-up, Katie said, "You don't have to wear a disguise, Freddy. You're not exactly a fugitive on the run."

"Not yet. They're watching everything I do. I shouldn't even be here with you. In fact, let's get out of here." He tried putting the car in reverse, but the gearshift was hard to maneuver. "Damn car," he muttered, tugging on the stick. There were CDs all over the seats and floor, and the ashtray was stuffed with cigarette butts.

"Hmm, what have we here?" said Katie inspecting the glove compartment. She removed a pair of g-string bikinis and a torn Trojan wrapper. "Looks like Fred Junior—this is Junior's car, isn't it?—is a chip off the old block." Freddy smirked. It was the only time during the past few days, ever since what's-her-name had started making her accusations, that he'd had a lighter moment.

They were driving past large concrete sound barriers that were supposed to protect the communities bordering the thruway. Freddy could never understand why anyone would build right next to a thruway anyway. It was one thing if the house was already there and they built the thruway afterward, but to build the house right at the edge of a six-lane highway didn't make any sense. The sound barrier was followed by open road with not much next to it until they came to a large development of light blue clapboard houses with white trim, sky lights, and lots of stairs leading to and from decks. Quite nice really. If the development had been somewhere else and the houses hadn't been all the same, you could actually imagine living in one of them. But their sameness had a numbing quality. Freddy wondered what it would be like to know that you were no different from your neighbors, to be completely ordinary, to have a mortgage to pay and medical insurance to worry about; in other words, to live like his constituents. His parents had lived in a row house in the Bronx, but that was different somehow, maybe because there was a community there. This was the middle of nowhere and kind of depressing. Still, it might not be so bad. It might be better than having goons like Artie and Vince breathing down your neck and getting hounded by the press.

The thought brought it all back to him and he started to breathe heavily. He tried inhaling diaphragmatically, but his bowels were beginning to feel loose and he was afraid he might have an attack of diarrhea added to his shortness of breath. He took the closest exit and swung into another gas station. Katie was surprisingly quiet through all of this. That was fine because he wasn't supposed to talk to her anyway. Hirschenbaum had told him to avoid even the slightest appearance of impropriety, and that—Hirsch had to spell it out for him because Freddy didn't really think that sex counted—included mistresses, past and present.

He went up to the counter of the utility store inside the gas station, got the key to the men's room, a blue-for-boys key hanging on a block of wood, and raced around to the side of the station where the toilets were located. He was still pulling on his belt buckle when he got back to the car, his pants slightly bunched at the waist, a small wet spot at the bottom of his fly. The spot was a visible sign of vulnerability and revolted Katie.

His little physical imperfections, the way he never noticed residual food on his face or the fact that ear wax prevented a certain kind of intimacy, had not really bothered her as long as he had been clearly in charge and his power uncontested. Then his imperfections even lent him a certain charm. But if power is like make-up for men and enhances a man's appearance, then vulnerability is like a strong astringent and shows things as worse than they are by magnifying every little flaw. As long as he was mayor, the spot on his pants was endearing moisture proving that even the most illustrious of men were flesh and blood like the rest of us; but if he ceased to be mayor, then his wet spot would just be the residual piss of a sloppy man. Back on the thruway, Freddy noticed forsythia and trees the tender green of early spring. It made him feel emotional, like he wanted to cry. In a rare gesture of tenderness, he took Katie's left hand in his own and held it in his lap as he drove. She wanted information, not emotion, but she left her hand there for a while in the hope it would eventually produce more than perspiration.

It did. Without prompting, without any cunning on her part, he started talking with what seemed like abandon about the injustice of his situation. He talked, Katie listened, waiting to hear what was unjust, waiting to hear how his opponent was making wild and irresponsible statements that would get her into trouble when he accused her of running a smear campaign and of making unsubstantiated charges. But he never got to it, never said exactly what was unfair. Mostly his emphasis was on everything he'd done as mayor and how people should count their lucky stars that they had someone in office who knew how to get things done. The new senior center, for example, was going to really make a difference to a lot of people. And then there was Meals on Wheels and the

Welcome Wagon, both programs he'd turned into very smooth-running operations, even if he hadn't introduced them. And hadn't he been in support of drug and alcohol programs in the schools, given the department of community mental health the go-ahead to place a counselor in the middle and upper schools?

Katie didn't interrupt, didn't say that his record wasn't the issue, but was smart enough to realize that if he'd been innocent, she would have known it by now. Little by little, evidence was accumulating, a picture was forming, and the verdict, not long in coming, was guilty: Freddy was guilty as charged, guilty as sin, guilty as anyone whose only qualification for office was a wife with rich and powerful brothers. Not that Katie had ever really doubted his guilt, but she had forgotten that he didn't know what people thought and that he would be trying to project a certain image. He was actually working very hard at it and had begun to think that by talking about matters unrelated to the accusations against him, he had succeeded in distracting Katie, that, figuratively speaking, he had driven by the wreck of his collision with Boxer-Stanton without even stopping. If he could talk about matters of indifference, according to this strategy, then it might be because the possibility of guilt was out of the question, hors de question, as Freddy Jr. once astounded him by saying. It had even occurred to him that one of the ironies of his situation was that he had finally become a very good politician who had mastered the art of double-talk and that, in a perverse twist of fortune, this might be his finest hour.

That was what he thought until Katie said "Listen, hon, I can help you with this."

Help him? Help him?! Who said anything about needing help? The statement totally threw him. It rattled him, and if he'd been in a position to get angry, it would have pissed him off too. Help him, the nerve! He sped along the thruway without responding, confused and irritated. He didn't know what to say to her. Was she bluffing, or had he fooled himself into thinking that he was giving a persuasive performance when in fact it was an obvious act, so obvious that she had simply and tactfully ignored it? He drove past a couple of lights and then turned left onto a road running past a large industrial park of glass and steel, a few cars in its lot, not a soul in sight. Who worked in these places anyway? he half-grumbled to himself. Shrubbery surrounded the parking lot, and Freddy saw what looked like a small, furry animal waddle away into its porous wall of leaves. It was either a beaver or a mole, he couldn't tell which. Skunks, raccoons, squirrels, mice, and rats he could recognize, but there was this other group of little animals—beavers, moles, otters, and hedgehogs—he couldn't identify. It seemed like he couldn't identify people either because he'd attended a meeting in one of these buildings a couple of years ago, but all he could remember about it was two trays, one of bagels and the other of muffins, and a stainless steel thermos/pitcher of coffee. That was it, not a single human being came to mind.

He was getting hungry. "Let's find something to eat," he suggested, realizing as he said it that he had ignored her last statement, just as she had ignored what he was saying earlier. But Katie decided to persevere, and once they were installed at IHOP, she said it again. "I can help you with this." A family in the next booth was extremely audible and enthusiastic in their examination of the menu, and the words blueberry blintzes kept making their way across the partition dividing their stalls.

"What makes you think I need help?"

Katie leaned forward, her freckled chest, blotchy with emotion, visible above the top button of her blouse. "Because you're under attack, Sherlock. Look, I'm not asking you to tell me anything, I'm just saying that when a gun is pointed at your head, it doesn't matter whether you're guilty or innocent: if you want to stay alive, you either duck or shoot."

Freddy liked what he was hearing. It meant that he wouldn't have to project an image of innocence with her. There was a big difference between discretionary lying in the service of power and defensive lying in the pathetic hope of preventing another turn of the screw; and he was not very good at the second, except when it came to Marie. No, this was much better: he was being hunted and that was all that mattered. He was a hunted animal, wounded, lame, retreating in search of succor, a civil servant who had made some poor decisions, perhaps, but overall a decent guy and effective politician with the public interest at heart. He felt such immediate relief that he decided to order buckwheat pancakes with bacon instead of the more nutritious, less caloric fruit platter IHOP had recently added to their menu. There were several syrup options in the middle of their table and, after a moment of debate, he decided on maple, tried-and-true maple. It was how he was feeling about Katie, too: tried-and-true Katie, his friend. He was actually a little surprised by her because, up until that moment, he hadn't known that they were real friends and would have expected her to act more like a reporter than like someone who actually cared about his well-being.

"Go on," he said expectantly.

"You have to protect yourself, but you can't do it by going on the defensive or by attacking," she said, and now he really appreciated her because she had figured out the problem without his ever saying a word.

"Your only alternative," she continued, "is a diversionary tactic."

This was interesting, very interesting, he thought, trying to imagine a tactic. Maybe he could arrange a diagnosis of prostate cancer. It was debilitating but not necessarily deadly, and, unlike Giuliani, he could soldier on. He could create a fund, bring prostate cancer to greater public awareness, like Dole had done for impotence. It seemed like the penis was making a comeback, only it was an older and somewhat defeated penis, limp and ailing, in need of medical attention. Maybe he could even get people to walk for prostate cancer; in Manhattan they walked for gay pride and AIDS, why couldn't they walk for prostate cancer in Bridge Haven? Prostate pride, they could call it. It might even be good for real estate. He'd have to be careful of the real estate angle though, especially if it involved any contracting jobs, he thought with some amusement.

"Remember the first Gulf War?" Katie was asking. "What do you think that was really all about?"

"Oil?" Freddy asked tentatively, feeling dumb because, as a politician, he thought he should know these things. Tip O'Neill had said that all politics is local politics, and Freddy, who fully agreed without fully understanding, had distorted the statement to mean that global politics was hardly worth his attention. As a consequence, he had very few ideas beyond Bridge Haven.

"Oil? C'mon Freddy. I mean oil figured, of course—this country is not about to forfeit its energy supplies—but it was really no more about oil than about Kuwait." Her piercing eyes were like drills boring into the dry, oil-free field of his brain. "The government had people spinning it to look like it was about oil because that was an explanation that went down easily and flattered the public into thinking it was savvy and had true understanding—that it hadn't been duped by the Kuwait explanation." Freddy was fascinated. The chorus of blintz, blintz coming from the next booth kept transmuting into blitz, blitz as he listened to her.

"The Gulf War," she said slowly and with complete authority and conviction, "was a distraction from the Savings and Loan scandal, the biggest and least examined financial trespass against the American people in our history." She paused for effect. "I mean, I'm no Clinton fan," she said, having steadfastly refused to consider the possibility that she and the mere intern Monica had anything in common, "but next to the Savings and Loan scandal, I mean, Whitewater? A monetary drip compared to the financial flood of the Savings and Loan, and yet Whitewater, piddling and pathetic as it was, got a whole lot more play in the press. I mean, come on, why?"

"Where do you get this stuff?" Freddy asked, full of admiration.

"Hey, I'm a reporter, " Katie said as if she had personally developed the theory instead of getting it from Dan Liebowitz, whom she had accused of paranoia when, in an inspired moment, he had passed it by the office staff. At the time, she had thought it was the kind of thing a Jewish intellectual like Dan would come up with, but now, in Freddy's Catholic company, it made a lot of sense. And, in addition, it served her. "The Savings and Loan scandal cost every single tax-payer, I forget the exact number, but think of it, every one of us paid for it. How could we have let a thing like that go so unnoticed and so unpunished? Why didn't it dominate the headlines for years on end?" she asked, now on a roll. "I mean here was this major scandal perpetrated by Jeb Bush, among others, and covered up by his father, our President, George Bush," her eyes were big and round, open to maximum aperture so they could take it all in and let it all out, "and yet…" she held up both hands, palms up, palm empty, as if to say, what happened, where'd it go. "It was a huge scandal, at least it would have been if they hadn't concealed it so effectively. It was so big they needed something even bigger to distract the public, and that was when the Gulf War began. What better way to distract the public than with a war? Not only that, it had the added benefit of turning criticism into support. As I recollect," she said, recalling Dan's diatribe against the Bush administration, "Bush's ratings were at an all-time high after the war."

"His son's too," Freddy observed contemplatively, as he considered the positive advantages of subterfuge

The waitress came around with their orders, and when Freddy saw his pancakes piled high, light brown saucers with golden rims, his mood, already improved, just kept on getting better. "Well, this is all very interesting," he said, after taking a big bite, the syrup leaking from his mouth, "but I'm not sure what it has to do with me. Do you think that Bridge Haven should wage war on Stamford?" he grinned, his next bite poised midway to his mouth, "That would be a novel approach to local politics. Nuke 'em!" He roared with laughter, starting to pound his fist on the table, but he stopped quickly, realizing from Katie's wan smile that this was neither the time for humor nor the moment to attract attention to himself.

She waited for him to calm down, for the gravity of his situation to re-establish itself, restored by her serious expression and by her refusal to respond until his mirth had become his misery again. "Maybe something a little less drastic," she said at last, her gaze level, her voice deliberate, almost conspiratorial, the rim of lipstick on her coffee mug like evidence.

"Do you have something in mind?" he asked, suddenly feeling as if everything had been leading up to this question. It was a seamless transition, and he had no idea how it had taken place, but he knew that he was less comfortable than he had been only a jocular moment earlier, as he realized that his question had been a request for help, that he had been asking Katie for help. How had she done that? How had she brought that about? He had to give her credit: the woman was a born manipulator. She should have been the politician, he thought, despondent again, as the pump she had used to inflate him was suddenly removed and his inflated spirits sagged.

For Katie, too, it was a critical moment. She'd done so well up to this point. She didn't want to blow the whole thing, and there was a real risk of that since Freddy smelled opportunism as quickly as a deer hears hunters. "I don't have anything in mind," she half-lied into her coffee cup, since a scheme, still in its formative stage, wasn't ready for presentation yet. "I just think that you need to divert the public's attention away from…" and here she paused, reluctant to use the word scandal. "I just think that you need to redirect the public's attention—" she recapitulated, intentionally correcting herself out loud so that he could see her sensitivity at work—"toward something else. Something that requires you to play a major role."

CHAPTER TEN

Murray was on the terrace of his apartment where a pleasant summer breeze was enhancing his good mood. It was August and warm enough so that he could stand on his terrace still wet from his morning shower. He loved the exclusivity of it. How many people, he asked himself daily, had the good fortune of enjoying their morning coffee under an umbrella eighteen floors above Park Avenue? How many people could say that? As a rule, he got up early, around 5:30 and, weather permitting, had breakfast outside. Every swallow of freshly squeezed orange juice and freshly brewed coffee had the purifying effect of quality, and he frequently looked down on the street and then up at the sky so that God would know what he was referring to as, palms raised, he said, "Thank you, thank you, thank you." He had lived well for years, but he had never grown complacent and had never taken his good fortune for granted, unlike, truth be told, his beloved wife and daughter. He was lucky; they were spoiled. But if that meant they had never known hardship, he preferred it that way.

And from the look of it, with the new account he'd just been given—a big complicated case with lots of rancor and billable hours—he might just be able to keep this thing afloat a while longer. It would certainly pay for their tenth, a blowout weekend in Paris culminating in the Eiffel Tower bursting into light at midnight. Someone told him that you could have the tower lit up for yourself if you were willing to foot the bill, and that's what he intended to do, to surprise Judy with a huge eruption of light. He would bring a bottle of Dom Perignon and two champagne flutes, and just as he was toasting her, the tower would come to life. It might be a bit extravagant, but as far as he was concerned, they had every reason to be proud. Ten years of marriage was nothing to sneeze at—a strange expression, he thought—and if he wanted to celebrate and show it off, that seemed to him his right. The only possible reason to avoid exultation was superstition; the moment you proclaimed yourself, especially if you did it very loudly, you were probably in for trouble. Both he and Judy were superstitious and believed in hubris, in the dire consequences of overstepping; and the question, which no one except maybe Judy could answer for you, was whether the boundaries of hubris were absolute or got redrawn in different countries and in different situations. It was just possible that hubris didn't exist in the United States where no one could ever have enough; in which case, was he, as an American outside the United States, exempt from its effects, or did its rules reassert themselves abroad? Would the tower's illumination be a little like celestial trespass, provoking some Greek god—Boreas, if he remembered Mythology 101—to fill his big cloud cheeks and with one huge exhalation blow out all the lights? They would call it a power outage but it would really be a power outrage, a warning to the hubrismacher not to tempt fate because Fate almost always accepted a dare and did exactly what it was best known for in these cases, which was to intercede on its own behalf.

The geopolitics of hubris were absorbing his attention when the kitchen telephone rang. It had to be his mother. No one else called at 6 a.m. to chat. "Hi, Ma," he said into the receiver. There was silence on the other end.

"You should have been a detective," she said after a longish pause.

"You mean because I was able to figure out that it was you." She didn't answer.

"Don't be offended. I'm not saying 'don't call'"—it was Judy who said that—"I'm just saying that there was strong reason to believe that the caller was the same person I hear from every morning at 6 a.m."

"You could be mistaken, Mister Detective."

He was tempted to agree by saying that it might be someone with a real reason for calling, but he didn't. Why hurt her feelings? She was lonely and she loved him.

"Did Rachel get her braces yet?"

"She's got a retainer."

"Poor kid."

"You can hardly notice it. All you see is a wire. Mom, was there some reason…"

"I'm calling," she cut in very decisively, "to tell you that Joshua, your sister's son, was accepted by Brown University yesterday." Murray only had one sibling and she only had one son, so it would have been more than sufficient to identify him by name, but whenever something important happened, his mother liked to insert a little genealogy.

"Brown. That's great. Good genes, the kid's got those Strongman genes. Miriam must be overjoyed."

"Yes and no."

"No? How could there be a no in there?"

His mother sighed. Her sigh, her legacy, which would last long after she died, preceded her explanation. "The 'no' got in when he said he wanted to go to Berkeley."

"He got in to Berkeley, too?"

"Not yet."

Typical. This was typical of his mother and sister: manufacture a problem, just in case. In case of what, he wasn't sure (hubris maybe?) but he thought it was the reason he had become a lawyer. "Berkeley's a good school too," he answered, playing along with the idea that a) Josh would get in and b) it would be a problem that he, Murray, should have an attitude toward. Mistake. He shouldn't have said that. Now he would have to hear the problem with Berkeley in painstaking detail when it could be summed up in three words: three thousand miles. He had to act fast, before he would be interrupting her explanation. "Ma, this is too important for a rushed conversation, and I have an eight o'clock meeting. Let me call you later."

"I understand. You have important things to think about."

"Don't do this, Ma," he said, a sentence produced by ten thousand dollars worth of therapy.

"I'm not doing anything," she said in a voice that seemed to crawl out from under centuries of oppressed motherhood. Another pause, then "Murray, remember to take an umbrella to work with you." Murray looked out the window at a bright sun. "I know, you think because it's sunny now and because it rained last night that it's going to stay sunny," she continued, " but it's not—it's going to rain. I can feel it in my bones. Trust me."

Judy shuffled into the kitchen on terry cloth slippers as he was hanging up. "How's Pearl?" she asked through a yawn, her eyes couched inside pouches like down quilts.

"Pearl is my mother," he answered in defiant anticipation of Judy's chronic complaint about his mother's early morning phone calls and in unnecessarily assertive acknowledgement of the uncertain emotion he had learned to embrace at the cost of another five thousand.

"All I did was ask."

"Yeah well," he said, sounding skeptical. "You might give her a call later. Josh got in to Brown and she wants to crow. You should call Miriam too."

"I knew I should have stayed in bed, but," she added with sudden energy, "I'm up, and the reason I got up is to tell you to take an umbrella."

"You too?" he asked. Judy looked confused. "Never mind," he said, unscrewing a jar of Sara Beth Preserves, his favorite. The preserves, along with Judy's reminder of an umbrella, were making him feel very affectionate. Funny. His mother's reminder annoyed him, but Judy's made him feel good.

"It's because I dreamt it was raining," she yawned, exposing a mouth full of fillings and crowns. "The rain was like an omen, or maybe it was more like a test of affection. Anyway, there was such a downpour that it was hard for us to get to each other. But we had to. It was very important that we find each other. I don't know—ever since the Tsunami and then Katrina, the weather's been freaking me out. The dream was turning into a nightmare. Then the phone woke me up, and I wanted to hug you before you left the house and we got separated by rain." He looked outside at the sunshine. There was hardly a cloud in the sky.

Judy looked at the sunshine too. "It was a dream," she said.

"A wonderful, touching dream," he said, pulling her toward him by the terry lapels of her bathrobe and, in an unusual show of daytime affection, kissing her on the lips. They didn't usually kiss during the day. Over the years, instead of becoming more physically intimate, they had become shy with each other, as if years of cohabitation had introduced an embarrassing element of the fraternal into their marital relations, and instead of kissing, they hugged. It was only in the privacy of their bedroom and with a sufficient build-up that they overcame their reserve, so when Murray kissed her in the kitchen before 7 a.m., Judy was surprised and not entirely sure what she thought of it. In her dream, she had had to get to him, but she didn't have morning breath in her dream; and a quick trip to the bedroom, which was what his kiss seemed to suggest, was not at all in the spirit of the dream, which she was still in the grip of. Luckily, it was not in the spirit of Murray's morning schedule either, which was timed to the minute.

The bedroom question hung in the air for a moment before the telephone rang again and spared them from spontaneous passion. "I'll get it," Judy said, thinking that if she took care of Pearl immediately, that would only leave Miriam, who she could put off till later. She picked up the phone, heard Pearl's voice, and nodded to Murray, who, as soon as he knew it was his mother, went back to the bedroom to finish dressing. When he came back into the kitchen ten minutes later, Judy was still on the phone and rolling her eyes. "Just a minute Pearl," she interrupted her mother-in-law, "Murray's about to leave and I want to say good-bye to him…No, he hasn't left yet. He's leaving now…He *was* leaving, but it's only been five minutes since you called the last time and it takes a few minutes to leave."

Murray wished that Judy hadn't said that he was still there, but Judy refused to be cowed by his mother and never cooperated in his little subterfuges. Her forthrightness made him uncomfortable, but he also admired it and had stopped pleading with her to be gentler with his mother. He particularly didn't want to say anything about it on his way out the door. They had just kissed and he wanted to start the day off on the right footing. He had been tempted to say "I'll see you later," in a way that implied that later would have sexual significance, but there was something a little ridiculous about talking to Judy that way, and he decided not to be stupid. Why be stupid? He was still fairly handsome, he was well educated, his prostate was fine, his tennis was strong, and he was very successful, so why be stupid? He kissed her a second time, this time in a more business-like fashion, took his final swallow of coffee, went out to the foyer where he picked up his briefcase, tucked his newspaper neatly into his armpit, and, with the confidence and panache of a man who lived in the building's only apartment that could be accessed directly from the elevator, he left for work.

"Good morning, Mr. Strongman," Juan intoned in the lobby. He was standing at his post by the concierge desk, his gray suit looking a little warm for August despite the air conditioning.

"Good morning, Juan," Murray smiled warmly. He always had an urge to say "top of the morning to you," but Judy insisted that he resist certain expressions. They might be misunderstood. In fact, considering Juan's English, they might not be understood at all.

"Beautiful weather, we're having, isn't it?" Murray said, loving the stock phrases of social exchange. Judy didn't like his saying that either because she thought that Juan was supposed to say that to him and not the other way around. But Murray didn't care. So what if he got it backward. Backward, forward, what diffcrence did it make? This wasn't England.

"Yessir, berry byootifool," Juan agreed. "But maybe we have some rain today. Maybe you better take an umbrella." Again, this irritating prediction of rain.

It was still sunny and clear after Murray's meeting, which ended at ten. It stayed that way for another two hours, until around midday. Then, looking up from the papers on his desk and out the window, Murray noticed that the sun had disappeared. He scanned the sky, but he couldn't find it. The New York sky was a crowded place, and he thought it might have become obscured by a building, but after looking all over for it, like something he had misplaced, he still couldn't find it. It would show up sooner or later, he decided, and went back to the papers on his desk. After a while, he looked out the window again. The sky was still empty, as if the sun had simply and unceremoniously walked off the playing field, leaving everything the same as before but missing its principal player. Without the sun, the sky was nondescript, a blank screen, pale and flat, a television that wasn't on, revealing nothing, concealing nothing, a businessman's sky. It was also, he thought, typical of August, which had none of the sparkle of June or intensity of July and really, as a month, without much to recommend it. The absence of sun and clouds left Murray with a slight feeling of letdown, although even if it had been a better month, a dull sky was not unusual for New York, where the skyline was the horizon and the atmosphere was more hue than sky, indistinguishable from the gray façades of New York's skyscrapers. Skyscrapers, the word itself a reflection of the abrasive relationship between the natural and the manufactured.

By mid afternoon, the sky had changed from blank white to a darker color, the same stage but with lowered lights. It was strange, Murray thought, how unlikely forecasts, like rain on a sunny day, for example, often seemed the most accurate. He gave Judy a quick call. She was having another cup of coffee and using an old Time Magazine—she had trouble throwing things out—as a placemat. The saucer's wet perimeter encircled Monica Lewinsky's mouth. A montage of all the key players in the Clinton story stretched across the top of two pages: Bill, Hillary, Monica, Paula, Kenneth, and Linda. Ken had a tight, brittle smile; Linda looked harried; and Hillary looked fierce. The other three, the ones who'd had sex, all looked sublimely insouciant.

"Thanks for getting up with me. Have you spoken to Miriam yet?"

"Not yet, but have you looked out the window? I told you it would rain."

He looked out the window again. The sky was in transition, developing a brooding darkness. "Yeah, it looks like it. You're clairvoyant. Either that or you're developing arthritis. Anyway, you don't have to worry. It would take more than a little rain to keep me from you, babe. Hey," he said as Judy braced herself for a metaphor, "who's the skipper of our ship? The captain," Judy joined in, "who has safely navigated his family through hostile waters?" the two now speaking in unison.

She wished he hadn't done that; she wished he hadn't used the sailing metaphor. He knew she was tired of his metaphors and particularly the ones that referred to getting old. It was true that he was quite a bit older than she was, eleven years actually, but that didn't mean that she was ready to "drop anchor in the final port of call," or to "spend the next twenty-five years watching grandchildren frolic in the sand as the tide lapped against their bow." They had even had a recent discussion about the different trajectories of their lives, about his need for a break and her need to be more involved. As someone who had never stopped working since the day he began law school, he thought he had earned the right to cut back, whereas she, a woman who had been spared daily combat with life's necessities, was still eager to achieve. At first Murray had joked about her "sudden bout of ambition" and told her not to worry, she'd get over it; but then, when he saw how serious she was and how well Second Hand Rose was doing, he got a little irritated. Why should he, as the one who had worked hard, followed the rules, and finally gotten to the point where he could take a couple of weeks here and there, be prevented from doing so just because Judy had gotten ambition? He was slightly annoyed, but he wasn't ready for head-on conflict and preferred the oblique reference and subtle engagement of metaphor. And it wasn't as if his metaphors were unfriendly either; after all, wasn't he talking about *their* ship and *their* final port of call? His metaphors might have been ever so slightly exasperating, but they were also quite loving, and he simply couldn't believe that Judy really found them offensive, especially when he grinned his famous grin, the one that implied she should love him anyway, warts and all, because his provocations were part of his boyish charm.

Judy was not charmed, however, and, by the conclusion of their phone call, she was considering whether metaphors were grounds for divorce. Their repetition was wearing a groove into her brain, and it had gotten so that every exchange between them seemed to be falling into that groove. She brooded for a while, ruminating on the condition of her life, its pros and cons, neither pleased nor depressed, and finally decided, as she always did at roughly the same point in her deliberations, to take a shower. Trying to reach a conclusion about marriage was like trying to decide about the ocean, so fluid were its moods and changes. Marriage, she decided, was a compost heap of organic matter whose decay was also fertilizer. She liked that description and, smiling to herself, realized that among its other attributes, the description was also a metaphor. Maybe she should try it out on Murray. Didn't one good metaphor deserve another? Fight metaphor with metafire.

It was beginning to rain. A few big drops landed on the kitchen window like water wrung from billowing, gray sheets hung out to dry. The sky was the color of dishwater. Judy was supposed to have her hair done at Davidoff's and was trying to decide whether to keep the appointment. The frosting would not be affected by the rain, but she didn't like having her hair colored unless she also had it blown, and there would be no point to a blow-drying if her meticulous "do," each hair the artistic decision of her hair consultant, was going to collapse as soon as she went outside. Even if she could get a taxi right away, the humidity would probably beat her to the door of the cab. She could, of course, reschedule, but Arnel was in demand and it could mean waiting another week with her roots showing. She tried calling her own private weather forecaster for advice, but Claire was on another line and Judy got connected with someone else.

"Katie O'Brien," the voice said.

It took her a second. Then she remembered who Katie was. Katie offered to personally deliver Judy's message, which was surprising and suspiciously helpful. Even the smallest businesses had someone to answer their phones, so why was this small-time big shot taking calls? Even if the receptionist was on her break, you still wouldn't expect an important anchorwoman to personally deliver messages.

"Why thank you. It's nice of you to take the trouble," Judy responded judiciously. "If you could just tell Ms. Day that it's a weather-related matter of some urgency."

You do the Hokey Pokey,
And you turn yourself around,
That's what it's all about!

Roland LaPrise, Composer

CHAPTER ELEVEN

Claire was on another line talking to Emmett Nelson of the National Weather Service when Judy called. Emmett's predictions were usually accurate, and Claire paid attention to what he said. On the few occasions they disagreed, one of them would refer to the other's last mistake as a way of bolstering his present position, but every time that happened they would also argue about the other's recollection of the previous so-called mistake. After a few such debates, which both of them enjoyed in the way that adults sometimes enjoy squabbling like children, they decided to keep score. According to the system they developed, barometric pressure was worth one point, wind speed was worth another, the national forecast and the next day forecast were worth two points apiece, and the five-day forecast was worth three. At the moment, Emmett had a slight lead, but the differences in their predictions were so minor and their abilities so evenly matched that their scores never varied more than a few percentage points, and each had begun to hope for a difference of opinion that could decisively tip the balance one way or the other.

It looked like that moment had come, at least judging by the intensity of Claire's voice, which Katie had learned to detect over the sounds of the news room and which seemed particularly loud as she approached Claire's work station. Of course, Katie could only hear one half of the conversation, but she was intrigued by Claire's vigor, and if Katie wasn't dreaming, if she was hearing things correctly, then the reason for Claire's pressured speech could be explained by the word hurricane. Could it be? If Katie properly deduced what was being said on the other end of the line then a hurricane was heading their way. Katie had been walking over to deliver Judy's message when she heard the word; and instead of stopping at Claire's desk, she continued on to the other side of Claire's monitors where, obscured by a bookshelf, she could listen without being seen. The shelves were full of information for JTF employees, so to look busy while she eavesdropped, she picked up a form…something to do with health care.

"Hurricane! Emmett, I know you're bored, but…I know, I know, when it rains it bores, but…a hurricane? There hasn't been a hurricane in Bridge Haven since, let me see…ever. There has never been a real hurricane in Bridge Haven." After she said that there was a long pause punctuated by two "yes, buts." Then she said "I'm talking about the eye now," which was followed by another "yes, but" and "you can't really believe what you're saying. It's too far-fetched, it's absurd. Okay sure, but…do I want to bet ten points on that? Absolutely, and I'll up the ante on the five-day forecast too."

Katie was spellbound. A hurricane in Bridge Haven predicted by the guy from NWS! This was too good. "Emmett," Claire was saying, "all we've got so far is a tropical storm in the Caribbean Sea." Claire paused for a moment and then, as if she were cutting in, she said "no" several times, her voice rising with each enunciation of the word. "Don't you think," she said, her speech highly deliberate, "your prediction is just a wee bit premature? This storm is just a baby...alright, a toddler, but still too young for us to know what it will become." Waiting for more, listening so intently that she didn't hear Dan approach, Katie absently leafed through a brochure on employee benefits until she heard a voice say, "Ah, benefits. The question is whose benefit, yours or ours?"

"Shit, Dan! Do you have to sneak up on me like that?" she asked with a startled jerk, her question a lame attempt to turn him into the culprit.

Why did it have to be Dan who discovered her, Katie thought with irritation. Why couldn't it have been Russo or Goodwin? They wouldn't have even noticed what she was looking at, but Dan—not only was he aware of what she was reading, but he had a better idea of its contents than she did.

"Let me see here," he said, looking over her shoulder and examining the page she was turned to, "COBRA? You're looking into the COBRA plan? Well, at least the species makes sense." He looked very thin, probably because he wasn't wearing a sweater or jacket, and his shirt hung limply from the wire hangar of his body.

Katie scowled and walked around the bookshelf to Claire, who seemed to be winding down with NWS. Damn it, Katie thought, irritated that she'd missed the rest of the conversation. Claire glanced at the memo Katie gave her—a pink slip with the words URGENT: WEATHER-RELATED MATTER in a large scrawl followed by Judy's number—and without any visible reaction, put it down on her desk. Katie was puzzled by Claire's apparent dismissal of what was, to all intents and purposes, an emergency and wondered whether this indifference to the opinions of others was what the poor guy at NWS had to deal with?

Claire was also wondering about the guy at NWS. What was Emmett up to? In 1938, a hurricane had hit Long Island, and there had also been Agnes—although she was technically a tropical storm—in 1972. But a hurricane, even a modest Category One, had never hit Bridge Haven, of that Claire was certain. She had given a course on tropical depressions, storms, and hurricanes and knew a thing or two about their behavior and history. For a storm to be healthy, the eye and a radius of roughly fifty miles had to be over warm water, and that was a condition that rarely existed in the Northeast. The tendency—strong enough it could be called a rule—was for hurricanes to get caught up and curve east if they made it up the coast at all and didn't strike in Florida or the Carolinas beforehand. True, weather patterns had been changing, and there were more intense hurricanes than there had been in the past; but so far, they had not traveled anywhere near Bridge Haven, and, according to the information coming in on the new, cutting-edge GFDL she had persuaded the station to invest in, there was nothing to suggest it was about to change.

Still, the weather's unpredictability had to be respected, as did the instinct of the seasoned meteorologist. Claire took Emmett seriously and so did Katie, who was on the alert for information that could be put to her own use, and who, within seconds of hearing Claire's telephone conversation, had a plan all but formulated. She could hardly believe her good fortune. This hurricane was a windfall, so to speak, a piece of providential good fortune tailor-made to her objectives. There were a few details that might prove sticky, but so long as the weather didn't suddenly change for the better, they were nothing she couldn't handle. Katie went to the ladies' room, which had one of the station's few windows.

THE FABUWEATHER FORECAST

The weather was unimpressive. Basically, it was drizzling. Still, there was cause for optimism, she thought, considering that it had been bright and sunny only a few hours earlier, and seizing the moment, she rushed to call Freddy.

• • •

Freddy was not in his office. The rain, just a sprinkle really, hadn't deterred him from leaving the municipal building and walking over to CVS. Marie had asked him to fill a prescription and, since he wanted to get some air anyway, he decided to hoof it. It was only a light rain, but he couldn't help thinking that a day that had begun with sun and finished with rain was a perfect description of his week: golden boy on Monday morning, scoundrel on Friday night, and he the same man he'd always been. He was so preoccupied with his problems—with figuring out whether and how to respond to the accusation Boxer-Stanton had made—that he wasn't thinking about anything else, and the bleak sky and drizzle had seemed to him the natural setting for his dark thoughts and no reason to stay inside. He was halfway to CVS on that rather desultory stretch after the patio furniture store but before the optician's when it started to rain more heavily. The absence of protection, the feeling that, once again, he had been ambushed, only this time by nature, upset him so much that he started to cry, his tears indistinguishable from the rain. The tears were prompted by genuine agony, but as soon as he gave way to them, the pleasure of release was such that instead of holding back, he allowed them to flow more freely, even coaxing them forward a little as the need to cry began to subside. Freddy was not made for grief, and, in keeping with his personality, his misery was short-lived and quickly replaced by the need to evacuate pain from his system, his crying akin to a man blowing his nose or coughing to relieve an itch. Boxer-Stanton's attack had required him to brace himself and be strong—both unfamiliar stances—and he had been longing for the kind of surreptitious relief that allowed transgressions to be easily and invisibly washed away, like tears in the rain and pee in the shower.

He was completely wet by the time he rushed into CVS. A few drops was all it took, not much, and his clothes were drenched, not unlike careers, he thought, which one or two scandals, even minor ones, could bring low by creating a stain that spread to everything else. He walked past a large bin with beach equipment—swimming tubes, goggles, kiddie flippers, and snorkels suitable for the ten-year-old diver—and down an aisle with school supplies—notebooks, binders, and lined paper, the aisles and prices anticipating the approaching change of season and the transition from summer to fall. He lingered over candy and junk food, the Pringles always hard to resist, and remarked upon the inclusion of more nutritious things on the shelves like raisins and Snapples. Prunes, what were they doing there? He walked past the hair products, wondering as he always did whether he should try Just for Men. He liked the name, although he couldn't imagine how men's hair dye was really different from women's unless it was thicker and stronger, sort of more virile. The trouble was he was going bald as fast as he was going gray, and a few dark hairs might do nothing more than attract attention to the fact, kind of like a spider on the desert of his scalp. Rogaine might be a better idea or, better still, transplants; but you could always tell when a man was getting transplants because of the even spread and location of the hair, which began at the forehead and extended back toward the crown. If he ever did it, he would have them start on the sides or in the back and work their way up toward the middle. The trouble was that he liked things that could not be detected—crying in the rain, peeing in the shower—and you could always tell when a man's hair was thickening.

He picked up the meds—Climara for the peri-menopausal woman—and thought about the change of life, a phrase Freddy Jr. had derided over breakfast that morning as lower class. He would have cuffed him, but he knew there was some truth to the remark and that, unlike more enlightened couples, he and Marie never talked about her experience. Who wanted to talk about things like that anyway? It was all so depressing, things coming to an end. Marie's child-bearing years had actually ended some years earlier when she'd had her tubes tied; but the change of life was different because it was not within her control, and, like his career, her body just seemed to be winding down. Like his career, he thought with a start, panic seizing him again. He went to the front of the store where, suddenly eager to get back to his office, he stood in line behind a woman he recognized as the saleswoman from the jewelry store. He was sure she had seen him too and was pretending not to. The same people who'd been thrilled to stand next to him a week or two ago were looking away, and practically overnight, he had gone from personage to persona non grata. That made him both angry and defiant: if that was the way it was going to be—no loyalty, no appreciation of the man who had upgraded the senior citizen center—then they were persons non grateful in his eyes and deserved whatever they got.

As he approached City Hall, he noticed that the same reporters who were standing by his car the other day were in front of the building entrance. The last thing Freddy wanted was to deal with reporters, so instead of continuing toward them, he made a sharp left. There was a small metal door by the side of the building which, miraculously, opened when he turned the knob. Freddy was inside the building, but where was he? There was nothing but concrete walls and floors and large pipes overhead. What a sorry state of affairs, the mayor wandering around City Hall's basement. He'd been down there once before—with Katie—but although he had no intention of ever telling anyone what they had been doing, he knew that it hadn't made him feel undignified the way he did now as he tried to figure out how to get to his office without being seen.

There seemed to be two routes: the freight elevator and the stairs. He entered the stairwell—gray cement, depressing—and walked hurriedly to the second floor. The door had a metal bar with a red sign across it. Emergency Exit Only. Alarm Will Sound When Pushed. He decided not to risk it and tried the third floor. Same thing. Shit. He had a hard time imagining that these doors were only used in emergencies, but he couldn't take the chance. He had no choice. He walked back to the main floor, which had the only door without a sign on it.

The group from the parking lot had reconvened just inside the building entrance and as soon as Freddie emerged from the door adjacent to the lobby news stand, they rushed at him. "Mr. Mayor, Mr. Mayor, is there any truth to the allegations that you gave sweetheart deals to relatives? Did DiMotta Construction receive preferential treatment? Will there be a press conference? What's your reaction to these charges?"

"No truth, no truth whatsoever," he said as he walked toward the main stairs. He usually took the elevator, but there was no way he was going to stand and wait for it with that pack of piranhas snapping at him.

He had actually been planning to start walking up the stairs anyway, as part of an exercise regime, but the lobby, which was the only part of City Hall that was stately, had a very high ceiling, and the staircase was correspondingly long. Right off the bat, he was out of breath. Half hauling, half climbing, he held on to the beautiful old mahogany balustrade until, when he was almost out of earshot, he heard someone ask why he was using the side entrance instead of the main one. Must be the same reason he's taking the stairs instead of waiting for the elevator, he heard someone else say to accompanying laughter.

Back in his office, he changed into dry clothes for the four o'clock meeting he had called. His staff was getting hounded by reporters and needed reassurance that the man they worked for was honest and above board. Of course, he would have to say a little bit more than that—they were his staff after all, and he was supposed to be more open with them. So he asked Hershie to join them for the sake of jumping in when he himself couldn't think of what to say.

Freddy's pants were wool, Eddie Bauer, and too warm for the season, but he'd brought them to the office in January, and he hadn't remembered to replace them with lighter ones when the weather got warmer. Well, too bad; if anyone had a problem with his pants, they could just go out and buy him new ones. At least that was what he told himself, although he no longer truly believed in his defiance. In fact, he was very nervous, and to calm himself, he tried deep breathing. Following the instructions in his yoga manual, he took a deep diaphragmatic breath, watching his belly expand to Buddha-like proportions and feeling the slight sensation in his spine as the air descended. Slowly, he exhaled, trying to follow the manual's recommendation that he simultaneously imagine his cares riding out on the wave of his exhalation. Maybe it was working, maybe that's what they were doing, maybe his cares were astride a little palomino; he couldn't really tell.

After he changed his clothes, he checked his messages. There were five from Katie: one she'd left with Francine, one on his voice mail, two on his cell phone, and one on his computer. He had never gotten so many messages from her before, and it irritated him. Everywhere he looked, she was popping up. It was a little like a house of mirrors, except that the image he saw was not of himself but of her, and because he was in trouble and she now felt free to importune him, her image reflected the vulnerability of his position. Two weeks earlier, she would not have dared to do that to the man whose motto had been "Make 'em laugh, make 'em cry, make 'em wait;" but that was two weeks ago, and, like it or not, things were different now. Undoubtedly Hershie was giving him good advice when he told him not to talk to anybody, especially ambitious television reporters, and he would not like it if he knew that Freddy was talking to Katie. But lawyers were always preparing their defense whereas he was still trying to run a campaign—a hobbled campaign perhaps, a campaign lagging behind the treadmill of events, but a campaign nonetheless, and Katie seemed to have some ideas about how to go about it. If he was going to be defeated, he might as well get nailed too, and whether it was for involving a reporter or for engaging in cronyism and racketeering, what difference did it make?

CHAPTER TWELVE

Katie was at home, pacing her Fortunoff living room, waiting for Freddy to return her call. Surely he had gotten one of her messages by now. Didn't he know that she would never have bombarded him with phone calls if it wasn't important? Timing was everything. If the wind and rain began to subside, it would be too late. They had to act while the threat of a hurricane still existed, and while preventive measures still seemed justified. Then, if there really was a hurricane, so much the better, and if not and the storm blew out to sea, then at least the mayor could say that he had done everything within his power to protect his community. Wasn't that what people wanted, she asked herself, rehearsing her pitch to Freddy?

She paused at her window to mark the storm's progress. It was definitely raining, but that was all. No thunder, no lightning, no intense winds. "Blow, goddammit," she said, clenching her fist angrily at her window. "Strike some terror into the hearts of men, why don't you?" her eyes accused the dull drizzle. "Look at you. You're weak, pathetic…just like the rest of us," she said, thinking of Freddy, their wuss of a mayor. Where was he, goddammit?

When he finally called, an interminable twenty minutes later, their conversation was brief. "Remember, our talk in the diner?" she asked. "Well…" and with a rush of barely concealed excitement, she explained the situation, making quite sure to avoid the phrase "diversionary tactics." It didn't take long to persuade him. After he'd asked a few questions, after she'd explained the seriousness of the situation and how this wasn't just a question of politics anymore but that, to the contrary, it was a time to put politics aside and attend to the needs of the community, in short, after she'd told him what to say and they'd tacitly agreed to pretend to conscience, he approved her plan. Although to say that he approved is suggestive of a personality without a persona and quite different from Freddy's. It would be more accurate to say that, with gravity in his voice and glee in his heart, he uttered the time-honored phrase, whose origins he was quite sure were Sicilian, that she should do whatever was necessary.

Easier to say than do however, especially since her plan's execution involved the help of others, particularly Louis Martin. Katie had been introduced to Louis at a re-election fundraiser—which the clever Dan referred to as a cocktail party with interior motives—but that was several months back and she had pretty much ignored him since then, never imagining that she would be needing his help so soon. The fundraiser was held in a converted shoe factory in Harris Falls, an industrial town southwest of Bridge Haven, and as the only television personalities in attendance, they had stood out, and after circling each other for a while, they stood together, each surveying the scene from an open bar near the apartment's entrance. As if his part were scripted, Louis asked Katie what she was drinking and, ordering the same for himself, they quickly discovered that they had more in common than the drinks they were holding. The similarities between them—his hair that unusual blonde and hers that rich red, his great build and her great body, his unmerited success and overweening ambition, her unmerited success and overweening ambition—led them to discover other similarities of a more personal nature. Tracking the course of those ambitions was what led them to confide in each other and to discover that for both of them, ambition derived from an urban childhood, hers in the Bronx and his in Queens. L(o)uis Martin(ez)' father was from Northern Spain and his mother was from Southern France, and despite the modest Ozone Park apartment he had grown up in, it had been maintained according to standards set by the Chateau Sur Mer in Biarritz, where his mother and father had met. Unfortunately, they met as custodial staff and not as guests, and Louis's exotic ethnicity was offset by its lowly working class status. The result, as he had laughingly admitted to Katie, was that when he talked about his background, he was highly selective in the information he gave. For some, he was the son of a French woman and a Spaniard, and for others, he was the son of a maid and a janitor, and very rarely was he both at the same time.

It was, he said, looking at her from over the rim of his martini, unusual for him to tell his whole story, and Katie, who was keenly aware of the risks of self-disclosure, didn't doubt it. She was, in fact, so deeply affected by his willingness to risk honesty that she responded with a confession of her own and admitted that in the tradition of the Irish family too large for its income, hers had been plagued by the double scourge of alcoholism and violence. That was their moment, and for both of them, it was almost unprecedented. But neither knew what to do with it, and, after a flicker of recognition and significant eye contact, they left it behind and moved on to an animated discussion of Hollywood, the Academy Awards, and their own celebrity-hood. That lasted for another few minutes of enthusiastic consensus before, having covered their two favorite topics—namely, their own difficult past and their own promising future—conversation sagged and then, after it sagged, it collapsed entirely, and they wandered away from each other in search of better social opportunity.

For Katie, who had felt the desire to retreat after her horrifyingly unfamiliar rush of candor, that was fine. Louis was nice, and they did seem to have a lot in common, even in the way they pretended to problem-free careers, but her relationships had always been vertical—older sisters, younger brothers, social higher ups, racial lower downs; and although she knew exactly how to use her star status with those she imagined above or below her, she had no idea how to talk to peers. As for romance, she didn't believe in lateral romance, even as a strategy, and as a mere weather reporter, Louis was altogether too much her equal. The similarity between them militated against romance but promoted collaboration, and Katie foresaw that the time might come when she would be needing Louis's help.

That time, however, had come sooner than anticipated, and Katie suddenly found herself in the uncomfortable position of needing a major favor. All along, she had assumed that, as the man whose ratings had been hurt by Claire's success, she could count on him to want revenge; but now that the moment had arrived and she was about to dial his number, she was confronted with the realization that her phantom ally was neither phantom nor, necessarily, ally, but a professional weather reporter who might take exception with her attempt to influence his report. Neither a difficult urban background nor a mutual desire to embarrass Claire guaranteed a willingness to act unethically, and if he refused, Katie would come up worse than empty because approaching him was not without its risks.

These were the thoughts she was having as, nonetheless, she called FYI. "Louis," she said, with more enthusiasm than necessary after she'd reluctantly identified herself to the receptionist, "Yes…long time…you know how it is, same old, same old…no time to breathe…listen, I don't want to take up too much of your time, I know you must be busy with this hurricane, but…oh, you're not sure it is a hurricane…what makes me think…oh …hmm…okay, but perhaps we should talk about this in person. How about Tattler's? In an hour?"

Katie would not have gone to Tattler's Bar and Grill without a very good reason. Hooligans was the bar frequented by JTF, and drinking at Tattler's was roughly equivalent to crossing enemy lines. But if she calculated correctly, it would be pretty empty in midafternoon and she could go there unobserved by anyone from either station. She watched for Louis from her car across the street until she saw a tall hunched figure dash into the bar, newspaper shielding his head, and allowing herself an extra five minutes, she swung her car around and made her own wet entrance. She was glad that the rain had picked up and that there was actually something of a downpour at the moment of their arrival.

It had not been Louis's intention to get there ahead of Katie. He had thought that by going over his charts one more time before he left the station, he would be late; but it didn't work out that way, and he was stuck with the next best thing to keeping someone waiting, which was being punctual. He greeted her with genial patience as she, breathless and panting, apologized for her delay. "Louis," she said, removing her raincoat and pulling her bar stool close, the sheen on stockings exposed to mid calf deliberately distracting, "just so you don't think I dragged you out in this weather for no good reason, I will get right to the point." She had decided on a direct, no-nonsense, nothing-to-hide approach and leaned forward, her physical proximity adding emphasis to her words. "I've been informed there is good reason to expect that a hurricane may strike Bridge Haven in the next few days and that the mayor is considering steps to protect the community from a possible disaster. He is asking for the cooperation of the media and particularly for the help of our weather reporters."

"Help?"

"Yes, in preparing people for the hurricane."

"How come no one from the mayor's office contacted me directly?" he asked, the light that illuminated her stockings also catching the shine on the well-maintained stubble of his beard.

Katie ordered a scotch. She rarely drank and never before five, but the occasion seemed to require a little extra fuel. "There's a problem with government interfering in how the news is covered," she said, looking at him levelly. "And in this case," and she paused to let it be known that she understood exactly what she was saying, "there's an additional problem. Claire Day doesn't seem to think this is a hurricane."

Louis was fascinated and trying to do mental arithmetic before he said anything else. If neither he nor Claire reported a hurricane, then things stayed as they were, with her ratings higher than his. If he reported a hurricane and she reported a storm, then his ratings for the day would be higher, but might subsequently drop even lower than they already were if the storm fizzled. If, on the other hand, there actually was a hurricane, then he would score big for having the courage to make a daring prediction and for advising people to take precautions.

Katie could practically see his mind at work and knew that he needed help. "The mayor acknowledges that there might be some controversy over this prediction," she went on, swishing the ice cubes around in her glass, "but he is very concerned about the potential consequences that might ensue from not even *mentioning* a hurricane as a *possibility*," she said absolutely deadpan, her emphatic tone suggesting that an omission of this sort would be the height of irresponsibility. "After all, the weather has not exactly been our friend these past few months, and perhaps we have a greater responsibility than we had in the past—what with global warming and the polar ice cap melting—to err on the side of caution and not take anything for granted," she concluded, practically dictating his report to him.

Louis reached over and, in a gesture that totally disarmed Katie, took her hand. "So a possible hurricane is reported and the mayor gets to take measures that protect and simultaneously distract the public?" he said, still holding her hand. "He goes on television, tells people what to do in the event of X, Y, or, Z and maybe even gets to set up shelters?" Katie was horrified. "Don't look so dismayed," he continued, as adept at reading her mind as she had been at reading his. "No one else has to know what you're up to. I guessed because I can't think of any other reason you would want to tamper with my weather report."

The bar was empty and quiet except for the sound of Celine Dion singing the theme song to *Titanic*. Busted and bested, Katie was totally incapable of any response except to wonder whether the remote stirring inside her breast was love or hate. She was half-tempted to pull her hand away, not sure whether he was making a pass at her (although she'd heard he had a partner) or simply letting her know that she was in his control; but instead she just sat in stunned silence, trying, as Louis had done only minutes earlier, to think through her options and, all the while, absently pondering her drink, whose gradations of color, beginning with ochre where the scotch was least diluted and paling to a lovely translucent caramel where the ice had melted, were mesmerizing. She could, in total violation of her principles, acknowledge the cynicism of the plan—or she could play it straight, even though he would know it was bull.

Her decision was made for her when Louis burst out laughing and exclaimed, "It's beautiful, it's too beautiful. Whoever thought this up is a genius. My only question is whether this is entirely a test tube hurricane or whether someone you know and trust thinks there's a basis for it. My numbers don't spell hurricane, and although it's possible it could develop, most hurricanes start to break up when they move inland or over cooler water. Unless there's warm sinking air in the eye, clouds fill the space and it weakens and dies. I'm not saying it can't happen, but it's unusual this far north."

Katie waited a moment, preparing to answer, when her cell phone rang. "What…" she said and paused, listening. "No kidding. Off Andros Island…" She was speaking into the phone but looking directly at Louis, "…three teenagers…three teenagers and a dog. Yeah, okay, soon." She put her cell phone back in her purse and said, "Three teenagers and a dog were out on their boat when the storm hit. The boat capsized and they are presumed dead." The call couldn't have come at a better time. "Four storm-related deaths, Louis."

"Off Andros Island? You've got to be kidding. Most people don't even know where that is. Listen, a hurricane in that part of the world, which incidentally is between Cuba and Florida," he looked at her for a moment, wondering why anyone would even bother to call with that information, "can be a summer shower in Bridge Haven. Look, I'm sorry about those kids, but that's weather-related news, not weather."

"Doesn't the fact that it's moving in our direction make it weather?"

"Only if it threatens our area."

"Suppose someone at NWS were calling it a hurricane?"

Louis looked surprised. He had really begun to think Katie and the mayor had cooked the whole thing up to save Coniglia's hide. He had no intention of making a fool of himself just because it benefited them, but if he had NWS behind him, that was different. Then he might, as Katie had suggested, be willing to say there was the possibility of a hurricane and promise to keep viewers posted with up-to-the-minute news. In a gesture that had become his trademark, he pushed a golden lock from his forehead. Katie was convinced that he had stolen the gesture from Claire, who was always anchoring her hair behind her ears, and that he hoped there was a connection between effective weather reporting and unruly hair. "If there's someone at NWS fool enough to corroborate, I'll go along with it, otherwise…"

"There is," Katie jumped in. Louis looked interested. His experience of NWS had been that they were cautious and conservative. "Just ask your contact at the service," she went on, "to get Emmett Nelson's opinion."

"Nelson?" Louis asked incredulously. Emmett Nelson was one of the most experienced and accurate weathermen in the business, and Louis could hardly believe he would go out on a limb with such a wild and irresponsible prediction. "Nelson works very closely with Claire. If he's predicting a hurricane, it seems unlikely she would predict a storm." he said, thinking out loud.

"Check it out," she said, "but time's a wasting. Better act fast."

He cocked his head and looked at her quizzically. "I haven't agreed to do it."

"Louis," she said imploringly, placing her hand on his forearm in an effort to get personal, although she was feeling more impatient than intimate, "do you know what this hurricane is called?" By enlisting one of the private weather services, Katie had managed to get insider information on the name of the storm and had been overjoyed to discover that it was none other than…"They named it Louis. The storm is Louis. It's named after you. It's Hurricane Louis!"

He clapped his hands together in childlike delight. "Louis! It's called Louis?!"

Louis was thrilled. Vain man that he was, the storm's name influenced him more that anything else she had said. What did he care about the mayor's troubles? What did he have to gain from cooperating with the mayor, who looked like he was on his way out anyway? And how would he benefit from making an inaccurate prediction, with or without NWS backing? But Hurricane Louis, that was another story. A story he could tell, one he could joke about, one he could really personalize. He could experience the weather in much the same way Claire did because this was *his* storm—it was named after him and he could do what he wanted with it.

CHAPTER THIRTEEN

The following morning was overcast and raining. The storm's co-ordinates had not changed since the previous day, and Claire was still puzzling over Emmett's prediction when Katie walked into her workspace. Her visit was almost as unexpected as Emmett's forecast. In fact, it was only the second time in two years that they had spoken to each other casually. The first time—a result of Mama Coniglia's advice to befriend one's enemies—occurred when they had lunch together at a local restaurant. Billed as country French, the restaurant was sandwiched between a Rite Aid and a Gap Outlet; and sitting amidst huge eruptions of fern in hammered copper urns, they discovered they had no more in common with each other than the restaurant had with its neighbors. Katie came from a large, working class family, Claire's was small and professional; Katie was the only member of her family who had gone to college, everyone in Claire's had an advanced degree; Katie had never been outside the country, Claire had spent her junior year in France; Katie's style was flashy, Claire's was understated. They laughed about their differences, ordered decaf cappuccinos, agreed they should go out together more often, and never did it again. Instead of collegiality, a distance developed between them, and it had lasted until that morning in Claire's cubicle.

"What's this I hear about a hurricane?" Katie asked in an offhand way, leaning diagonally against the bookcase next to Claire's computer. "There hasn't been a hurricane in Bridge Haven in, gee, I can't remember when. But if there ever was one, it was a long time ago."

"What makes you think there's going to be a hurricane?" Claire asked, hardly taking her eyes off her screen. She couldn't imagine what was going on. First Emmett, now Katie; it was all very strange.

"FYI." Katie discretely chewed gum while she talked. "Heard Louis say something about it on FYI this morning."

"Well," she answered, resolute in her opinion, "there's very little hard evidence of a hurricane heading our way. There will be continuing rain, but beyond that it's too soon to say. If Louis Martin is forecasting a hurricane, then he knows something I don't know." She anchored an obstinate strand of hair behind her ear.

After Emmett Nelson, Claire's best source of information was Susan Spiegel, and as soon as Katie left her workspace, Claire gave Susan a call. Susan was a former student interning at the Hurricane Research Department's Florida headquarters, and as part of her training, she sat in on the division's daily map discussions. There was no better place to get up-to-the-minute information.

"There's a wave," Susan said into her headphone, "that seems to have broken off a monster wave, and the smaller one is the potential player. There's closed circulation in it and falling air pressure. The National Hurricane Advisory is placing it south of the Carolinas by Thursday, but it's still dicey, and no one is putting his career on the line. Even so, it meets definition, and they've named it. They're calling it Louis after Joe

Louis, in the hope it will deliver a knockout."

"Is it moving?"

"That's one of the reasons it's a hard call. On the satellite imagery it's fairly stationary. Right now it's parked in the Straits of Florida between Andros Island and Cuba. There's a whole bunch of thunderstorms on top of it, but they're not sure where its center is. From what they can tell, the center might be well out in front. They're looking for a good storm to fly, but they're not ready to chase this one yet, and they haven't put anyone on standby either."

"What's the weather in Florida like now?" Claire asked.

"Sunny and bright," Susan laughed

Everything Susan said supported Claire's belief that a hurricane forecast was way premature. When the bottom half of an incipient storm was out of whack with the top then everything else—speed, intensity, and location—was thrown into question. What made the prediction particularly strange was that it wasn't based on a threatening wave. Dead waves had, of course, been known to spawn major disturbances in the same way that dramatic waves had been known to fizzle, but their unpredictability, if nothing else, was more than sufficient reason to hold off making dire predictions. Like everything else in nature, the creation of a hurricane depended on proper growth conditions; and in the case of hurricanes, those conditions included an African wave as seedling, a hot sea as nourishment, an unstable atmosphere as maintenance, the Coriolis effect for motion, and a low vertical shear for maturation. So far, there was no evidence those conditions existed, and Claire was making no progress in detecting them either.

After a while she decided to take a breather. The moist air outside was warmer than the air in the office, but the absence of air conditioning or, perhaps, the absence of human intention made it refreshing, and despite the drizzle, Claire opened her car window as she left the building parking lot and drove toward the shore. The ride was like a lesson in suburban sociology, beginning with the relative desuetude of Bridge Haven's downtown followed by a neighborhood of modest houses, which grew in size and scale with the approach of waterfront. Some of the houses had fences, but most had nothing more than a narrow walkway separating them from each other. As the houses grew further apart, so did Claire's thoughts, as if some sort of distillation of her brain were taking place, a watering down which might, if she retreated to the country altogether, be watered rather than watered down and promote eventual blossoming. She passed a ranch house with a bicycle recklessly abandoned beside a hedge and a metal pruning fork still clinging to the base of a sapling. A partially deflated swimming pool lay limp on a flat stretch of yard, a loosely coiled hose dangling over its edge snake-like.

On the far side of the freeway, the houses were larger and more distinctive. After the old firehouse, which was something of a landmark, the aluminum façades of neatly aligned two-family houses were suddenly replaced by Victorians, Colonials, and Tudors. They, in turn, gave way to mini estates—five, six, and seven bedroom mansions that bordered the Long Island Sound in that eternal and lucrative embrace between water and real estate. Claire was familiar with the area, having explored it several times during her lunchtime peregrinations, and after slowly driving down empty streets too exclusive for street parking, she turned onto an unobtrusive road leading to the water. Or almost to the water. The road ended abruptly, existentially, at a Cyclone fence, with nothing beyond it but an outcropping of rocks tumbling down to a small stretch of apparently unclaimed beach. The road was flanked by a Bauhaus ranch made from industrial materials on one side and a white stucco Mediterranean-style villa on the other, and with her motor still idling, the houses like massive blinders within her peripheral vision, Claire drove up to the fence and watched the dark heft of ocean rock back and forth against the shore, the ping of raindrops barely noticeable on the water's surface. Long Island was visible, and the Sound, like a sullen and recalcitrant reminder of nature's power, waddled lumpily between the docks of exorbitant real estate.

As she looked at the water, the lines of a poem by Carl Sandburg came to her. "Pile the bodies high at Austerlitz and Waterloo./Shovel them under and let me work—/I am the grass; I cover all." Grass…water… nature was mounting an attack, and the world was experiencing a season of death. In recent months, there had been tidal waves, floods, and hurricanes, and more than ever, Claire felt the weight of her responsibility to give the public accurate information.

Russo and Goodwin were also thinking about what Claire was going to tell the public. Russo had just received a phone call from the mayor's office, from the mayor himself actually, who wanted him to persuade Claire to forecast a hurricane. Somehow the mayor had found out that Claire was not convinced the weather would be so severe, and Coniglia was concerned about her reticence. Russo wasn't sure the mayor should have been calling or asking him to do that; but ethics apart, he loved getting the phone call, loved the idea that the mayor needed his help. Russo's belief in his own importance was shaky at best, and every little acknowledgement gave added if temporary support to his fragile sense of self-worth. It would have been better if he'd been the only one to get the phone call, and he wished that Goodwin hadn't gotten one too; but since they'd both been contacted, he was glad that Goodwin had suggested that he be the one to talk to Claire. Any reason to be alone with her appealed to Russo, and the fact that in this case, his task was not particularly desirable or that he might regret its consequences only occurred to him later on.

But not much later because once she was in his office and actually seated in front of him, Russo found her composure unsettling and didn't know what to say. If only he thought things through beforehand. He kept looking out the window, outside to where it had practically stopped raining, and began to have a sense of foreboding. He repeatedly cleared his throat. Eventually, finding no subtle way to either withdraw from the situation or to say what was on his mind, he unburdened himself bluntly. "I hear that Louis Martin's predicting a hurricane, and that you're predicting rain. Not even a thunderstorm, but rain."

Claire didn't say anything. She saw the direction he was heading and had no intention of making his job any easier for him. He walked over to the window and leaned against the sill, his back to the outdoors. "There's an awfully big discrepancy between your forecasts," he said, repeating himself, and then stopping again, not comfortable asking her to justify the difference.

Claire just sat there, composed, silent, her hands folded on her lap.

"Well aren't you going to say something?" he asked, his hair falling limply over his brow like a curtain lowering to the floor of his protuberant jaw.

"I don't know what to say. My prediction is based on the information I have."

"Then how come your reports are so different from each other?"

"I wish I knew. August is hurricane month, and there's always that potential, but crying wolf is a risky business, and right now..." she shrugged, "we'd be crying wolf. There's a probability threshold in hurricane prediction, and, so far, we haven't crossed it. If I forecast a hurricane at this point, I'd lose credibility in the long run."

"Yeah, but if you're both making the same prediction..." he said, implying that if both reporters lost credibility, then neither station would really suffer. There was a moment's silence before he realized that Claire might be insulted by the suggestion that she think about her report strictly in terms of comparative ratings. "The risks," he said, quoting Freddy and trying to find a more acceptable way to make his case, "the potential damage to person and property is too great to allow ourselves excessive caution."

"There is no potential for damage right now," she answered pointedly. "We have plenty of time to evaluate what will happen next."

"We could wait too long," Russo squirmed, "and when public safety is at stake, that's probably not a good idea."

"Public safety is not at stake," Claire countered again, wondering if there had been some government directive to exhibit extreme caution when it came to the weather. Ever since Katrina there was a heightened interest in preparing, or at least in seeming to prepare, for the worst. "It seems as if, for some reason or other, you *want* me to report a hurricane."

Russo was about to lie and deny her accusation when Goodwin walked in. He had been standing near the watercooler and heard their entire conversation. "That's true," Goodwin acknowledged, ignoring Russo and directing his comment at Claire. "The mayor is concerned about what will happen if the town isn't prepared. He thinks Bridge Haven should be alerted so that if there is a hurricane, we can minimize the damage."

Russo was pissed. He would never have mentioned the mayor, and now Goodwin had blundered in and messed the whole thing up.

"Wait a minute," said Claire, anchoring a curl behind her ear. "What's the mayor got to do with this? Am I to understand that the mayor is telling us how to report the weather?"

"It's not like that," Russo jumped back in. He knew that they couldn't alienate the mayor, but he didn't want to alienate their star reporter either. "He's just concerned that if there *is* a hurricane and we haven't said *en-nee*-thing at all, then there may not be enough time to prepare for it." He couldn't resist looking out the window again. The sky was a yellowish-gray, dark and bleak if not exactly threatening.

"Then let him report the weather," Claire snapped back, surprising both of them with the sharpness of her response.

No one said anything for a moment. Within minutes of Goodwin's entry, they had reached the point that Russo had desperately wanted to avoid, and it wasn't clear where to go next. At least, it wasn't clear to him. Goodwin didn't have that problem. Claire was a media sensation and great for the station, but as far as Goodwin was concerned, he was boss, and neither Claire nor anyone else was going to tell him how to run things. Not her and not Katie either. The women at JTF had gotten altogether too high and mighty, and he was tired of it. He had no objection to treating the matter delicately, and if Russo could enlist Claire's support without offending her, so much the better. But you couldn't run a television station on the basis of feelings, and there were times when you couldn't run it on the basis of ethics either. Someone had to lay down the law and that, Goodwin thought, was where he came in.

A tall, bony New Englander, Goodwin was a man who rarely spoke, and when he did, it was with the expectation he would be listened to. Sitting cross-legged in a low chair, which forced his knees up and exposed his summer argyles, he said, "This is not going to be precedent setting." He seemed quite confident that the mere fact of declaring himself was enough to settle the matter. "The mayor's not going to start interfering, I promise you. Actually, it's really unusual for Coniglia to call. I don't think he's ever done it before. To be honest, I really don't know why," he continued, relaxed now that he thought the confrontation was over, "he's so convinced there's going to be a hurricane. I guess he listened to Louis's report and got himself all worked up over the possibility of a hurricane washing away Bridge Haven and his job along with it. Just look at how that guy, that mayor in New Orleans, screwed up. Coniglia doesn't need any bad publicity, especially now that he's got that messy corruption business to deal with. He probably thinks this hurricane is an act of God specifically targeting his house...punishing him for his crimes. What did you say the other day? Something about Zeus? Anyway, that's not the point. The point is that we need his support, especially when it comes to covering other stories, like the election, and if we alienate him now, we may not get access later."

Claire listened impassively. She had a lot to say, but there was no point. This was not a consultation, it was a command, and her only decision was whether or not to follow it. Russo kept sneaking furtive glances at her, shifting uneasily in his chair while Goodwin settled comfortably into his. It was dawning on him that he was much more allied with Claire than with Goodwin, but his insights came to him too late because in what seemed like an abrupt rejection of both of them, Claire got up. "Well gentlemen," she said looking at the two of them, one concave and the other convex, Goodwin cramped and slightly knock-kneed, his shoulders hunched forward and inward, and Russo contrastingly bulky and protuberant, his belly and chin asserting his presence, "it looks like this meeting is over," and without elaborating, she walked out.

Neither Russo nor Goodwin understood: did that mean she was agreeing or not? "You asshole," Russo said as soon as the door closed behind her. "What'd you have to walk in on us for?" he sputtered, furious.

"You were making a balls of it," Goodwin answered with somewhat less authority than he had shown only minutes earlier.

"How do you know? Were you listening in?" Russo glowered at Goodwin. "And speaking of making a balls of it, you should never have mentioned the mayor. We might have persuaded her if you hadn't told her about the mayor."

"Maybe we did persuade her," Goodwin defended himself. "She didn't say she wouldn't do it, did she?"

CHAPTER FOURTEEN

No, she hadn't, and at the moment Claire wasn't sure what to do. She had no doubt that her responsibility was to the public, but she also knew that she answered to her boss, and for the first time since she began working, she was in a position where ethics seemed like a luxury she might not be able to afford. Slightly dazed, she walked down the corridor to the restroom to douse her face in cold water.

Michelle, the new makeup artist, was leaning over the washbasin, getting as close to the mirror as she could. "Contacts," she said, pulling down her eyelid and then releasing it and blinking repeatedly. After inserting her lens, she removed a large makeup pouch from her pocketbook, and leaning in to the mirror again, her chin up, her back convex, and her knees locked above tip-toed feet, she reversed a small bottle of makeup into a cotton ball and gently applied it to her skin. Claire watched in fascination. She couldn't help marveling at the difference between their experiences, and as Michelle's face emerged from the blank benignity of her personality like an angelic fresco in relief, Claire felt as if hers was fading from view and disappearing behind the situational ethics of Goodwin and Russo.

She had, of course, known all along that television was based on ratings, but even so, she didn't understand how they could ask her to deceive the public. They should have argued with the mayor, taken her part, lined up behind their employee. Instead, ratings pimps that they were, they had knuckled under, played ball, and all because the mayor had taken it into his head that a hurricane was coming.

Where had he gotten that idea? Louis Martin's forecast? Maybe, but since Louis based his reports on the National Weather Service, Claire had to assume that indirectly his information was coming from Emmett Nelson. Claire was totally baffled. The equipment at the Weather Service was cutting-edge and much more advanced than what she had to work with, but it was still highly unlikely that her information could be so different from his. The discrepancy was all the more troubling since Claire and Emmett almost never disagreed. Right from the start, Claire had recognized Emmett as a kindred spirit, the type who, like her, would forget to eat, sleep, or dress until he got things right. He was the man who had flown a Twin Otter inside the rim of a hurricane's eye, the man who had *been there,* and in contrast to the new breed of meteorologists who relied solely on data, Emmett had that special, tactile, finger-in-the-wind feeling for when a storm was coming. Ever since his Florida childhood when he watched the roof of his parents' house turn to matchsticks during a Category Four, Emmett had felt a tremendous respect for nature; and an intentional distortion of information seemed no more likely to come from him than it would have been coming from Claire.

Or so she had thought. Claire's ideas about Emmett derived solely from the one thing they had in common, and based on it, Claire had imagined an entire man. It never occurred to her that although they were like-minded meteorologists, the resemblance ended there, and that while she was trying to figure out what was going on with him, Emmett was hurrying over to NRD where he wanted to create the impression that Hurricane Louis might make landfall.

He was eager to get to NRD early, before their daily lunch meeting at 12:30, which was when they always met so that they would have time to alert Macdill to get a plane ready if they were going to fly a cane. He was not so foolish as to imagine that his input would affect their decision, but he wanted to be on the record just in case his subsequent behavior was ever investigated. Rushing out of the office, he grabbed a sandwich at the lobby lunch bar, put on his sunglasses—polarized lens with a wrap frame and side shields—and braced himself for the Florida sun. It wasn't even mid-morning, but the Miami sun had been shining for several hours and was already very bright and demanding. Renee said that, as a native Floridian, he should be used to it; but the sun and Renee were both relentless co-conspirators, and he had begun to feel stalked by the sun, the way it was always there, waiting, anticipating his every move. It even occurred to him that some of the secrecy that had begun to describe his behavior might be interpreted as his private retreat from the intrusive Florida glare, but he knew that if he got caught manipulating the numbers, the sun's rays would make a very poor defense.

There was a group of about thirty scientists, support staff, and PhDs huddled around a rickety table in front of two monitors when Emmett got there. Emmett spotted Susan, the Columbia graduate student that Claire had referred for an internship, and made sure that she saw him too before he pulled his chair up next to Pete.

"Anything good?" he asked. Pete was hunched over a pastrami sandwich, mustard dripping on tin foil.

"Hey buddy," Pete looked up and smiled, "I thought you quit this place?" When Emmett left NRD for NWS, Pete thought he wouldn't see too much more of him.

"Hey," Emmett shrugged, "once a chaser, always chaser."

"Well, you won't find too much chasing going on here," Pete leaned in toward Emmett and spoke in undertones. "El Jefe, over there," he said pointing his head in the direction of their new lab director, Derek Bolton, "is very budget conscious. He won't call Tampa unless a cane is practically guaranteed. He's more interested in staying on good terms with the powers that be than with the Powers that Be, if you know what I mean."

"If you were in charge," Emmett asked, "would you be checking that out?" he asked, pointing to a red and orange mass on the top right corner of the monitor.

"Tough call. It's what we've been talking about for the past fifteen minutes. The numbers coming off the Cray," he said referring to the supercomputer in Suitland, Maryland, "are ambiguous. I'd probably wait, at least till tomorrow."

Emmett thought that was what he would do too. At least it was what he would have done if he had been in charge of research. But it was his own personal budget not NRD's he was worried about, and at the moment he wanted them to take a potential hurricane seriously enough so that they could justify chasing it and he could justify predicting it.

"Is there so little money in the kitty that you can't gamble on a cane's development?" he asked.

Pete looked at him incredulously. "When did we ever have any money? Have you been over at NWS so long that you've forgotten what a tight budget is? The problem," Pete continued, "is that, at the moment, it's not clear whether the storm will make landfall. Bolton's only interested in the ones that serve the dual purpose of research and prediction, and so far, this baby looks like it's staying in the swimming pool. The public doesn't care about storms at sea. If we flew this one, we might find out something about how storms strengthen over the ocean, but Bolton wants to know how the wind field behaves when it comes on shore." He took another bite of his sandwich. "In any case," he continued, his mouth half full of pastrami, "as a matter of intellectual curiosity, what do you think it's going to do? Any hunches?"

Emmett was really glad Pete asked. It would look better if he'd been consulted than if he imposed his opinion. "This one's a sleeper," he said with conviction. Pete was really surprised and was getting ready for a good debate, when Emmett, whose visit had only lasted a few minutes, got up, one arm in the sleeve of his windbreaker, and started to leave.

"Been to Hialeah lately?" Pete asked, implying that Emmett's prediction had about as much science to it as a bet on a horse.

"Yes, as a matter of fact. Been there and won. Trust me," Emmett continued, "this one's a road warrior."

Pete looked back up at the monitor, confused. If it hadn't been for Emmett's record of accuracy, he would have dismissed the prediction as way premature.

Traffic had begun to thicken near the toll as Emmett headed back to NWS. A black Lexus was in the lane next to his, and Emmett was imagining himself in it. He had never even dreamed of owning a desirable car before, but things were different now, and it was just possible that the time had come for him to join the world of people who could afford things. In his previous life as a simple meteorologist, the purchase of a car would have been a very big deal, and there would have been months of car research and comparative pricing, not to mention discussions with Renee, before he finally made his first installment. But that time seemed to be coming to an end, and even purchases like the Lexus began to look within his reach. The irony was that before he and Renee started making money, even though there had been many desires Emmett couldn't indulge, he had been able to pursue his one true desire, which was to lead a life of the mind. And if it hadn't been for Renee, he would have stuck with that life and never given any thought to making changes. Renee, however, was not an intellectual but a housewife—which is to say, a bookkeeper—and her life, the life that preceded their acquisition of wealth, had not been particularly gratifying. She'd had to constantly worry about what things cost, and even the simplest pleasures involved budgeting. Unlike Emmett, who found fulfillment in his work, her life was mindless and sterile, and it made her angry that someone as knowledgeable and talented as her husband should make less money than an MBA thirty years Emmett's junior and fresh out of business school.

The change in their circumstance had begun innocently enough, which is, perhaps, the way most things come about. Innocently and with a financial underpinning. It all began with their daughter's college tuition, which was unbelievably high because, despite their relatively modest income, they were homeowners and that disqualified them from scholarship money. He and Renee could have handled the tuition if their daughter had gone to Miami State, but she was accepted at Princeton and Emmett simply couldn't deny her the opportunity. Up to that point, he and Renee had been meeting expenses, but with the cost of a private university, they were forced to take out a second mortgage, and the second mortgage practically led to a second marriage because Renee was convinced the mortgage wouldn't have been necessary if Emmett had agreed to do a little moonlighting to cover the extra costs. She had gotten wind of great opportunities for meteorologists in energy consulting and desperately wanted Emmett to sign on.

"It's obvious," she would say, adopting a business-like tone, which gave the appearance of equanimity when, in fact, it concealed an unfortunate propensity toward shrillness and accusation. "All you have to do…" That was where the conversation usually ended. All he had to do? All he had to do! What did she think he'd been doing for the past thirty years if not working to support them!

The debate about money might have continued indefinitely had it not been for Emmett's mother. But less than one month after their daughter's graduation, the moment Emmett had identified as their release from financial obligation, his mother had a stroke. The stroke didn't leave her paralyzed, but her left eyelid drooped, and, as if it were a blind partially lowered on her brain, she suffered from severe memory loss and paranoia and began needing help with basic functions. The effect on Emmett of her decline, more an event than a process, as sudden as the slap of a wave in an otherwise calm sea, was to view life as urgent, something that should neither be put off nor lived with a constant and wary eye on the wallet. For the first time in his life, he started to think about money, and not just money to pay the bills either, but enough so that he could fish from his own boat instead of off the pier. Why not? If he was going to make changes in order to make money, then he might as well make enough to justify altering a lifelong routine.

He didn't say anything to Renee at first. The subject of money would come up again, there was no doubt of that, and when it did, after it had taken its usual route to the phrase "all you have to do," he would let her explain what she had in mind. It wasn't long before the opportunity arose. The board of his condo had decided to make some necessary building improvements, and each apartment received an assessment, ranging anywhere from one to several thousand dollars. The money was intended to fortify the foundation of their building, which was beginning to show the effects of land erosion, and that really irritated Renee because their apartment was in the back, a small two bedroom unit that had none of the benefits of waterfront. They might as well have lived in the desert for all the good their location did them. It was okay for Emmett, who was interested in fishing and not in views, but from Renee's perspective, it made no sense at all to live on the water and look out onto a service road.

She had been emptying a grocery bag of Slim-Fast Optima when Emmett walked in to the kitchen, the assessment in his hand. The kitchen counter, like everything else in the apartment, aggravated Renee. It wasn't its peeling aluminum edge so much as the old-fashioned vinyl—which could have been tile or marble if only Emmett had shown a little initiative—that got to her. She was wearing gym clothes, an elasticized body suit that confirmed the need for diet drink, and waited silently for Emmett's comment. She fully expected him to defend the building assessment.

"Twelve hundred dollars" he said despondently. "Well, I guess there's some advantage to an assessment over an increase in carrying charges. But still…" To Renee's surprise and delight, he wasn't defending the assessment. In fact, he seemed dismayed by it. Could it be that keeping her own mouth shut was the way to get him to open up? She saw her chance. She knew she had to go slow, not overdo it, but for the first time since they had begun to argue about money, they seemed in sympathy with each other. Very slowly, very carefully, and with very little of the opposition she had encountered in the past, she explained how they could get out from under. It was really quite simple. The insurance companies were crafting all sorts of monetary instruments to protect business from the ups and downs of the weather. A whole industry was developing around climate modeling, and Emmett, with his superior skills and access to equipment, was uniquely positioned to take advantage of it. "Emmett, you could earn more and work less. All you have to do…"

CHAPTER FIFTEEN

"All you have to do," Judy was saying, "is give them their damned forecast. What is the big deal?" It was early evening, and instead of going home after her afternoon broadcast, Claire had taken the long drive to Manhattan. They were sitting on Judy's terrace enjoying the little bit of sun that had broken through the clouds. "Do you think it's clearing up?" Judy asked.

"No, this is very temporary, I assure you. Just look at the sky. It's going to rain, probably for the next few days, but there is not—and you can quote me on this—there is not going to be a hurricane." She was extremely emphatic.

"Hey, lighten up. Will you forget your forecast for a minute?" Judy said irritably. "There are other forms of nature besides the weather, you know. There is, for example, sex. There is also childbirth. Have a kid and then you'll realize what's *really* important. Your eggs, your little *unfertilized* eggs could get into the single digits pretty soon. Don't forget that they're in there, a little shrinking pile of them, calling out to you, waiting…Mama, Mama."

Claire smiled at Judy, whose bulk—the twenty pounds she couldn't seem to lose—no longer looked like overweight but like exuberance, each pound her offspring. The sun was momentarily bright as it hovered between gray clouds, and Judy put on the sunglasses dangling in front of her effusive cleavage. "The sun wins."

"Thank goodness for that, the sun's my employer." Claire closed her eyes and turned her face serenely upward like a black-eyed Susan.

"You should have married Murray. For him, everything's a metaphor too. We are now, in case you didn't know it, sailing into the harbor of our tenth anniversary. We're not just having our anniversary, mind you, but we're sailing into its harbor, where we will drop anchor and watch the tide." She started to laugh. "It's funny, but I can't stand it. If it's not one metaphor, it's another; if we're not sailors, we're stockholders, in which case we have shares in the mutual fund of our marriage."

"I think it's wonderful. What bothers you about it?" It was hard for Claire to imagine any fissures in the Strongman marriage, which appeared completely packaged and sealed, the only seam where they were joined.

"It's hard to explain, but he's like a waiter careening around a restaurant with our marriage on a tray, showing it off. Our marriage has become a reproduction of our original attachment to each other. We're spewing out carbon copies of ourselves, and even though our affection is real, it's also simulated; we're a fifteen-year editing job." Judy appeared weary, and her added weight, which only moments earlier had looked like exuberance, now seemed like repetition, her double chin a visible sign of her own redundancy. "To tell you the truth, I envy you. You still have everything before you." She paused, as if some disturbing aspect of what she had said was just sinking in. "Even so," she continued with a vigor that rejected self-indulgence and sentimentality, "it's time to get on with it. It's great to have a lot of admirers, but they're no substitute for a lover," she said, returning to the original theme of Claire's private life. "And don't tell me about that guy Jesse, either. Trust me, he's a fiction of your imagination."

That was entirely possible. Claire hadn't seen Jesse for years, and there was no reason to believe they would end up together. She should have given him—the idea of him—up a long time ago. But he had stayed with her like a barnacle on the underbelly of her heart and wouldn't go away. A *mature* woman, Judy insisted, would have realized it was over the moment he had left the country. The moment he had set foot on that plane, she would have moved on with her life. The guy had expatriated, for God's sake, settled in another country, and as far as Judy was concerned, Claire's so-called loyalty was really a form of denial, a way to *avoid* relationships.

"At least the men I know live on this continent," she had said when the subject of Jesse first came up. "And they're available *now,*" she continued, referring to the fact that Claire hadn't seen this Jesse for years, and that, for all practical purposes, he was nothing more than a few lines in Claire's high school year book. The few lines were actually only three words, but they'd given Claire's past a magnetic hold on her future. The words "don't forget me" written in a small neat hand with no capitals and no punctuation described a feeling that had no beginning and no end, as if they were infinite and had always been there, a phrase let loose in space. The words were also instructions, and Claire had followed them: Jesse had left the country and gone to live in Italy, and Claire had not forgotten.

She remembered as far back as elementary school when he had come to her house to do a science experiment with her. They were in third grade, and he was cute in that special way best recognized by little girls of the same age. Their project had been to make a cloud, and they had poured hot water into a jar, placed a tray of ice cubes on top of it, and lain stomach down on the floor with their eyes riveted on the jar. After elementary school, they had been divided by school district, one for the better part of town where Claire lived and one for kids who lived near the center, and they didn't see each other again until four years later when their schools recombined like Siamese twins who were joined at the head. But their lives had changed during the interim, and somehow the nebulous, molten relationships of middle school had hardened into the igneous social strata of high school. Had it not been for a graduation party, they might never have been in the same room together again. However, in an unusual display of open-mindedness, the entire class was invited to the party—kids who were going to college, kids who were going into the trades, and kids like Jesse, whose fate was undetermined, and it was there, on the back patio of Ricky Scott's house, dancing to "Let It Be," that they fell in love.

The party was already in full swing when Claire walked through the living room of the big house on Myrtle and onto its back patio. A small group had formed around someone playing the guitar, and when Claire got close, she saw that it was Jesse, his stooped frame deeply cradling his guitar, his head hanging way down over it. At that time, guitar playing was considered the way to social success, and there were all kinds of teaching manuals promising that if you learned to play, then you, too, could be the life of the party. Boys supposedly played the guitar and girls supposedly played the piano, but nobody actually played in public, and when Jesse started to play, not to strum but to really play, and then, as if that were not enough, to sing, the room went completely still and he became something of a teen idol, especially to the girls who had never known any boys other than the conservative preppies and juvenile delinquents of Richmond High, dubbed Monde Riche by the French students.

After a while, Jesse made his way toward Claire, and later that night, when Claire's father went to pick her up, he found the lights to the patio dimmed, soft rock on the stereo, Claire's cheek resting against Jesse's chest, their arms entwined like vines spiraling down the sides of their bodies. Until that moment when the lights went back on signaling the presence of parents and the end of evening with their rude, intrusive, autocratic glare, Claire and her friends had been slow-dancing in the dark, their hearts beating in rhythm to the music, their minds and bodies dedicated and floating. It was the best evening of Claire's life.

How could Claire explain to Judy the meaning of that night? How could she make anyone understand that fifteen years later, she remembered its passion and the eagerness of the ensuing weeks as if they'd had a steamy affair, when, in fact, there had been nothing more than two stumbling hearts reaching out to each other? It had been late spring. Claire was going to Maine in July and college in September, and Jesse was going to Italy to study voice. All that remained was August, but the pulse of their passion was about to be interrupted, and both knew that they couldn't build up and wind down at the same time.

For a while, there were letters, and a small bundle of airmail envelopes bordered with Italy's national yellow and green stripes was tucked away in a drawer where it later bore testimony to what Claire, after a semester of French lit, referred to as the denouement of their short love story. Then the letters became postcards, and for several years, when she expected it least, she would receive a postcard from some far-flung place—Bahia, Katmandu, Cape Town. But eventually the postcards dwindled down to one or two a year, and then there were none at all. The following years brought other boyfriends—several casual, one serious—who for one reason or another didn't work out, and Claire was beginning to despair when, out of the blue, only days before her most recent visit with Judy, she got a postcard from Italy.

Word of your success has traveled as far as Rome. Congratulations! I look forward to seeing you on television on my next trip to the States, or maybe, if you can find the time, we can see each other again in person.
Gone, but not, I hope, entirely forgotten, Jesse

Claire read the postcard over and over. Over and Over, even though there was nothing hard to understand in it. Then she put her hands one on top of the other and both on top of the postcard, which she held to her heart. She didn't tell Judy about it, although the temptation was strong, especially as they relaxed on Judy's terrace. But there would be plenty of opportunity to talk about Jesse if things worked out, and if they didn't, there would be no need to subject herself to the exhortations of common sense.

"Let's go back inside," Judy said, completely unaware of what Claire was thinking. "It's getting overcast again."

Every time it rains, it rains
Pennies from heaven.
Don't you know each cloud contains
Pennies from heaven?

Johnny Burke 1908-64: "Pennies from Heaven" (1936 song)

CHAPTER SIXTEEN

Famous last words: "All you have to do." To Emmett, it had sounded like there might be *a lot* to do and that he might end up in a shitload of trouble for doing it. The potential for a calamitous domino effect resulting from those five words had kept Emmett from agreeing to anything for a long time, but when he finally let Renee steer him into some independent consulting, he found out that she had been right and that for someone with his experience, the work itself was remarkably easy. In addition, *there was absolutely no competition out there!—no one else was doing what he was doing!*—and within two years of going into business, he and Renee had managed to pay off the second mortgage and even to buy a few things. Not only that, it was Renee who, in her capacity as the entire support staff, did practically everything.

The idea was that Emmett should be spared as much work as possible—after all, he did have a full-time job—and like the surgeon who comes into the operating room after the patient is prepped and anaesthetized, "all he had to do" was to make the requested prediction: if it was an amusement park that needed to know what weather to expect for its grand opening, Emmett could tell them, and if it was a wine grower who needed rainfall levels, Emmett could help them with that too. Some of this information could be gotten without a high-priced consultant, but the insurance companies insisted on expert opinion and, as a scientist of some renown within the small world of meteorology, Emmett fit the bill.

Fit the bill, but at what price, he had asked in the beginning, unwilling to openly admit that his participation was anything but reluctant. The price, he said in answer to his own question, was to his im-meteorological soul—his im-meteorolgical soul, which risked becoming a shooting star in the milky way of morals. So what, Renee had responded, quite convinced that his im-meteorological soul, as he put it, had been allied with the heavens so long that no one could doubt that it would ultimately end up in them one day. If he hung out in corporate America for a while in the meantime, what harm could there be? What harm indeed? How could an extra ten thousand a month be considered harm? How could he complain when his life had improved immeasurably and when, instead of feeling like Atlas perennially carrying the earth on his shoulders, the earth was effortlessly bearing his weight? And the weight of Renee, his daughter, and his mother, too. Not only was the earth carrying them along, but its rivers and streams had begun to seem like waters through which his own thirty-foot boat might float, its decks a place from which to admire the waterfront home he would buy.

Their first job had come from Emma Brown, a friend of Renee's who had moved north to Stowe, Vermont. Emma's husband had a sporting goods business that had been hurt by an unseasonably warm winter and sales were way down. People said global warming was behind the temperatures, but Emma didn't care what the explanation was—it wasn't the environment she was thinking about. Renee broached the subject of weather insurance gingerly, a little uncomfortable suggesting a business deal to a friend, but hopeful that, under the circumstances, Emma would be grateful. "It's just an idea," Renee said, "but it's something I've been thinking about for a while, and it might be good for both of us. Have you ever considered buying weather insurance?"

Emma hadn't. She had never even heard of it. How did you insure against the weather, she wanted to know. "You don't," Renee explained. "You insure against weather incompatible with your business. If warm weather negatively impacts Stowe Ski, the insurance company has to compensate you. If, on the other hand, you buy protection and it turns out to be a snowy, cold winter, you're out the cost of insurance, but at least you're not out of business."

They worked something out with a local insurance company, and that was the beginning. What followed was success, and the not the kind that takes years to develop either, but meteoric rise, a short, direct ascent to financial comfort. What accounted for its rapidity was the existence of a market, almost untapped, waiting for someone with the precise tools to mine its rich veins. The desire for a hedge against the weather had existed since the time of Lloyd's coffeehouse in London; however, Renee—who increasingly spoke in the language of finance—explained that there had never been a product to trade before. Now, thanks in large part to the deregulation of energy, there were weather derivatives—costless collars, strangles, straddles, swaptions—all tradeable products—not to mention their marriage, which, Emmett had begun to perceive, was a financial product as well.

It blew Emmett's mind, his wife, talking about weather derivatives. He would sit in their living/dining room and, in utter amazement, listen to her from her office in their bedroom. "Ben," she would say to some stranger on the phone, "it's alright if I call you Ben, isn't it?" And then she would make her pitch. It made no difference who she was talking to, a ski resort or an airline, they all had weather-related needs, and Air Waves—the name was Emmett's idea—could meet them. Where did she get this stuff? Swaps, options, futures...she talked about it with the hard-edged abandon of someone who, after a lifetime of manners, had suddenly taken to cursing. Except that she was crowing, and with good reason: they were all signing on, even big names like Goldman Sachs and CIGNA.

Emmett found the work itself remarkably easy, but working for corporate giants was different from working for a national service, and it almost felt as if they were metaphysical rivals. "What do you care who you work for?" Renee had asked, agitation planted deep in the furrow of her brow. "You're still predicting the weather. The only difference is that now you're well paid. And," she added slyly, "for someone with so many scruples, you sure cash those checks fast enough."

There was no denying it: Emmett liked the money, and he felt that a great burden had been lifted when the second mortgage was paid off. The big difference was that if it hadn't been for Renee's persistent badgering, he would have stopped as soon as their debts were paid, unlike Renee, who wanted to grow the business.

"Emmett," she continued, "no one is asking you to change your life." She was clearing the dishes from their new dining room table. "You could do this in your sleep," she continued, unaware that Emmett had moved to the living room. He didn't hear what she said after "life," but he knew that it wasn't true and that his life had changed. Even the sofa he was sitting on had changed. Renee had bought it to sustain the spirit of the new dining room table, which was visible from the L-shaped living room. The sofa had changed, the dining room table had changed, and if he didn't hold on to what he believed, he would change.

Renee had already changed. She was a woman come alive, her newfound identity as risk management rep the vital nutrient missing from her Slim-Fast diet. She came into the living room, wiping her hands on her apron and looking up at the ceiling as if she could actually see the hammering in the apartment overhead. The building had thin walls and every little noise, now that they had more money, was increasingly irritating. "Emmett, do you know how hot this stuff is?" she asked, waving her arms around as she accompanied herself to the Macarena, "we—you and me—are on to something BIG!"

And even she had no idea how big it was. Even if there had never been a Katrina, Emmett's services would have been very much in demand, especially from the energy companies who needed someone who could index the number of heating degree days against the number of cooling degree days, or, as they said in the business, HDD's vs. CDD's. But after Katrina, everything changed and what had simply been a lucrative sideline became a business bonanza. Risk management was the order of the day, and Hurricane Katrina, which had ruined so many lives, was the best thing that could have happened to them. If they were going to stay in business, information that distinguished wind from water was absolutely essential to the insurance companies, and no one was better equipped than Emmett Nelson to write those distinctions into their policies. Nelson's credentials were iron-clad, and whether he turned out to be right or wrong, by using his services, the insurance companies were protecting their own interests and saving themselves millions. They, in turn, were willing to pay him substantial amounts for the savings.

Renee was thrilled. "This isn't just about money anymore, Emmett. It's about people's lives; it's about their jobs and homes," she said, trying to talk her husband into one more contract. He had been working almost round the clock and had pretty much reached his breaking point. But Renee wasn't ready for him to pack it in yet, not when there was still so much money to be made. If only he would continue a little while longer, they could get one of those amazing waterfront properties advertised in *Luxury Homes Magazine*. Her appetite had become insatiable, her mind a rubber band that, no matter how far it stretched, always snapped back to its original, opportunistic shape. "I have a feeling that you never thought of it this way, but you are performing a public service when you work for the insurance companies." She was sitting on the edge of the sofa and leaning in toward Emmett, who had switched to his old chair and was leaning back, his legs crossed like swords on a shield of armor. She was right: he did not think of it that way, and even though he was the first to admit that he liked the money, he did not like the insurance companies, which he thought of as fear-mongering vendors in a market of human misery.

"Renee, honey," he laughed, feeling neither humor nor pleasure, "I'm not one of your customers. Don't try to sell me on something." There was a photograph of him on the end table next to his chair, and he was looking at the picture instead of at her. He was standing at the end of a dock holding his fishing pole upright, a fish dangling from its hook. Renee saw the glance and knew what it meant; but she wasn't interested in his longings, not when there was a potentially huge contract in the works.

"Emmett..." she said, in that way she had.

"I'm not interested..." he said in that way he had and got up from his chair. He felt it coming, her demands like ice crystals on clouds, building up positive electrical charges at their top and negative charges at their base; a thunderstorm was brewing.

"Please. One more contract, just one more." She actually looked kind of cute when she pleaded, her head cocked to the side, more human than when she was in business mode.

He turned away and looked out the window. It was unseasonably hot, even for Florida, and sweat was staining the armpits of his guayabera, which, thanks to the Cubans, had become a popular style of dress.

"... they insure *all* the hotels on the Florida coast," she continued, apparently elaborating on whatever she had said in the kitchen "Need I say more?"

Emmett didn't need to know what she had said—all she talked about was the business. "No, no, no need to say more," he muttered with obvious irritation.

Renee backed off momentarily. He had become like another customer, and she knew the risk of a hard sell, especially with him. But she also knew that she had to tell the insurance company something and couldn't just wait for Emmett's mood to change "Look, Emmett," she started again, more business-like this time.

"You don't give up, do you?" he interrupted sharply, putting his keys and wallet in his pocket. More and more, he was feeling the need to be alone, and although he used to like the idea of an evening stroll with his wife, he stopped suggesting that they go out together and made for the door.

It was getting to be twilight, and he didn't want to miss the sunset. It was his favorite hour, the moment when the relentless sun began to close shop on the day, and the building elevator, a glass box inside steel girders, afforded a perfect view of the sun's descent. On that particular evening, with either ominous or auspicious coincidence, he was descending to ground level at the same moment the sun dipped below the horizon, and it was with a sense of rebirth that he stepped from the elevator and onto the green cement walkway that led to the front of the condo where two plastic palm trees flanked the building entrance.

The building itself was a largely glass structure whose cinder blocks stood on pilings reaching into native marl. Front and side were surrounded by cactus, palm, and mangrove. The back of the building, which faced the service road running into the thruway, had no plantings because, at least according to management, it was too shady; but it was hard to avoid the impression that its barren state could be more accurately explained by prejudice against the rear and impecunious side of the building than by growing conditions. Renee had even planted something herself just to prove that things would grow, but management felt no need to defend their position, even after a little green shoot had emerged.

A creature of habit, Emmett took the path toward the water with its thick, high hedge of punk trees on one side and little flat stones on the other. It was quiet, with a soothing stillness punctuated only by the rhythmic putter of the sprinkler system and someone's repeated efforts to start a motor boat. Emmett followed the path around a small field dotted with cabbage palm, and as he walked, he thought of all the times he and Renee had taken this stroll together. It was on those occasions that he had begun to realize the extent to which she was a dissatisfied woman. Whereas he looked forward to the walk as a pause in the day, a tranquil moment of relaxation, Renee saw it as an opportunity to strategize and find ways to upgrade and improve their lives. He had never really understood the passion to own. The moment the roof flew off his parents' house during Hurricane Donna had truly been a great moment for him. It had confirmed nature's grandeur, revealed God's power, and formed the basis of his desire to become a chaser. He sat down on a bench facing the ocean and stared blankly in front of him. How could you protect yourself against this, he thought, looking at water and sky. The very idea offended him.

A pelican standing on a bit of marsh by the dock suddenly poked its head down. Seconds later, it re-appeared with a fish flapping from each side of its long bill. That was what Emmett was going to do too: he was going to exploit the confidence he had earned during his career and make one score so big that it would obviate the need to ever work again. Year after year, he had submitted reports predicting a disaster in Louisiana, and they had been ignored. Now, he would predict a hurricane that would dissipate, and they would heed his warning.

Renee said he was much more powerful than he realized, and that one statement from him could dramatically affect the economy. "A pronouncement from you will be as influential as anything Ben Bernanke has to say. People will buy and sell when you predict a rise or fall in temperatures same as if you were raising or lowering interest rates." Well, if she was right and he was truly the Ben Bernanke of the weather, then in a very short time, they would be extremely rich, she would have her house, he would have his boat, and life would return to normal.

CHAPTER SEVENTEEN

While Emmett pondered a return to the simple life, Louis prepared for a life of fame. His preparation began with his hair and wardrobe, each requiring a degree of care and attention he rarely gave his actual weather report. He didn't write his own reports anyway, whereas he selected his clothes himself. He actually expended a great deal of time and energy on his choice of outfits, studying each suit, shirt, and tie both individually and in combination to make sure they were well coordinated and that they conformed to the day and the season. Regis, his personal hair stylist and sometimes partner, vehemently disagreed with Louis's assertion that you couldn't wear midnight blue, dark brown, or charcoal in spring or summer. "My darling boy," he remonstrated, turning his head almost ninety degrees from a stiffly elongated neck and looking at Louis from under eyelids fluttering with theatrical indignation, "you must be true to yourself. To thine own self be true, sweetheart, especially when you're about to become a star," he said, brandishing the paste of peroxide and cream developer he was about to apply to Louis's almost illustrious forelock.

"Not too light," Louis said, always a little nervous when the bleach was applied.

"Trust me, darling. Have I ever let you down?" Actually there had been one time when his hair had come out more caramel than ash, but Louis didn't say anything. He wanted Regis to concentrate.

"So when exactly is this hurricane going to strike?" Regis hunched his shoulders together and shuddered. Louis gave his standard non-answer, citing current conditions and offering various alternatives to how the storm might develop. In other words, pretty much the same thing he'd already said on the news.

"Tell me something I don't already know, darling. What good is an inside track if you don't know any more than I do?"

As soon as Regis left and Louis had decided on his greenish twill suit, he lay down on his Aireloom mattress, his only major indulgence besides the installation of a California closet, and turned on the weather channel. When there was severe weather, the weather channel's information came directly and exclusively from NWS, so if Emmett Nelson was predicting a hurricane, there would certainly be something about it in on the news. But there was nothing. Instead, Dr. Steve Lyons, the weather channel's main reporter for extreme weather, led with a story about unrelenting heat in the Southern Plains and lower Mississippi Valley. He went on to describe a low-pressure front drifting across the Gulf Coast states. The front was bringing a lot of rain with it, but that rain had nothing to do with the hurricane. When he was almost finished, he mentioned—merely mentioned—hurricane activity in the Caribbean. Louis turned up the sound as Lyons explained that the satellite imagery was inconclusive and that late season storms were hard calls, something to do with their being closer to land and developing in fragmented atmospheric environments.

Louis grabbed a pen and tried to get Lyons' report on the back of an envelope, but he couldn't write fast enough. While he was scrambling to copy what had just been said, Lyons continued with a short piece about tropical storm systems, which, he explained, were only given names when they reached the storm stage, or, technically speaking, when they involved rotary circulation and constant winds of over thirty-eight miles per hour.

One such storm, he went on to say, had been baptized Louis. Louis's heart skipped a beat. Hearing his name in this way, in connection with the birth of something powerful, a potential force in the universe, had a profound effect on him. He had never thought of himself as someone with real impact, and his reputation as a male model who had become a rip and reader (they said he ripped instead of stripped) bothered him a lot. It didn't bother him enough to induce him to study meteorology; but he nonetheless craved respect and wouldn't have minded in the least if he was effortlessly delivered from his current reputation to a better one. Then, like Neptune rising out of the water—or was it Poseidon—trident in hand—he could face his critics as Hurricane Louis, the human dynamo.

That immensely satisfying fantasy was interrupted by more hurricane news. Louis, it turned out, was not the only system of indeterminate fate swirling around the Caribbean. There were others, rival systems, all vying for a promotional spot on television. Louis felt betrayed and angry, crestfallen. His own personal hurricane, his idealized self, was not the redemptive force he'd imagined, but a mirror image of himself, neither grand nor special in any way, just your basic storm hoping for a break that would lead to hurricane status: his namesake was a potential stillbirth. Petulant, his first impulse was to call Katie and complain, but that seemed kind of childish. The more mature and sensible thing was to wait for developments. Unless he could find a way…then it came to him. Why not imitate Lyons? He could give a brief weather report followed by a more extensive description of the activity in the Caribbean.

That way, he could talk up Louis as the principal player in a constantly changing situation and come across as an expert at the same time. He could explain how hurricanes developed and disappeared, give a lesson in hurricane history. He might even tear a page from Claire's book and do something creative. But what? All he did was work out in the gym and go to his water ballet class. Regis said Louis's problem was that he rejected his interests instead of exploiting them, and that he should… he should what? Louis asked impatiently. Lift weights on television? Do a water ballet with the women in his class? Yeah, why not? said Regis, all huffy.

• • •

At the very moment that Louis was trying to come up with the kind of imaginative thing Claire did, she was at her desk staring at her computer monitor. Only one day had passed since she'd met with Russo and Goodwin, and she was desperately hoping for some decisive storm activity that would give her a scientific reason to cooperate with them. Louis had become a Category One with bands of torrential rain spiraling north through southern Florida, but Claire was still quite certain that a weak Category One down south—which at seventy-six miles an hour, was only two miles over the seventy-four required to achieve hurricane status—did not spell a hurricane in Bridge Haven. The much greater likelihood, and the pattern that had always prevailed, was that it would either change course altogether or, if it continued north, peter out when it reached cooler water.

While Claire stared at her screen, a hand belonging to Russo reached around the side of her and pointed to the storm's coordinates. Claire was so absorbed that she hadn't known he was there and started when she heard him say, "What's that?"

"Why good morning, Don. What?" Claire put her hand over her eyebrows, as if to scan the horizon.

"Very funny," Russo said, pulling up a chair that looked far too small for his bulk. He had nicked himself while shaving and there was cream on the cut to stop the bleeding. The whole night before, he had thought about what he wanted to tell Claire, even talked it over with Barbara, and as if he were preparing to come clean, he had shaved too close. "Yes, that. That Category One hurricane."

"It sounds to me like you know what it is," said Claire, anchoring a loose strand of curl behind her ear.

"Claire," he said, leaning forward, his large stomach propped up by his thighs, his tie hanging down between his legs. The folds of his neck were gathered like a bouquet inside the top button of his shirt. "I don't like interference any more than you do. It's not just an assault on the integrity of your weather report, but it's also a challenge to the integrity of the station. And to my authority," he added. That was what Barbara had told him to say. She actually thought that Claire was kind of naïve in thinking that the station could simply rebuff the mayor, and she also thought that Claire was arrogant in assuming that it was only her integrity that was under attack. Russo didn't quite see it that way because his own integrity was a rather obscure thing, something he didn't have much contact with or reason to protect, but once Barbara mentioned the insult to his standards, it seemed like it might be a good idea to defend them and to ally himself with the honorable and the aggrieved.

"In that case," Claire said, "I don't see why you don't just tell the mayor that you cannot oblige him."

"I wish it were that simple. But in this business, the name of the game is ratings, and your competition over at FYI has already begun racking up with his hurricane hype."

"I wonder what he'll say when it turns out to be a dud?"

"He'll say," Russo responded with the alacrity of someone completely familiar with media subterfuge, "that he'd rather have egg on his face for excessive caution than be responsible for ignoring a possible threat to the public." Russo searched Claire's face as he talked, hoping her response would be reflected in her large, clear eyes. His hope, however, was not to be realized, and he once again discovered, as he already had on several other occasions, that clear and revealing are not the same thing, and that her integrity was as clear as her purpose was obscure to him.

A new set of numbers indicating a change in Louis's position moved across the monitor. Even though the storm was still a fledgling, it was picking up speed and moving in a northerly direction. "How about one more broadcast?" she suggested. "How about letting me do the five o'clock news before we make a final decision. As you can see, the storm's still pretty far south. If it continues to intensify, I'll cover it at eleven," she suggested. Claire knew that even she couldn't flatly refuse Russo, but she hoped that she could at least buy some time.

"No can do. I've got too many people breathing down my neck."

"Okay, boss," Claire reneged with a sigh, "you'll get your hurricane advisory. But," she added, "and here's the fine print—I'll tell it straight. I won't dismiss it, but I won't play it up either. No poetry, no prose. Just the facts." She looked at him levelly. "Deal?"

"Deal," he said, responding like a poor parishioner so grateful for receiving alms that he didn't even stop to think about the implications of what Claire said. They'd made a deal, the matter was taken care of, and the fine print, well, to hell with the fine print. It would all get worked out later, he thought, having decided only the night before that he worried too much and that his blood pressure, already on the high side, could not withstand the aggravation.

He was back in his office talking to his wife on the phone when he was distracted by the sound of laughter. It sounded like it was coming from Dan Liebowitz' desk. With sudden foreboding, afraid that his clever weather reporter had introduced so many qualifiers and circumspections into her broadcast that she had managed to turn her forecast into a farce, Russo rushed down the hall to see what was so funny. He found Dan stomping his feet and pointing to one of the televisions on the wall. Russo looked at the monitor, and after he figured out what he was looking at, he started to laugh too.

Within minutes, Reed, Katie, and Fletcher were all staring at the screen, but instead of JTF it was FYI they were watching, spellbound by the sight of six or seven women in a swimming pool. The women were identically clad in bright yellow swimsuits and yellow bathing caps, which were offset by the brilliant blue of the pool. They raised and lowered joined hands in a motion that, seen from overhead, created the impression of expanding and contracting circles. A yellow beach ball was introduced into their midst, and, in an attitude of gleeful frolic, the ball was batted from one to the other. There was much smiling, laughter, and splashing about. Had it not been for the FYI logo in the upper right corner of the screen, anyone might have thought they were watching a Busby Berkeley water ballet instead of the weather.

The scene progressed with the yellow representatives of fair weather and good cheer keeping the sunny ball aloft as it was thrown high from one swimmer to the other. Meanwhile, six more women appeared by the sides of the pool. They were also identically clad, except that their suits and caps were black and each had a white ribbon extending from right shoulder to left hip. The ribbons were inscribed with the names of the potential hurricanes Muriel, Nestor, and Odilie. They dove into the pool and, like forces of evil foreshadowing doom, remained under water until they surfaced inside the yellow circle where their emerging black heads brought about a great deal of shrieking, shuddering, and flailing of arms among their yellow counterparts. Their cries provoked renewed laughter from JTF's management, which now included Goodwin as well as Russo.

The water ballet continued with the swimmers in black diving over the joined hands of the swimmers in yellow, weaving in and out of the inner circle like porpoises. The swimmers in yellow put the palms of their hands on their cheeks, fingers facing backward toward their ears and elbows extending outward, and rocked their heads back and forth in a "woe is me" posture. After the harbingers of stormy weather had exhibited their superiority over the forces of sunshine, they dove into the middle of the pool again, where they raised joined hands in a circle of triumph. Then, just when everyone thought the show was over, a man in tight fitting black trunks burst from under the water into the middle of the circle of bathing beauties like a rocket from a cannon, water flying from his body.

Was that a trident in his hand? Was his hair blonde? Was that Louis?!!! Dan could hardly believe his eyes.

Louis's triumphant appearance brought the ballet to dramatic conclusion, and seconds after it was over, he re-appeared by his chroma-key, his combed wet hair a testimony to what had preceded. His co-workers at the news desk were all laughing, and Louis was laughing too, his blue eyes twinkling merrily. The first comment, "What a bod," came from Katie's counterpart at FYI, a Filipino woman with a slightly British accent. More laughter. "I bet the terrible twos were no picnic with a stormy kid like you," she added, the temptation to make weather puns irresistible. More banter, more laughter. "So, Louis, can we really expect a hurricane?" again the anchorwoman.

At that point, Louis's mood changed, signaling that the fun was over and that it was time to become serious. "One of the ideas behind that little sketch was to show that there are many forces at work in the ocean," he said, his earnest expression an indication that he was a man of parts—a versatile man, a talented man, a man able to clown around on the one hand and do the serious stuff on the other. "At this very moment there are several storm systems at play out there, any one of which could develop into a hurricane, but," he added, his mischievous smile back again for a seductive second, "in all likelihood, they won't. The only one we have to worry about right now is, yes, you guessed it, that rascal

Louis, which is currently moving in our direction at a rate of seventy-six miles an hour. Now, according to the Saffir-Simpson scale, which is used by meteorologists to categorize hurricane strength, at this moment Louis is the weakest category of hurricane. But all that could change if the right conditions prevail." As he said that, he realized that "right" was the wrong word and that he didn't want to sound as if he actually hoped the hurricane would intensify. "If, for example…" and he went on to describe the conditions that might contribute to worsening weather and the possible effects of a severe storm in Bridge Haven.

It wasn't until Louis had finished that JTF watched their own broadcast. Then, as soon as Claire was on the television in front of them, Russo was reminded of the deal they had struck. "Just the facts," she had said, and he had agreed. He had agreed and he had screwed up. He should never have gone along with her. But how could he have known that Louis—vain, stupid, and turgid Louis—was capable of such delightful entertainment? Goodwin was going to be pissed. "Just the facts" was not at all what Goodwin had in mind when he told Claire about the mayor's request for a hurricane advisory. To the contrary, Goodwin had wanted her to do the kind of thing that Louis had just done. He didn't want anyone to *even notice the actual facts.* What he'd wanted were drum rolls, cymbals, lightning. Strobe lights flashing on and off. In short, what he wanted was for Claire, who was great at dreaming stuff up, to do what she did best.

Claire was standing beside a satellite map and pointing to an air mass heading across the Gulf Coast states. To Russo's suddenly apprehensive eye, she looked plain, uninspired. Her tone was muted, her voice flat, her eyes without sparkle. By any standard, Claire was a good-looking woman; but her beauty came from somewhere else, and at that particular moment, she appeared ordinary to him. Precipitation, she said, was expected to continue locally and regionally. There would be intermittent showers, and rain would be heavy at times. A Category One hurricane in the area of Cuba might affect the Northeast, but it would have to become a whole lot stronger if it were to have an impact on Bridge Haven. The current downpour they were experiencing was unrelated to the hurricane in the Caribbean and had originated east of the Rockies.

As if a role reversal had taken place, Claire delivered a weather report as dull as Louis's was dynamic. Her report was a dud, a potential firecracker that fizzled before it even got off the ground—and very much like, Claire would later argue when Goodwin asked her to explain herself, the hurricane itself. So anticlimactic was her segment of the news, that there was an awkward silence before anyone even realized it was over and before Reed was ready to resume the smooth, glib patter of news-speak. After an instant, which lasted just long enough to register the report's obliquity, Reed cleared his throat and re-established the news to proper levity where, like verbal water-skiing, it skimmed the surface of the serious and the sincere without ever making contact with either. "And on that note, we switch to a brighter topic and to the Mets victory at Shea…Fletcher…"

"What was that all about?" Goodwin asked, still staring at the screen. "What's going on here anyway? First water ballet and then…then the drabbest, most boring report I've ever seen." The nostrils of his pinched nose flared. Dan found the question infuriating and was very inclined to say that what was "going on here" had been going on daily for all the years before Claire had come on board. He would have liked to point out that a bad day for Claire was the equivalent of every day for their previous weather reporter, Norwood Fossil, and that the only reason Goodwin could even ask that question was because Claire had created something so special that the ordinary looked like failure.

Dan was the only person in the room even tempted to argue with Goodwin, but something prevented him from speaking up, and when he didn't defend her, Katie experienced the first moment of relief she had known since the day Claire's ratings had topped hers. Who was there to be afraid of? Goodwin was totally fickle; Russo had the right impulses, but he didn't have the intelligence to support them; Reed was more interested in protecting his own turf than in defending Claire's; and Fletcher didn't really count. Dan was the only person left, and, to her surprise and delight, it turned out that he wasn't the threat she had imagined. After allowing Goodwin's remark to linger a little longer, Katie reluctantly added that she could not understand how Claire could have treated a potential hurricane so lightly. Didn't she have a greater responsibility to the public? Again, no one said anything.

CHAPTER EIGHTEEN

Now that Louis's water ballet had gotten the ball rolling, Freddy wanted to build on the momentum. The five o'clock news had just aired, so if he held an emergency press conference right away to announce his plan for a storm shelter, then there could be a recap at six and the public would get a really heavy dose of him being mayor-like. He felt like a surfer catching a wave. He had to act while anticipation was high and before there was reason to believe the hurricane might not materialize. Actually, he was in luck because it was raining steadily, sometimes hard, and severe gusts of wind were littering the streets with debris. Moist air from the Great Plains was dumping buckets along the Connecticut and New York coast, and, simultaneously, humid air was moving up from Florida. The converging systems were drenching the area with water, and while a storm surge was unlikely, Bridge Haven's Flats flooded easily and were capable of causing considerable damage to surrounding property, particularly to the bridge area adjacent to the thruway. Anyone foolish enough to drive through its underpass when the water level was high could have a very rough time of it, and during the hurricane of 1938, a drowning had even occurred there. The headline had read "Manor Resident Drowns in Flats," which somehow said it all, at least to the people who lived in the Flats and were convinced that chronic flooding would not have been allowed in the Manor and would not have been considered an outrage if the deceased had lived in the Flats.

Privately, Freddy agreed. The rich always had it easier. It was poor Blacks, not the rich, who had been corralled into the super dome in Louisiana while everyone else hightailed it out of town. Oh my God, he thought, a sudden pang interrupting his scheming. Suppose people thought this situation was like that one? *He* knew it wasn't the same because Katie had concocted it, but suppose *other* people thought it was the same? Suppose they pointed out that the shelter would most likely be used by the poor? Suppose they said the Flats was a ghetto inhabited by Blacks, and that, not coincidentally, it was the most likely part of town to flood? Suppose they said that although he was taking precautions, precautions would not have been necessary if he had adopted the water diversion system proposed by his predecessor? Oh my God, the water diversion system! People would compare the water diversion system to the levees, and say that in both cases there had been no political will. What would he say then? He couldn't admit that he preferred old people to poor people; he couldn't say that the senior center had taken precedent over the water diversion system because old people voted for him and poor people didn't vote.

That, really, was his grievance with the poor. As far as Freddy was concerned, people who didn't vote got what they deserved. The residents of the Flats complained plenty when they had problems—which was all the time—and were only too willing to mouth off against the government—local, state, and federal—when they had the chance; but when it came time to vote, for some mysterious reason, they were nowhere to be seen. In this particular instance Freddy was glad they hadn't gone to the polls because if they had, they would almost certainly have supported the construction of the water diversion system; and if they had done that, then there would be no risk of the Flats flooding, and there would be one less reason to set up a shelter.

Of course, the residents of the Flats were likely to point out that it flooded every time it rained, hurricane or no hurricane, and there had never been a shelter before. They would say that by investing in the senior center, Coniglia had, in effect, *allowed* the Flats to flood again. But that was a criticism he could handle because in politics, as in comedy, timing was everything; and *after* he set up the shelter, *after* he did his levelheaded best to protect Bridge Haven from the *mere possibility* of flooding, *after* he promised that never again during his tenure as mayor would he allow the good people of Bridge Haven's Flats to suffer from flooding and that the very first order of business of his second term would be the implementation of the water diversion system, *after* all that, it would seem kind of petty, almost mean-spirited, to criticize the building of the senior center. We all learn from our mistakes, he would tell the public, and now that we've seen the kind of devastation that flooding can cause, I think everyone in office has to take stock and re-evaluate their priorities. That was what he would say, and *after* a statement like that, it would be very hard for anyone to condemn him.

After, he kept thinking *after,* but that was only because he didn't want to think about *now* and what lay immediately ahead. Even in grade school his teachers had said that he had a tendency to procrastinate, but now, he advised himself, *now* was the moment to act. Leaning as far toward his left shoulder as his short, thick neck would allow, he slowly rolled his head from one side to the other. Then he inhaled deeply, letting the air out to the count of five, and called his aide John on the office intercom. Ten minutes later, the local news stations had been informed that in response to hazardous weather conditions, the mayor was setting up an evacuation shelter in the high school. He would be making a live broadcast shortly.

"Shit," said Russo when he heard about the shelter. He had felt confident that the excitement was pretty much over: Louis had scored some points, but Claire would be proven the more accurate of the two and the whole hurricane brouhaha would just blow over, so to speak. The last thing he expected was shelters. He didn't quite get it, didn't quite understand the point to the shelter, but their job was to report the news, not to evaluate the mayor's motives; and this time he couldn't let Claire get away with "just the facts." Persuading himself that he now had the right to give Claire a clear directive, he called Dan on the office intercom.

"Say whatever you want to her," he admonished as soon as Dan had closed the door to Russo's office behind him, "but get Claire to cooperate. And by cooperate, I don't mean merely alluding to the *possibility* of a hurricane. We can't have our news team covering a live broadcast of the mayor in an evacuation shelter at the same time our weather reporter is forecasting showers. Showers just don't justify shelters. It's like we're making a fool of the mayor."

"He is a fool," said Dan morosely, privately wondering how he'd ended up in this two-bit television station. True, he'd only gone to Queen's College, but it was actually a very good school at the time that he went there. The only thing wrong with Queens was its middle-class Jewish image, the one he had, despite himself, adopted, and the one that, even graduating magna cum laude, he could not shake. It was school name and not class rank, he discovered, that mattered in the end.

Russo was standing by his window. "He may be a fool, but he's a smart one," he retorted, trying to understand the import of his own words and wondering if he had described himself as well as the mayor. He sat down to concentrate. Sometimes he had the strange feeling that his mind was running a few laps behind his mouth and that if he could only catch up and examine his statements, he would know whether he was smart or not. He had once described this feeling to Barbara, who said she could answer that question for him and walked out of the room laughing. "I mean," Russo added, in case what he had said was dumb, "he's probably got millions—what with all the money he and his relatives have been skimming—and he's now about to weasel his way out of a corruption scandal."

"Yeah, with our help," said Dan who was still berating himself for letting Goodwin's comment about Claire pass.

"What do you mean?"

"The hurricane. The shelter. There's something fishy about the whole thing."

"Well what should we do about it?" Russo asked, impressed at how quickly Dan caught on.

"Nothing," Dan looked at Russo impatiently. He had been studying the age spots on his hands. "It's news and we cover it. If the mayor wants to make an ass of himself, that's his business. It's no more up to us to tell the mayor what to do than…" and here he paused, "to tell Claire what weather to forecast." He looked at Russo defiantly. Somehow, it was easier to stand up to Russo than to Goodwin. "I am sure," he added in a more conciliatory tone, "that she will find a way to word her report so that it's not an embarrassment to anyone, but I, for one, am not going to tell her what to say."

Having expressed himself on the subject of Claire, Dan felt immediately better. And so, actually, did Russo, who, after listening to Dan, changed his mind about how to deal with Claire and felt relieved of some terrible burden. "You're a good man, Liebowitz. My wife always tells me that I worry too much, and I think she's right. We cover the news, that's all. We don't dictate and we don't censor," he said, mostly to himself. He picked up the paperweight on his desk—a Christmas present from his son—turned it upside down, and watched the little white flakes create a snowy landscape inside its glass hemisphere. The moment of magic was in the descending snow, and once it settled, it lost its allure. "What do you think?" Russo asked, watching the snow land anti-climactically on a plastic woodland scene. "Is this hurricane for real, or is it a figment of someone's imagination?"

"Beats the hell out of me," said Dan, running his hand over hair that, now that he had begun wearing it in a pony tail, was smooth beneath his touch.

• • •

Three crews of television reporters descended on PS 141. A lot of people seemed involved in the preparation of the shelter, coming and going and milling about, and the mayor was at the center of it all, answering questions, directing traffic, making statements. The gym was lined with cots, a folded blanket at the foot of each one, and a long narrow table was stocked with flashlights, first aid equipment, and water. The mayor was consulting with a Red Cross nurse and a policeman, each conspicuously outfitted in the costume of his profession. From a public relations standpoint, the preparation of the shelter was at least as important as the actual press conference, and cameramen were roaming around the room, cameras on their shoulders, filming the hubbub.

Jason Fremd was JTF's reporter on the scene and a dialogue was taking place between him and Katie and Reed, who were asking questions from the anchor's desk. An attractive young man whose cheeks were prematurely headed toward jowls, Fremd was explaining unfolding events as the camera, as if to reinforce the need for a shelter, turned to film the steady pelting of raindrops against the schoolroom windows.

JTF had been told that the mayor would make his address some time after the five o'clock news, but since he didn't appear to be ready, coverage temporarily switched back to the studio where Reed and Katie were in conversation. They were partially addressing each other, partially addressing the viewer.

"Have we ever seen anything like this in Bridge Haven before, Reed?" Katie asked, her expression a picture of solicitude.

"Obviously, there have always been serious weather conditions to deal with," said Reed, who, as the more senior of the two, was the one entitled to generalize, "and if the past few months have shown us anything, it is that we can never be absolutely certain what to expect. We have only to think back several weeks to Katrina to be reminded of the risk of complacency."

Reed's nose had become a complicated thing, which, despite liberally applied pancake, was darkened by veins, ridges, ruts, and stray hairs growing out of enlarged pores; and Katie, who had seen the same kind of nose on her alcoholic father, was momentarily distracted by the possibility that she had not gotten as far from her origins as she imagined.

"Yes, that was so terrible…all that suffering. And you are so right about uncertainty. Do you know whether any power outages are anticipated with this storm?"

Reed gratefully fielded the question, which, as Katie already knew, he was prepared for. After briefly acknowledging his co-anchor, he looked directly into the camera: "The loss of electricity is a common feature of thunderstorms and, uh, hurricanes. As we all know, there has been a lot of talk about energy conversation, excuse me, conservation, and it will be interesting to see how the present administration handles things if this storm causes major shortages and blackouts." A message announcing that a hurricane watch had gone into effect in Florida ran across the bottom of the screen.

Katie was about to agree when the camera cut back to the high school. "It appears," said Fremd, "that the mayor is ready to make his address now." A gaggle of reporters was hovering near the mayor who looked frazzled and very irritated with the person he was talking to. His head was lowered, and he was moving belligerently toward the other man, who was backing off, his hands slightly raised as if to defend himself. The camera lingered before returning to Fremd, who said that it looked like the mayor wasn't ready yet after all. Then he deftly choreographed a transition back to Reed and Katie by asking whether there was any more news on the hurricane.

"We've just gotten word, Jason, that a hurricane watch has gone into effect in Florida. That means that a hurricane can strike this area any time within the next twenty-four to thirty-six hours. We'll have more on the actual specifics of the storm when our meteorologist, Claire Day, brings you her detailed report, but in the meantime, people should be aware," and she repeated herself a second time, "that *a hurricane watch is now in effect.*"

Fremd was about to ask the difference between a watch and a warning, just to keep the patter going, when, mercifully, he got the signal. "It looks like the mayor is getting ready to make his address now. Yes, he's sitting down and signaling for silence." Like a dutiful watchdog, the camera followed Fremd's directive and shifted to the mayor, who was seated at a little table near the entrance of the gym. It had originally been suggested that reporters sit in the first rows of the bleachers, but Freddy refused to sit below the press, so chairs had to be set up in a semi-circle around him.

Freddy had learned a lot about being mayor from watching Ed Koch on television and always tried to address a crowd as if it were made up of friends and relatives. When he was growing up, he was constantly getting dragged off to christenings, communions, and confirmations, and it helped him to think of his audience as a large familiar group that he could kid around with. That was what he usually did, but this time, he thought the best approach would be absolute seriousness.

"The people of Bridge Haven have a tendency to think that it can't happen here and that it won't happen to us," he began, once absolute quiet had been established and reporters had been instructed to save their questions for later, "that weather devastation only affects other parts of the country," he continued, resisting the urge to itemize the afflictions of other states, although in his private moments, it had occurred to him that floods, fires, and earthquakes were a contemporary scourge visited upon states gone astray, like California. He had even allowed himself to privately consider the possibility that he had been chosen to shepherd the people of his great state through a desert of ignorance, profanity, and New Age Idolatry, and that it was no accident there were lots of Jews in the suburbs of Bridge Haven.

"But that isn't true, and that attitude could get us into a lot of trouble. According to meteorologists, we along the East Coast can expect a dramatic increase in the frequency and destructive potential of hurricanes in the first decade of this century. A researcher at the University of Buffalo is predicting that this year alone there will be ten tropical storms in the Atlantic, and that six or seven of them will develop into hurricanes," he said, ignoring the fact that in 1995, there had been almost twice as many storms and that none of them had posed a serious threat to the region. "An assemblyman from Westchester, New York, has said that if we don't view Katrina as a wake-up call than we are fooling ourselves, and the Office of Emergency Management has called New York the third most vulnerable city in the nation—New York, a mere stone's throw away from us.

"Unpleasant though it may be, we all have to heed the lessons of Hurricane Katrina and accept the idea that none of us is invincible or immune to danger. Hurricane Katrina with its terrible destruction and loss of life is, of course, foremost on our minds, but there was also Hurricane Floyd," he said, taking a quick glance at his cue card. "Hurricane Floyd killed fifty-six people in 1999 and fifty of those deaths were the result of inland flooding. That just goes to show that even though hurricanes don't come our way very often, they can cause a lot of damage when they do, especially to neighborhoods close to the coast like ours."

At that point someone in the audience started to interrupt, possibly to point out that Hurricane Floyd had struck Florida and that by the time it had made its way up the East Coast, it was downgraded to tropical storm status, but Freddy waved him off with the promise of a question-and-answer period following his statement. "The infrequency of hurricanes is all the more reason for us to avoid the complacency of an it-can't-happen-here attitude and all the more reason for us to be prepared for en-nee-thing en-nee-time," he said. "Anyone who has ever been in a car accident or been struck by disease or been victimized by crime can tell you that life can change in an instant," he snapped his fingers, "and that more often than not, the change was not what you had in mind. But," he said, his index finger raised, "there are ways to prepare for adversity. We may not be able to prevent it, but we can prepare for it. And *if it should happen that we're over-prepared,*" he said, alluding to the possibility that the storm might blow out to sea, "isn't that better than having our windows shattered by gale winds, or than having our cars parked in three feet of water, or, God forbid, than risking the well-being of our children. If the worst thing that happens," he said, taking a sip of water, "is that our concerns are over-stated and we are a little inconvenienced, I can live with that."

The room was quiet, and for one brief moment even Freddy's critics seemed impressed. Freddy knew that he had hit his stride, and pausing only long enough to achieve maximum effect, he continued with a lesson in hurricane preparedness. "Now in cooperation with FEMA, I have an extensive and, I believe, thorough list of what everyone needs to know to prepare for the hurricane. I'll go over it with you, but again, please save your questions and comments till later." He put on his glasses and began to read the exhaustive list one of his staff members had gotten from the

FEMA Web site, interrupting himself only once to joke about how they should pay attention because they were going to be tested on it later. The audience laughed cooperatively, glad for any excuse to break the tedium of the dos and don'ts list.

When Freddy was finished, a bunch of eager hands shot up. Everyone assumed that he would be answering the questions himself, but to their surprise, the mayor said that to help him with some of the more technical questions, FYI had been kind enough to let him borrow their weather forecaster. The choice of Louis Martin was at odds with the recommendation of his staff, who thought Claire Day was the better choice; but Freddy vetoed her on the grounds that he had more of a relationship with Louis, never mentioning, of course, that Claire's prediction was far more equivocal than Louis's, or that he was afraid Claire would upstage him if they shared the floor.

"I am sure that everyone here is familiar with Louis Martin, the man who some are saying is responsible for all this bad weather we're having," Freddy quipped by way of introduction as Louis walked forward from the back row of chairs. Smiling pleasantly, Martin put his hands up in an it's-not-my-fault posture and said, "Hey, blame Mother Nature, don't blame me." The first question came from a diminutive woman in the front who wanted to know why there was a discrepancy between his report and JTF's. "Who are people supposed to listen to when one station is saying one thing, and the other is saying another?" Freddy moved his chair off somewhat to the side and folded his hands on his lap. It was Louis's show now.

"I haven't heard Ms. Day's report, but all I can say is that each of us studies the information that comes in to us. Sometimes it happens that there are differences in how we interpret the information we receive. Next," he said, pleased both with his response and with his power to summarily dismiss people. He pointed at Fremd without knowing who he was or that this young man with an unfortunate jaw had recently been hired by JTF and was eager to show his support for his own station's weather reporter.

"During his talk, the mayor mentioned Hurricane Floyd, which I believe made landfall in Florida and subsided into a tropical storm by the time it reached the mid-Atlantic states. By the time it reached New England, it had petered out altogether. That seems to be the case with most hurricanes affecting our area—that is, they seem to do their worst in southern coastal states like Florida and the Carolinas."

"Is there a question?" Louis cut in.

"My question to you is whether there has ever been a hurricane that has struck Bridge Haven directly?"

Louis had studied hurricane history earlier in the day and was delighted to have the opportunity to show off. "First off, I would like to comment on Floyd whose sixty-mile-an-hour sub-hurricane winds caused flash floods in inland towns and brought ten to fifteen inches of rain to parts of this state. Property damage forced thousands of people to leave their homes, and several people died when their cars were overtaken by flood water. Other flooding caused by hurricanes in the region include Hurricane Gloria, whose gusting winds led to millions of dollars worth of damage in 1985, and Connie and Diane, two earlier hurricanes that also caused massive flooding." He pushed his forelock away from his eyes and was about to move on when the young man asked whether Connie and Diane hadn't occurred as long ago as 1955. Jesus, this guy had really done his homework.

Louis said he couldn't remember the exact year, but if it really was that long ago than we might be due for another one; and simultaneous with his response, redirected his gaze and said "next" to an older, sympathetic looking woman in the back. But Fremd wasn't ready to give up, and although Louis had already shifted his attention, the entire audience heard the aggressive, well-informed, and highly audible reporter ask whether, in fact, there had ever been a hurricane to strike Bridge Haven directly, not just near it, but the eye, making landfall, in Bridge Haven.

He side-stepped by remarking that if other people in the room were going to have a chance, he would have to move on; but the older woman in the back said that although she'd originally wanted to ask something else, she was now kind of curious to know the answer to the young man's question. "To the best of my knowledge," Louis said with a candor that felt more like the failure of deceit than honesty, "Bridge Haven has never been in the eye of a hurricane. But if I understood the mayor correctly," he continued, deflecting responsibility for this absurd situation away from himself and back to the mayor, "then our concern is to protect Bridge Haven from the damaging effects of severe weather conditions, whatever name we give them."

"That's right," the mayor jumped back in, eager to take over again, "This is not about definitions. This is about…"

"Getting re-elected," said Dan from his desk at JTF. A group had formed around him, and a tentative silence followed the press conference. No one knew quite what to what to make of it. It had to be admitted that the mayor had handled it skillfully, and even Dan, whose dislike of Coniglia was such that he never found anything positive to say about him, had to acknowledge the mayor's political adroitness. Taken individually, the contributing factors to this talent might be seen as less than desirable—a blend of cynicism, sentimentality, simplicity, and ambition; but taken as a whole, they were the qualities of the true politician. Yes, the mayor had been effective, but so was their man Fremd, who had made it very clear that there was good reason to question the utility of an evacuation shelter.

"Fremd was great," Dan observed to no one in particular.

"What was so great about him?" Goodwin barked angrily. Goodwin was mad because it was Louis sitting next to the mayor instead of Claire, and he was sure there was a not too subtle message in the choice. "What was so great about him?" he asked again belligerently. "His questions embarrassed the mayor. I don't see anything so great about what he did." Goodwin focused his cold, crystalline gaze on Dan.

"The mayor embarrassed himself," Dan shot back. "This whole shelter thing is a transparent scheme and Fremd saw through it."

"I don't know that. Didn't you notice that a hurricane watch went into effect? When was the last time that happened?"

"Probably the last time Coniglia got into a situation he couldn't wriggle out of."

Everyone snickered, except for Goodwin, who took him literally. "Are you suggesting," Goodwin lowered his brows and sharpened his focus, "that this hurricane is made up?"

That, actually, was not what Dan had been thinking, but he smiled enigmatically. For a moment, his face looked like punctuation, his eyes like periods set beneath the carets of his brows and his smile set within the confines of deep parenthetical wrinkles.

"It's not possible," Goodwin stated in decisive answer to his own question. "The mayor may cook the books, he may engage in racketeering, tax evasion, and cronyism, but even he can't invent the weather. There are definitions for these things—a storm has to be, I forget how many, but it has to be going a certain number of miles per hour to qualify as a hurricane and then it has to strike within a certain number of hours…"

"Twenty-four to thirty-six," Katie cut in.

"Yeah, twenty-four to thirty-six hours."

"That's true," said Dan, warming to the idea of an invented hurricane, "but within thirty-six hours of…of where? Maybe it just has to be twenty-four to thirty-six hours from the place where the forecast is made," he laughed in wicked delight, "and that place is Florida."

"That's nonsense," said Goodwin, shaking himself as if something had landed on him. "Obviously, when you say something could happen within a certain amount of time, you aren't talking about some other part of the country."

Katie was horrified by the turn the conversation had taken. "In the interest of setting the record straight," she said, eager to squelch the speculation before it got really out of hand, "let's just ask Claire to define the phrase 'hurricane watch.' There's no point to our debating something we know nothing about."

"You can do whatever you like," said Goodwin, who had had enough and was heading back to his office, "but to tell you the truth, I don't care whether this is a real hurricane or a Disney creation. As long as it's news, that's how we're going to treat it. If any one has a problem with that, they should see me in my office."

CHAPTER NINETEEN

Claire was still looking for some indication of how the hurricane could be expected to behave when, like eager pupils, Katie and Dan stuck their heads into her work space.

"We have just been having a debate," said Katie, "about the meaning of the phrase 'hurricane watch.' The question is when a watch is in effect, could the predicted hurricane make landfall somewhere other than at the site of the announced watch?"

Claire looked confused. "Of course it could."

"No," said Dan, "that's not the question. The question is why would you announce a watch in one place if you live in another? In other words, is there any reason to expect that a hurricane watch announced in Florida will have an effect on us in Bridge Haven within the next twenty-four to thirty-six hours?"

"Ah," said Claire. "Well, what we can expect and what is possible are two different things. That is why a watch is distinguished from a warning. When there's a warning, certain behavior is expected, but a watch only serves to let the public know that certain behavior is possible."

"You see...eee," said Katie, who somehow found vindication in Claire's statement.

Ignoring Katie, Dan asked another question. "Right now, a hurricane watch is in effect, and that simply means that one is possible. Correct? Theoretically then, since the ocean is a cauldron in which hurricanes are constantly brewing, a hurricane watch could always be in effect, whether we are actually at immediate risk or not. Right?"

"Almost," Claire smiled this time. Dan seemed to be following a scent, and judging by the nature of his question, it was a rat that he smelled. "I suppose that you could make a technical argument for a constant watch, but the reason the watch was created was not technical but social, so that people would be more attentive to weather conditions than they usually are. If it were simply a matter of informing the public of the existence of hurricane activity in the Caribbean, then, yes, you could pretty much justify a constant watch from August to October, which is peak hurricane season. Actually, The National Hurricane Center goes fully operational on May 15 for the East Pacific, two weeks later for the Atlantic, and there can be hurricanes at any time during that period; but strictly speaking, the time of greatest activity is late summer. Does that help?"

"Absolutely," they both said and walked away in continuing debate, with Dan making the argument that anyone cynical enough to exaggerate the possibility of a hurricane for political motives would have no scruples about setting up a hurricane shelter, while Katie simply rolled her eyes and shook her head in implied disbelief.

Alone again, Claire went back to her monitor. The hurricane was meandering along the Georgia coast, starting, stopping, flirting as its winds noncommittally brushed the shore. It was as beguiling, passionate, and unpredictable as any lover, but steadfast too; despite its modest speed, this cane was hanging in there, a tenacious trooper fearlessly soldiering on. Claire took a sip of the cold coffee on her desk. You're a sly one, she said, with love in her heart for this force that was every bit as independent and resistant to programming as she was. Stay where you are; go back out to sea; you're better off out there, believe me. If you come on land, they'll sell you to the public, first as a potent force, then as a menace, as heir to Katrina; then when you fade and die, they'll pretend you didn't achieve your potential and say how lucky we were to escape unscathed.

That could happen to her too, she thought, angrily twisting her hair into a tight knot, and jabbing it in place with a pencil. If she didn't hype the hurricane at eleven, especially after the mayor's press conference, the public, whom she had already disappointed once that day, might begin to consider a more entertaining alternative to her. The stage had been set: water ballet, a press conference, a storm shelter. Nothing remained but her report, and if she stayed true to her reputation, then it would be mind-blowing. Perhaps she would deliver her forecast to the accompanying trumpets of Wagner's "Ride of the Walkyries," or maybe she would hold forth from the heaving prow of a sea-faring vessel in a tempest-tossed sea. She had built her reputation on dramatizing the weather, on "making the air tremble with the season," as she had once put it, and now that she had a real hurricane to report, people would be dying to see what she would do with it.

The late night news began with a sound bite of the mayor in the evacuation center followed by Reed's summary of the day's events. After Reed had finished, the catch in his throat barely audible thanks, he believed, to a new form of therapy called reflexology, Katie picked up with a list of things the public could do to prepare for the hurricane. They were all seated at the news desk, Reed, Katie, Fletcher, and Claire.

"Mayor Coniglia has urged folks to keep informed. He said they should know what supplies to have on hand and when to call 911 or EMS. He also urged people to shop for provisions and to board up their windows if necessary. You can find the complete list on our Web site; however before we continue any further," her brows were knit in concern, "let's hear from our own Claire Day, who is here to tell us how bad it's going to be. Claire?"

Claire was now beside the weather map. She looked directly into the camera. Its Cyclops eye stared back at her. Up until that moment, the camera had been her friend, her assistant in a joint venture enthusiastically undertaken; but now, as if it had switched camps and joined the prosecution, the camera had become her interrogator and she was on the stand. Like any witness, she could withhold information, she could tell the truth, or she could lie.

The decision she made, the decision she always made when she felt under attack, was to stiffen her resolve. She knew no other way, and she thought it was the right way. Her life had not been about placating philistines or kowtowing to politicians. Still, it was with a pounding heart that she proceeded, and taking a deep breath, she said that converging weather systems were producing heavy rain. There was none of the usual excitement in her voice. No energy, no bounce. The water table was beginning to rise and cause flooding in poor drainage areas. Still deadpan. There was flooding all the way up the East Coast and across the Great Plains, and rain could be expected throughout the area, she continued, without once making mention of a hurricane.

A voice-over announced that Claire would be back with full details on Hurricane Louis following a word from the sponsor. When she came back, nothing had changed. Rain, she reported, had been coming down fairly steadily for the past five hours and was continuing to saturate the region. A hurricane watch had gone into effect, and severe weather could affect the area any time within the next twenty-four to thirty-six hours. That was it, that was all, no poetry, no props, no prose, no further mention of a hurricane. Another commercial and the news was almost over. The biggest weather day of the year and…nothing.

"What is the likelihood of a forced evacuation?" Katie asked in an effort to rev things up again.

"At this stage, it's a little too soon to say; however, hurricanes are unpredictable and just as they can change course or lose their impact, they can also develop in strength and speed. Hurricane Louis has already reached Georgia and is showing no sign of abatement."

"At what point should people, especially those in low-lying areas, begin to consider leaving their homes?" Katie persisted, loving every minute of a situation in which she was more dominant and dynamic than Claire.

"People should listen to their local news for instructions. Inland flooding can lead to washed out roads, mud slides, downed electrical wires, and fallen trees or branches, so if those conditions should arise," she said, addressing Katie now instead of the camera, "people should be careful." She made no mention of the shelter or of a forced evacuation. "Overall, it's always better to expect the worst and hope for the best than to wait too long and run the risk of encountering difficulties." That was it—that was as far as Claire was willing to go, as much of this charade as she would participate in.

"Valuable advice," said Katie, with an approving nod, which summarily dismissed her colleague. "Thank you, Claire. Needless to say," she tossed her head buoyantly, "we will be following the hurricane's progress with up-to-the minute news, and you can also get more information by logging on to WJTF.com/hurricane. On a final and, I think, significant note," Katie wrapped up, "it is worthy of mention that Mayor Coniglia is not the only politician who is concerned about the devastating impact of storms threatening the East Coast. In a special address to the Executive Chamber of the New York State Assembly, Governor Pataki has decided to proclaim May 20th through May 26th Hurricane Awareness Week.

• • •

Freddy was watching the news from his den, which had been his favorite room in the house until Marie started making improvements to it. He noticed that a riding saddle had been placed on the floor near the sliding glass doors to the back patio and wondered what a saddle was doing there, especially when no one knew how to ride a horse. It had to be part of Marie's fixation with rustic decor. He hadn't known about Pataki's proclamation and when he heard the announcement, he got so excited that he began pounding the cushion of his armchair and overturned his bowl of tortilla chips. The chair was hunter green and the tortilla chips, a new variety called Rancho Mexicano, were a bright yellowish orange and stained the chair a chartreuse color when he pushed them back into the bowl. He went to the utility closet for the power vac, thinking that if he was re-elected, he'd buy Marie new furniture, or, at least, slip covers. What incredible luck, he thought, feeling the old confidence refill his veins. He couldn't get over it, the governor of New York announcing Hurricane Awareness Week. He wondered why he chose a week in May instead of in September, when Katrina struck. Anyway, it didn't matter. What mattered was the bandwagon. As long as politicians were falling all over each other to show their concern for the public, he could climb on too, and the worst thing anyone could accuse him of was playing politics. His crimes would get lost in the shuffle.

He got up and crossed the den to an antique secretary on the far side of the room. There was a large mirror above it framed by crossing swords with gilt-edged handles at top and bottom. They did not exactly go with the western look of the room, but he decided not to say anything to Marie because the Louis XVI-style secretary had cost a bundle—even though it was an imitation—and he didn't want it to end up in the basement alongside the modern Danish furniture she had collected during her Scandinavian phase. The mirror was several feet above the secretary and too high for Freddy to really get a good look at himself. The only part of him that was visible was his head, and its position directly above the swords made him look like he'd been decapitated. He had asked Marie a hundred times to lower it, but she insisted it was the proper height and, stubborn woman that she was, resolutely kept it where he had to stand on tiptoe to see. What an indignity, he thought, wondering if that was the idea since Marie was convinced that he had gotten arrogant since he became mayor. Too big for his britches, but on the other hand, too short for the mirror. The decapitated head did not feature the face of a movie star, not even an ugly star like Charles Bronson. To the contrary, the face reflected in the mirror lacked any kind of true distinction:

neither strength nor dignity nor even gentleness returned his gaze. Simply a mild, dull head, more pudgy than bony. He looked at himself a bit longer, scrutinizing the details of his face, trying to see whether he couldn't invest it with some sort of magnetism, but that was hard to do, and the more he tried, the more he was reminded of the other thing wrong with his looks, which was, according to his son, that he didn't blink right. Trust kids to tell you that kind of thing. Apparently, instead of blinking, he squinted fast. No one else had ever said anything, but ever since Freddy Jr. mentioned it, he felt self-conscious.

It was dark and gloomy outside, and there was a steady downfall of rain against the Andersen doors to the patio. First the raindrops hit the glass, and then they meandered down its surface in a sheet of tiny silver rivulets that obscured the lawn. He couldn't even see his hedge. The sight of the rain reminded him of confetti, and Freddy had a momentary image of himself, the re-elected mayor in an open convertible, Marie at his side waving, the raindrops like ticker tape. That was fantasy, but re-election was still possible, and if he continued to handle this hurricane correctly, then he might have a pretty good shot at it. After all, when it came right down to it, nobody really wanted a soccer mom for mayor.

There was a chess set with squat little ivory pieces resembling Mayan gods on the coffee table. Freddy had thought he'd be good at chess because he liked strategy, but the trouble with the game was that the moves were absolute, whereas Freddy thought that true strategy involved deliberate but flexible moves, such as the kind that were governing his handling of the hurricane. He called his brother-in-law.

"Yeah," the voice responded.

"We need to talk."

"Yeah?"

"Can you come over? Now?"

"It's raining out."

Freddy didn't say anything.

"Yeah. Okay."

"Bring Vince too."

Freddy was asleep in his chair when Marie ushered her brothers into the den. She was wearing a new pair of glasses with a diamante trim and a long dress made of some gauze-like material. It had beads sewn into the fabric and looked vaguely Indian. Marie had gotten stocky with menopause and tried to conceal her plump midriff and thick thighs with long, loose dresses, which only served to emphasize her shortness and to remind him that his wife was a certain kind of woman and not another kind. He couldn't describe the difference between these types, but he thought that Claire Day could probably wear flowing dresses and that Katie probably couldn't. Or maybe he was just used to the arrogant and self-assured sexuality in Katie's short, tight, look-but-don't-touch skirts—except that he touched. He wondered who touched Claire. Marie said that he was always jumping to sexual conclusions about people, mostly that they were gay; but he wasn't jumping to any conclusions about Claire, and he liked that about her. It wasn't so much a matter of sex with her as of class; the woman had class.

When Artie and Vince walked into the den, they were decidedly less aggressive than they'd been a few days earlier, their swagger replaced by shuffle, their bravado reduced to grudging, mumbled respect. They had heard about the press conference in the high school gym and they knew that things had changed.

"It's lousy out there," said Artie irritably, dropping onto the sofa. "I hope there's a good reason you couldn't wait till tomorrow. What's with the saddle?"

"That's Marie's idea," Freddy waved his hand in dismissal. "She thinks she's living on a dude ranch with Ralph Lauren." Vince cocked his head slightly. He'd never heard of Ralph Lauren, and he wasn't sure his sister should be having such fantasies.

"He's a designer," Freddy explained. "He has a suntan and wears blue jeans, but forget about him. Listen," he said to both of them, although Vince had his back turned and was looking at himself in the mirror, in which he was tall enough to see both his head and upper torso. "This storm's a godsend, but it wasn't exactly sent by God." They both looked confused. "There's a hurricane further down the coast, but so far there's no real reason to think it will reach us up here. We exaggerated the bad weather so I could go on television, and, you know, set up the shelter…"

It still wasn't clear.

"Be the concerned mayor," he elaborated. "Take things in hand."

There was still no sign of comprehension in Vince's beady eyes, but Artie's face was beginning to show signs of recognition. His crooked, little mouth was expanding into a grin. "That's not bad," he acknowledged. "So what happens next?"

"What happens next is where you come in. I need storm damage. Tonight. It has to happen tonight in case the whole thing blows over by tomorrow. I need enough damage to justify the evacuation shelter and to give me an excuse to work closely with city officials—with the water superintendent, with the service technicians, with the police, and with the shopkeepers. I've got to work round-the-clock," he said, "quoting an imaginary headline, "to restore the city's services."

"So what are we supposed to do?"

"I don't know," said Freddy, pretending that he hadn't already thought the whole thing through. "Maybe a water main could burst, or something."

"Water mains are hard to break, especially if they're in good condition to begin with," Artie observed. He looked inquiringly at Freddy, who shrugged in ignorance, indicating that he had no idea what the condition of the water mains was. "They're made of twenty-inch cast iron," Artie continued. "Do you know how thick that is? We could blow some fuses and down some power lines—that's not as hard, although it's pretty dangerous. Technicians aren't supposed to go into the cherry pickers—you know, up to the power lines—when the winds are this strong. The electricity crawls all over their skin. Someone told me that it even gets inside their gloves." He scratched his head.

"But you can do it? Can you do it tonight?" Freddy asked eagerly. He really wanted a water main to break, but he'd settle for downed power lines if he had to.

Artie didn't say anything right away. He looked at his watch. Then he went over to the glass doors and, feet apart, looked out at the rain. For a moment, he seemed transfixed by the night. It was an uncharacteristically contemplative moment which, as such moments often do, came to an abrupt end. Turning around, he pounded his chest with his fists, and exclaimed "All this thunder and lightning, it makes me feel like a criminal. You know, 'enters the villain'…" Vince snorted in appreciation and Freddy momentarily wondered whether other animals, like bears and bulls, also had a sense of humor.

"Do you remember a guy named Donny Esposito?" Artie asked Freddy. The question was an apparent non sequitur, but Freddy had a pretty good idea of what was coming next.

"Sort of. Tall, mean, ugly?"

"He's looking for a job," Artie retorted, ignoring the characterization.

Freddy didn't respond.

"If you're re-elected, you'll be making some changes in your staff, won't you?" Artie persevered. "Maybe taking on some new people?"

Freddy hesitated. He had known that there would have to be a payoff—there was always a payoff—but so far no one on his staff could have been described as what his mother, God rest her soul, had referred to as the criminal element. He had promised himself that if he got out of this situation, if he didn't come up on charges and if he got re-elected, then he was going to do things differently—become a better man, a better mayor, and yet here he was, getting in deeper then before.

"Does he have any skills?" he asked lamely.

Artie looked at Vince and the two of them burst out laughing. Freddy was too much, a real joker! "Yeah," said Artie, with that little bit of menace that had haunted Freddy ever since he'd married Marie, "the guy's a good mechanic."

He took his cell phone out of his pocket and dialed. "Donny? Yeah, me, Artie. Yeah, I know it's late. Listen…"

CHAPTER TWENTY

It was after 1 a.m., and Claire was still at the station. She was determined to stay there until she got solid evidence that she had made the right decision. Louis had turned eastward away from the coast, but it had done that once before and there was no way of being sure it wouldn't turn back again. At the moment, it was stalled almost equidistant between Georgia and South Carolina; but Claire didn't think it would stay there for long and, like an obstetrician monitoring each centimeter of progress, she waited for its next move. After a while she got up and went to the watercooler. While she was away from her desk, during that brief moment, the hurricane's position changed dramatically and turned in the defiant direction of open ocean. Totally vindicated, feeling the deep satisfaction of having been right, Claire gave a triumphant whoop of victory and left for home.

The rain was coming down hard as her car emerged from the parking lot. Leaning into the windshield, the steering wheel gripped in her hands, she drove down Main Street, wondering as she passed the turnoff to the high school whether anyone had used it as a shelter. Ordinarily, Main Street would have been completely deserted at that hour, but as Claire peered through her windshield, she noticed activity at the top of a nearby pole. At first she thought it was an animal, but as she got closer, she saw two shadowy figures who looked like men at work. Slowly, she drove past them, straining to see ahead, and then, as they receded into the distance, straining to see behind. What could they be doing there? What was particularly perplexing was a flash of light, more like a sizzling firecracker than lightning, near where they were working. Further down the road, past City Hall and CVS, two more darkly clad figures stood beside a manhole. One of them turned his head in the direction of her car and then turned away again quickly, almost as if he wanted to avoid detection. Again, Claire could only wonder at their presence.

When she got home, her dog, Mario, skidded across the kitchen linoleum, his paws preceding his body as he came to a halt in front of her. She gave his soft, large head a hug, dropped her handbag on to her kitchen chair, and without bothering to turn the lights on, too tired to go upstairs, she went to the living room and lay down on her sofa. The room's only light came from the luminescent pearls of rain cascading down her windows. She closed her eyes and thought of the air that is never still, rising and falling like the chests of the sleeping. As she drifted off, her thoughts wandered to the people she knew who were sleeping beneath this same maternal blanket of rain: to Judy and Murray, snuggling next to each other on their 600 thread count sheets; to the mayor tossing and turning as he thought up re-election schemes; and to Goodwin and Russo, dreaming of fame and fortune, the raindrops like stardust on their houses.

The rain also fell on the man in her dream, the man who was standing in the entrance to her living room. What was he doing there? When he saw that she was looking at him, he wordlessly crossed the room. Who was he and why was he in her house? Not wishing to be impolite, Claire sat up. He walked toward her and instead of sitting in the armchair, he sat on the sofa next to her, as if the space had been intended for him. He reached around to the back of her head and removed the pencil holding her mass of unruly hair in place. Her hair fell in a knot onto her back, which he untangled by slowing separating the strands. Then he placed his hand on the back of her head and gently pulled her toward him until her face was in front of his and they were kissing.

No decision had been involved. She simply fell to kissing him as passionately as if they were lovers who had been separated for a long time. While they kissed, he began to unbutton her blouse and unfasten her bra. It fell limply from her as his hands traveled under her bra straps and over her shoulders. Drawing her half-naked body to him, he massaged her back. It was smooth and muscular and, to Claire's surprise, grateful. Traveling up and down the caravan of her spine, he lingered for so long that it began to seem as if the front of her body was the reward her back would deliver. Eventually, he continued over the summit of her shoulders and circled the orbs of her breasts in narrowing spirals as her nipples became taut and erect. Rising deeply from within, he lowered his hands inside her slacks, and simultaneously undressing himself, lowered his body over hers. A leisurely lover whose pace was becoming their prison, he timed it so that by the time he eventually moved on, their muscles had banded together, their nerves had joined forces, and the two of them had become a trapped pair, desperate to claw their way out of his languor. He was masterly and knew how to stoke desire until it roared with passion, and then with passion on the verge of frenzy to thrust himself inside her until all love broke loose. They were on her sofa, but somehow they found their way to her bed, where inside and out, up and down, surfing the waves of their passion, they lapped against each other's bodies and rode their bodies to shore. On the crest of her blood, she slid down its steep slope, over and over to where he waited, his arms open wide.

After a while, Claire became conscious of her ecstasy and began to feel as if she was being watched. She looked out her window and saw that the rain had stopped. A break in clouds framed by a black sky had been filled by a glittering assembly of stars. For a moment, she wondered whether the stars could have been drawn out by the sight of her and her lover, who, like stars themselves, were heavenly bodies aglow. She marveled at the phenomenon of the stars until, with slow reluctance, she became quite certain that she was dreaming, and simultaneous to that awareness, her lover began to fade.

Who was that man, she wondered? Was he simply the ghost of her longings, or was he Jesse, the only man she could imagine dreaming about? Maybe they were one and the same?

• • •

Patchy fog, hazy sunshine, sodden earth, wet leaves. That was the weather. There had been no hurricane, no storm surge, and no need for shelters. The storm had blown out to sea, and for the first time in days, Claire looked forward to going to work. She had just passed a test that everyone else had failed, and she thought she should be rewarded. No big deal, no fanfare, just a nod in her direction. It was the least they could do.

They didn't. There was no nod, no sign of approval, no indication that Claire had heroically held out against group pressure. There wasn't even grudging respect. To the contrary, nobody was paying much attention to her at all. Even Michele, who was a fan and could be counted on to look up from her novel when Claire passed her desk, appeared indifferent to her presence. What was going on? Was the disregard intentional? Was it a slight? The question was partially answered by the Post-it on her computer screen. "See me this a.m.," it said. No "please," no "when you find the time;" just "see me." The absence of a signature made it even more offensive. It was a clear statement of rank because only two people in the office had the authority to leave a note like that, and only one of them would do it.

"Is it just my imagination," Claire asked Dan, "or is something going on? I feel like Icarus on his way down. My wings are melting."

She was on her way to Goodwin's office. Dan shook his head in disgust. "Don't let that asshole get to you. He's just pissed because you didn't play up the hurricane yesterday."

"There was no hurricane yesterday."

"That, my dear girl, was why you had do play it up."

Goodwin had gotten to the office at seven. He was taking the afternoon off and wanted to set a good example by arriving early to compensate. He did not believe in special privileges for management, and in fact, he thought it should be the other way around with those in charge establishing a good work ethic for the rest of the staff. But he had forgotten that there would be no one at the office to notice when he arrived, and that he couldn't even make business calls at that hour. So, eager for a little catnap and ready to jump up at the first sound of office activity, he lay down on the sofa he had recently retrieved from his basement. He had not slept well the night before—he never slept well the night before his hair treatments—and within minutes, he was snoring like an idling diesel that occasionally backfired. He woke up with a loud snort when Claire stuck her head in the door, Claire, the last person in the world he wanted to see him sleeping on the job!

"Why don't I come back in a little while?" she asked, discreetly closing the door before he had a chance to respond.

Had he left the door open? He never left it open. The only possible reason for leaving it open would have been that he wanted people to see him at his desk and hard at work when they got to the office; but, for the life of him, he couldn't remember if that was what he had done. Maybe Claire had come in without knocking, or maybe she had knocked and, getting no response, stuck her head in? The whole thing was annoying, the sleeping, Claire's discovery of him, his forgetfulness.

What happened next is what usually happens when people burst in on you, which is that they retreat in embarrassment and give you way more time than you need to recover. Goodwin was ready to see Claire almost as soon as she closed the door behind her, but she discretely allowed him an extra half hour, which, of course, was about twenty-eight minutes too long and only added to his impatience and irritation.

When she came back to his office, he was on the telephone. He gestured for her to sit down in the leather and chrome chair across from his desk, but was in no hurry to hang up, especially since the call had to do with ratings, which was the reason he wanted to see her. She looked around while she waited: Navajo prints on the walls, a Persian rug on the floor, and a series of black-and-white photographs over the sofa.

"I know, I know," he said looking at Claire but responding to the invisible voice on the telephone. "But man cannot live by ratings alone," he responded, his face muscles almost relaxing into a smile, but stopping short as a preventive measure. "Oh, I see, I'm mistaken. Man *can* live on ratings for at least a week, and then he only needs bread and water. Well thanks for the tip. I'll pass it along to my staff, who will, I'm sure, appreciate the information."

"This," he said, when he got off the phone, "is what I'm up against. They're relentless. Our ratings slip a little and you'd think the stock market had crashed." The comparison gave him a slight jolt because it reminded him that his utilities stock had unexpectedly sky-rocketed and then plummeted that morning. It was the largest holding in his portfolio and very disturbing. The analysts were still trying to figure out what had happened. "Claire," he said after beating around the bush a while longer, "I'm going to get right to the point. The reason I asked to see you is that I've perceived a change in your reporting style."

The condensed timing of television—the idea that one or two broadcasts could constitute a change in style—was something Claire still had trouble getting used to. She had to resist the urge to point out that style was a unique composite developed over time and not the result of isolated incidents. "Now, as you know," he continued, encouraged by her silence, "I have made a point of not interfering with your reports." Claire cocked her head to the side and looked at him quizzically. Could he actually have forgotten that he'd told her to play up the hurricane? "From the beginning you've had a free hand and, I might add, done things in a very unorthodox manner. It made me uneasy in the beginning—I won't deny it—but you've more than justified our faith in you." He paused to see what kind of impression that made on Claire.

There was no sign that it made any impression, no indication that she thought Goodwin was even more slow-witted than she had imagined, and that his carriage—upright, starched, and stern—masked a mediocrity only apparent on the rare occasions he let his guard down.

"You have won me and the public over, and we've been more than happy to have you on the team."

"Thank you. It's been a good experience for me too," said Claire, still waiting and wondering why he had asked to see her.

"The problem," he continued, satisfied that having shown overall support for Claire's performance, he was now free to criticize her, "is that when you establish a certain style, it's what the public expects from you. You might almost say you get stuck with it. It's the reason they watch you instead of the next guy. I mean, imagine going to the theater to see a comedy only to discover that on the night you go, the lead actor has decided to bring out the play's tragic elements. You'd feel ripped off. It's the same with television. The public thinks of you a certain way, and that's how they want you to be."

"I suppose you are talking about last night's report?"

"Yes," he said with alacrity, relieved she had brought it up. "What happened?" He was hoping they could both agree that something had, in fact, happened, and that her dry delivery had not been deliberate. Maybe she would make his life easy for him and say that she hadn't been feeling well. "It was so sterile. Where was Zeus? Here we're having the biggest weather day of the year and you treat it like, like I don't know what, like April showers."

"Does it make any difference that my prediction was accurate?"

"Honestly? Not much. Claire, we had a story building—a possible hurricane, an emergency press conference, an impromptu hurricane shelter. A great story was developing, and our job is to tell it."

"I thought my job was to report the weather."

It was now Goodwin's turn to look bemused. "You've got me stumped. I thought you were the one person who really understood what this business is about. I mean the animation, the poetry, the woodland settings and autumn leaves. You'll do anything to get a rise out of people."

Goodwin's comment was a torch to Claire's inflamed mind. "Not anything, apparently," she shot back. "If I were willing to do anything then I would have pretended there was going to be a hurricane. I would have exaggerated its likelihood and downplayed the storm system from the Great Plains, the one, incidentally, that we were actually experiencing. I would have talked about the damage a hurricane can create and the destruction caused by previous hurricanes. In short, I would have parsed, feigned, dissembled, and misrepresented." She was leaning forward in her chair, her eyes aimed at Goodwin, who would have liked his response to be equally impassioned, but had no idea how to summon that level of intensity and was stuck saying the only thing that came to mind.

"Well...why didn't you?"

His answer caught her short, and for a moment she didn't know whether to laugh or cry. Instead, she simply persevered. "Let me try saying this differently. Apparently, I'm not being clear. Enhancement and fabrication are not the same, surely we can agree on that." Claire was still looking at Goodwin intently, her gaze a searchlight scanning his face for a sign that she had reached him; but he looked back blankly, his face a still-life. Of course, he was thinking, enhancement and fabrication aren't exactly the same, but so what? Why put this ethical overlay on everything? It was bad for business.

When he didn't respond, Claire remembered her attempts at teaching unresponsive students and suddenly felt defeated and drained. She had left teaching to go into television, and now it looked like they were following a similar course: deceptive success followed by decisive defeat. Her statement about the distinction between enhancement and fabrication represented two years of hard work, two years during which she had read every poet and researched every philosopher in an effort to make people's lives more vibrant, and yet, it had only led to this moment of self-justification. "The hurricane wasn't a threat to us," she said calmly, almost wearily. "All I did was tell the truth about it." She anchored a loose curl behind her ear.

"And we're not opposed to that," Goodwin jumped in, ready to reassure her, "we're definitely not opposed."

Claire smiled, which confirmed Goodwin's suspicion that Russo had never known how to deal with her. "Yes, absolutely, as much truth as possible, just so long as it doesn't negatively impact ratings. That's what happened yesterday: people were looking for drama, they got drab, and they voted with their remotes. That's what we have to avoid."

Claire gave it one last shot, more to be thorough than in the hope of reaching an understanding. "Phil, during the entire time I've worked for JTF, it's been my goal to create a heightened awareness of the weather based upon actual facts. To heighten without hyping."

If their meeting had ended there, both of them would have been better off, but much like Claire, Goodwin wanted to get his point across and he wanted to prevail. He was, after all, the boss. "Heighten, hype, hogwash, and hair-splitting."

Claire reddened. "What you call hair-splitting I consider a dividing line. On one side of it, you're a legitimate reporter, on the other side, well you're Louis Martin."

"Martin's ratings topped yours yesterday," Goodwin shot back. "And yours have been heading south. For the first time in months, he beat us out."

Claire ignored the comment about her ratings, although she was truly shocked to discover that they had dropped. "Look," she said, struggling to maintain composure, "you just said it yourself: 'for the first time in months.' I'd call that a pretty good batting average."

"It's a great batting average. The best. But in this business, you've got to guard against complacency all the time, or before you know it, a bad day becomes a bad week, and that dividing line you were talking about becomes a Maginot Line."

"If I recall, it was the bad guys who crossed it."

"Bad, good, I don't give a flying f—. The point is they crossed it." It was now Goodwin trying to get a grip on himself. It had been a long time since anyone had challenged his authority, either at home or at work, and it set off something he couldn't fully control. His face twitched, he became slightly flushed, and he had to wait a moment to respond. Look, all I'm trying to say here is…"

"I think you're saying that I'm only as good as my last broadcast," Claire cut in curtly.

"Exactly," he straightened himself, determined that, if nothing else, he would have the last word. "This is a tough business."

CHAPTER TWENTY-ONE

While Goodwin was delineating his position on acceptable levels of distortion, Emmett was at Cole's men's store trying on a jacket. He had been eying it for a long time. The jacket was very expensive, too expensive, and he would not have even considered buying it if he had not made a killing that morning on the derivatives market. It was amazing: one call to his broker followed by the magic word "sell," and his fortunes were changed forever. The trade involved an upsurge in the sale of generators. They had been purchased by hotels and restaurants all the way up the coast in preparation for an enigmatic hurricane that had threatened to make landfall as far north as Connecticut. Energy shares had also traded sharply higher, and, there too, Emmett had sold at exactly the right moment.

He reached his arm into the cool silk of a beautifully lined sleeve and took another look at himself, trim, dapper, and rather handsome despite skin too fair to achieve a tan. He was not in the habit of looking at himself and felt as if his inner and outer selves were meeting in the mirror. Or perhaps it was the crime he had just committed that accounted for the slight unfamiliarity of his face. Stock manipulation—that's what he would be up for if he got caught. The salesman was pinning the cuffs, which Emmett thought was a rather clever sales technique since he hadn't actually agreed to buy the jacket. It made him feel trapped, almost as if the sports jacket had become a straight jacket and he had been locked inside its sleeves. He was trapped and cuffed too, a criminal identified by his reckless behavior. Suddenly, he wanted to leave the store in a hurry. But an abrupt departure would attract attention. He was quite sure that the men who shopped in these stores did not just up and go. Maybe he should buy the jacket on the installment plan to counteract the impression he was rich, but that, too, might seem unusual. The best thing would be to buy the jacket outright and not make any more purchases for a while.

Back on the street, the glare of the sun obscured everything. Emmett walked to his car slowly, stunned to discover that his crime had an aftermath. He had been so focused on pulling it off that he had not really thought about what lay ahead except in the most general terms: he would have his boat and fish; Renee would have her house and paint. That was all. Anxiety, fear, thrill, elation, he had not expected any of those things.

Initially, he had planned to keep the whole thing to himself and not tell Renee what he was up to. That way, if anything went wrong, she would be protected. But it wasn't long before he discovered how much he depended on her financial skills and ended up asking for help. He was a little nervous about her reaction and afraid she might be appalled by what he was doing. Greedy as she had become, all their money had been made honestly, and there really was no reason to commit a crime.

To his surprise, however, she thought his plan was brilliant, sure-fire. If it were not for insider trading, Renee argued, the rich would be no better off than anyone else. How did he think they made their money, she had asked. According to her, it was *all* insider trading; insider trading was the norm. The only difference between Emmett and everyone else was that he wasn't sharing information so much as creating it.

Emmett wasn't entirely reassured by his singular status as the man who had exaggerated a hurricane for the purpose of trading short and spent the whole day—after selling his shares and buying his jacket—nervously considering the bad things that might happen to him. When he was finally able to relax somewhat, he gave Claire a quick call. Holding the phone between his cheek and his shoulder, he raised both his hands as if he were under arrest and, admitting defeat, said, "'No lo contendere.' You win, I lose, I owe you. I forget, how many points did we bet?"

Claire was at her desk when Emmett called. She was really glad to hear his voice, especially after having listened to Goodwin's for the last half hour. "Well of course I win, what did you expect with such a far-out prediction?" she asked, expecting a lengthy defense from him. She started to make herself comfortable, eager for the kind of in-depth discussion only he was capable of; but before she could even wriggle out of her shoes, he was already ending their conversation. "Sorry," he said, as soon as they had tallied up and adjusted their score cards, "gotta run. Wish I could talk but duty calls." What duty? Where was he running to? It was almost as if he didn't want to talk to her.

Claire was puzzled and disappointed. She had really been looking forward to Emmett's call. More than anyone else, she wanted to talk to him, but more than anyone else, he wanted to avoid her, and as soon as she had said good-bye, he called his wife. Talking to Claire was like facing his conscience, and he couldn't bear to do it; but Renee made him feel as if he had entered a world of adults in which things like stock manipulation occurred regularly and were no big deal. No longer merely married, he and Renee were now complicit—partners in crime—and as the one person who knew what he had done, she was the only person who could calm him down. For the first time in months, it was his wife that he needed.

"What do you think of this one?" Renee asked, happily leafing through a real estate brochure when he got home. The brochure was folded in half so that the page featuring Luxury Homes and Estates was face up. She pointed to a picture of a ranch with lots of glass. "Look, this is the front—it has its own gate—and there's a dock in the rear of the house. There's a separate picture showing the dock. That's very unusual, you know. Most houses only get one picture. If they're giving this house two pictures, it must really be special." She was very eager for Emmett's reaction, but as usual, she had forgotten who she was dealing with. He walked past her to the fridge, hardly looking at the picture. The air-conditioning felt like it was freezing his sweat, and once again he felt trapped, embalmed in the frozen perspiration of his anxiety.

"We can't go looking at houses right now, Renee. We can't do anything like that for a while. We've got to be very careful to avoid attracting attention to ourselves." He looked her directly in the eye to let her know he meant business and noticed that she was wearing eye make-up. It also looked like she had a new outfit on, but he wasn't entirely sure. "New dress?" he asked tentatively.

"I got it today. Do you like it?"

"Sure, it's fine," he said, irritated that she was already spending their newfound wealth, but inhibited from comment by his own extravagant purchase.

"Sure, it's fine?" she repeated. "Is that all you have to say? How does it look on me? Isn't this color green becoming?"

"Yes, it's great, you look terrific, but I have other things on my mind right now. And you should too."

"I do. I'm thinking about the house I just showed you."

"Renee, you amaze me. You never stop. Don't you realize that what I did today could land me in a whole lot of trouble if I get caught."

"And your naivete amazes me. Don't you know that yesterday's crime is today's career move?"

Emmett stared at her, transfixed. He was astonished and dumbfounded by her cynical worldliness. As the family breadwinner, the esteemed professional with a national reputation, he had always thought of himself as the more worldly of the two of them, but ever since they had started Air Waves, he had experienced her as a mysterious, fascinating, and slightly disreputable stranger with insight into a world he knew nothing about. It was that world she was leading him through, and, without her guidance, he would have been completely lost in it. Did she really understand it? Was corruption truly a dated concept? There was no one to ask but Renee, Renee the sphinx—the half woman, half lion, who, according to fable, killed those who could not solve its riddle.

She saw the way he was looking at her and knew that it was not her dress that was holding his attention. "Come on," she laughed, thrilled to be an object of fascination, "forget your silly scruples and put on your new jacket. Let's go out to dinner and celebrate."

How did she know he had a new jacket? The woman had magical powers, he thought, still rooted to the spot. It was another moment before he realized that he had not put down the bag with the Cole's logo on it and that the trademark was a giveaway.

CHAPTER TWENTY-TWO

Unlike Emmett, no one ever accused Freddy of having too many scruples, silly or otherwise. To the contrary, Freddy had enough things to think about without worrying about scruples. His "to-do" list was too long as it was. True, his list did include a category for ethics—"think of (and then do!) something ethical;" but that was toward the bottom of the list, when, presumably, he would be free enough of other responsibilities to engage in some leisure time activities. Later, he thought, remembering that he had to prioritize, after the election was over, he would do something that showed him to be a man of conscience. In the meantime, however, he had other things on his agenda, and scruples, like dieting, would just have to wait.

His first order of business was to get down to the office to make sure his staff was working the phones. He had hired a couple of temps to make early morning calls so that he would be on voters' minds from the time they left for work to the moment they arrived at the train station. His name was everywhere, on television, on the telephone, and on lawns, where placards in red, white, and blue were stuck in the grass like for sale signs: *Freddy Coniglia, a Vote for Experience.* Boxer-Stanton had shown early promise, but she was running out of money, and instead of coming on strong during these last few days before the election, she was fading from view. All that seemed to be left of her campaign was one late night ad plus a lot of hand-shaking. Her ad was a direct response to Freddy's: *Experience, sure he's got experience. But is this the kind of experience Bridge Haven needs? Experience in graft, fraud, and corruption? Think about it.*

That was Boxer-Stanton's slogan: *Think About It.* Freddy thought it was a dumb slogan, and so, apparently, did voters because his numbers had started pulling away. Actually, his lead was a very recent development, which probably had a lot more to do with the downturn in the weather and his appearance on television than with her ad. Before Katie's brilliant manipulation of the impending hurricane, the race had been a dead heat, but thanks to her inspired handling of what turned out to be nothing more than a thunderstorm, Freddy had gotten a chance to distract the electorate. What a woman Katie was. They should put her in charge of the Environmental Protection Agency. Somehow she had gotten Louis Martin to predict a hurricane, and that had put Freddy's whole campaign back on track. How she had managed to persuade Louis was another matter, but this was no time for conjecture or jealousy. Or for complacency. Freddy's lead was within a 3 percent margin of error, and he could still lose.

The thought put him into a panic, and he tried to breathe to the count of four at the same time that he searched for his galoshes. He hadn't worn galoshes in years and had no idea where they were, but he needed rain gear for the walking tour. The tour had been organized to survey the storm damage, and even though a quick glance at his driveway and lawn confirmed what he already knew, which was that the storm had blown out to sea and left little in the way of destruction, the tour would still be good publicity. His only concern was that people might wonder why a water main had broken and a power line had come down considering the storm's low intensity. They might think it strange that there had been no other damage—no property damage and no forced evacuations. Needless to say, with no evacuations, no one had used the shelter. Even Bridge Haven's two or three homeless people had found other places to go.

"Thank God it wasn't worse," he said when he met with local officials downtown. They were waiting for him in a huddle outside the courthouse, and despite the warm weather, each of them held a steaming container of coffee. No one responded. The town's chief engineer shook Freddy's hand and, putting his other arm around Freddy's back, steered him out of earshot.

"There was damage last night," he said, "but I'm not sure that it's storm damage." He stopped walking. "It might be vandalism." He did not look at Freddy directly. "The water main that burst—you know about that don't you?"—Freddy nodded—"the water main that burst was definitely a vulnerable pipe, but it came apart in a very unlikely place, and I think it might have been cut."

"Vulnerable?" Freddy asked, eager to talk about the vulnerability and not the unlikely place. "How so vulnerable?"

"Well, it had some leaks and there was internal corrosion. The pipe was unlined cast iron, which is more subject to corrosion than the ones that have a Thermopipe system. The thing is," he scratched his head, about to explain that despite some corrosion, there was no structural damage or other indication of advanced deterioration, when Freddy interrupted.

"Now this corrosion you're talking about. How long have you known about it?"

"Hard to say. I'd have to look at our logs."

"The pipe was unlined cast iron. Would the Thermopipe system you just mentioned have spared Bridge Haven the aggravation and expense of a burst pipe?"

"It would have lasted longer, but…"

"Well, then let's install it," Freddy bellowed. "An ounce of prevention…" he said, raising his right forefinger as he turned and walked back to the others.

The group continued to the site of the downed power line on Main Street where they were joined by several reporters, Katie among them. Goodwin had decided that Fremd was too provocative and that, at least until the election was over, Katie was going to be their reporter on the beat. A cameraman filmed Freddy wearing a hardhat while he answered Katie's questions.

"We were lucky," he said with the earnestness of someone who had come to believe his own lies. "It could have been a lot worse."

"Do you regret setting up the shelter?" Katie asked, sensing that the only way to legitimize the interview was by asking a tough question.

"Absolutely not. What does it cost," he asked rhetorically, "to set up some cots and blankets? Nothing. Not a thing. The school supplied them anyway. But I think it was important for the public to know that, in the event an evacuation turned out to be necessary, there was some place to go."

Another reporter was trying to ask about the rumor that the water main had been tampered with, but as soon as Freddy finished with Katie, he turned back toward the group of local officials. They were piling into a car that would take them down to the Flats to inspect the flooded basements. He hated going to the Flats and did not expect a particularly warm reception, but at least the house they were visiting belonged to a registered republican, one of the few in the neighborhood.

An attractive African-American woman surrounded by several children answered the door. Was she their mother or sister, he couldn't tell. A semi-circle of little diamonds lined the arch of her earlobe and another diamond pierced her right nostril. Her hair was braided into neat little rows, irrigated like a vegetable garden. She graciously invited them in although she seemed somewhat embarrassed by the visit. A man standing by the entrance to the living room—husband? brother? father?—was less welcoming and didn't say a word when Freddy and his entourage entered.

"De wader done sunk back in de groun," the woman explained on their way to the basement. "You could still smell it, but you cane see much."

The woman was right: the basement had the dank smell of water and mildew, but there was nothing to photograph. Was that a rat? Freddy wondered, shrinking at some scurrying sound. "You could see how much wader was here las night," she said, raising the corner of a rug that was completely water logged. "We got vermin too," she continued, "on accounta all de wader, but so far dey stay in de basemen." Yes, it probably was a rat.

Back upstairs, Freddy was photographed at the woman's kitchen table having coffee. "If I'm re-elected," he said, as much to the camera as to her, "a water diversion system will be my first order of business. It will be at the top of my agenda," he promised, "and after it's installed, let's hope you won't be having any more wet basements." He got up, gave her a big hug à la Bill Clinton, and left the house, relieved to get out of there.

"Not so fas, brothuh," said a man at the bottom of the steps leading to the front porch. He was surrounded by his own entourage, and the two groups looked like the posse and the bad guys facing off in a western. "You inna rush? You jus got here."

This was exactly what Freddy was afraid of. "Is there something you wanted to ask me?"

"You might say that," the man drawled insolently. He had viscous eyeballs laced with veins and a slow, leering smile. "I wanna know why de only tahm you come down here is raght before an election?"

"Are we having an election?" Freddy asked. Everyone laughed dutifully except the man asking the question. He was thrown off course, but only for a moment.

"Seems to me de only tahm you got an ineres in de Flats is when dere's some votes to be gotten." His groupies—The Lord is my Savior First Baptist Hallelujah Choir—grunted in assent.

One of his aides was getting ready to shepherd Freddy into the car, but Freddy put his hand up to stop him. "What's your name?" he asked.

"James," the man answered tentatively, as if it was a trick question.

"Well James, I got very few votes from African Americans in the last election and, according to recent polls, I'm not going to get too many in this one either. And do you know why that is, James?"

"Yeah, it's because you doan give a rat's ass 'bout dis neighborhood."

"Amen," someone in his group nodded.

"No, that's not why," Freddy said steadily. "I don't get your votes because you don't vote for anyone, not for me, not for anyone. You don't vote, and as far as I'm concerned, people who don't make themselves felt, don't exist. If you want to get my attention, you're going to have to vote. You can even vote for my opponent, although I'd rather you voted for me, but whoever you vote for, that's when we'll have something to offer each other and that's when we can do a little horse-trading. Now if you'll excuse me," he said and walked past the startled group to the open door of the black Lincoln used for official business.

During his term as mayor, Freddy had learned to bluster and throw his weight around, a stance that had earned him more sarcasm than respect; and while no one had actually thought of him as a criminal until Boxer-Stanton had made her allegations, the prevailing sentiment was that he was slightly ridiculous and profoundly unworthy. No one had ever seen him take charge of a difficult situation before, and his unexpected ability to rise to the occasion produced a stunned moment of reconsideration before the members of his group followed him down the steps and into the street. Once the car was pulling away and beyond the reach of meaningful response, James could be heard yelling at the departing vehicle. "Yo Freddy, you leave yo' wing tips at home? Hey, Mista Mayuh, you wanna buy my house? It got an indoh swimming pool." But it was too late, and everyone knew it. Freddy had triumphed, and he had done it by invoking candor, of all things.

CHAPTER TWENTY-THREE

The next day the local paper quoted Boxer-Stanton as accusing the mayor of bigotry. Mayor says people in Flats don't exist, was how the line read. But Freddy wasn't worried because the quote was on the third page below the fold, and the accusation was taken out of context and unfounded. If his opponent had been smart, she would have stuck with allegations of corruption, but she got greedy and kept heaping it on. It made her look bad, almost desperate. Not only that, her original accusations were getting lost amidst the new ones and obscured by the hurricane furor. Clearly, the lady had no political instinct. Instead of hammering away at the allegations of graft and fraud, she had lost focus and switched gears. Freddy was delighted. If he could mislead her, he should certainly be able to keep the public distracted a little while longer, maybe by re-introducing his predecessor's legislation for a water diversion system—maybe even long enough to get re-elected.

It was generally agreed that Freddy had acquitted himself well on the walking tour, and that the events of the past few days had done a lot for his campaign. They had certainly done more for him than for Claire, whose ratings had slipped noticeably since her lackluster hurricane report. Apparently Goodwin and Russo had been right, the public wanted entertainment no matter what, and when they didn't get it, they immediately started to look for it somewhere else. Two or three dull broadcasts on her part and one dazzling report on Louis's were all it had taken.

Despite all the warnings, Claire was genuinely astonished. She had not really, deep down, fully believed that Goodwin or Russo had a true understanding of the public; and she was quite persuaded that just as they had been mistaken about its tolerance for poetry and prose, they would be wrong about its capacity for loyalty too. Viewers would stand by her, and she would once again enjoy the supreme pleasure of proving the experts wrong. What a fool she had been! How arrogant and vain of her to imagine that she—who hardly even watched television!—knew what the public wanted. Two years on the job, and Claire didn't have the foggiest idea of who she was talking to. All along she had been swimming in shallow water and never once had she bothered to look down. Judy had always told her that she lived in a dream world, and it turned out Judy was right. Her relationship to viewers was a virtual relationship about as real as—was it true? could it be?—as her relationship with Jesse? Was Judy right about that too?

• • •

A couple of teenaged girls were going through the racks when Claire walked into Second Hand Rose. "You were right," she said, walking up to the cash register and getting straight to the point of her visit. "You and Goodwin were both right." She put her backpack down on the counter and moved in close to avoid being overheard. She was wearing a short white denim skirt and flip flops, her legs so long that the skirt's mid-thigh hemline was not the least bit risqué.

"Ye..ee..es," said Judy, waiting for more.

"My ratings have dropped." Claire spoke in the hushed tone of someone speaking in confidence. "I didn't hype the hurricane—the non-existent, totally fabricated and invented hurricane—and my ratings dropped."

Judy listened with one eye on the teenagers. She was expecting a more dramatic explanation of Claire's unannounced visit.

"It's amazing. It didn't even take a week," Claire continued. She was twisting a tissue into a thin, frayed strand of rope.

"People are so annoying," Judy said cooperatively when she realized there wouldn't be more.

"Annoying? Is that all you have to say? I mean, Judy, come on. I've put my heart and soul into these broadcasts. My entire education is reflected in their content. You would think that they—the viewers—could at least cut me a few days slack." She was burning with the indignation of the unappreciated and misunderstood. "And Goodwin...what a jerk. I can't believe that *I* work for him, and that *he* can tell *me* what to do. I would really love to cut him down to size."

Judy raised an eyebrow. Humility had never been Claire's strong suit, but "cut her boss down to size?" She took her eyes off the teenagers for a minute to examine a hangnail. "He's just doing his job," she said, fishing around her pocketbook for an emery board.

"*'Just doing his job?'* Are you defending him?" Claire asked incredulously. "Don't tell me that you agree with him?" She was so angry that anything less than total indictment was a betrayal of friendship.

"No, of course not. The guy's an idiot. I just think that you are getting sidetracked."

"Do you remember that time you were dissed by that salesgirl at Bloomingdale's?" Claire asked, looking for the fuse that would spark Judy's anger. "You were so mad you could have bombed the store. And that was because of a total stranger. Imagine if it were *your boss* dissing you!" she said, her whole being shaped and hardened by indignation.

"Please don't use disrespect as a verb."

That did it. The whole world was against her, and all Judy could think about was grammar.

"I may have to quit," Claire said, going for shock value. It worked.

"Because of a drop in ratings? That's crazy. How low did they go, for God's sake? Are they threatening to fire you?"

"No," said Claire impatiently. "It's not like that. It's just…it's too…I don't know if I can do this job anymore. The public has no interest in what I *derive* from the weather. All they care about is what *I impose* on it. They want entertainment, *no matter what.*"

Now it was Judy's turn to be irritated. "You mean it's television."

Claire was momentarily silenced. The teenagers were still going through the racks and one of them held up a dress for her friend to look at. "This is *soooo* cute. Tell me, is this adorable, or what?"

"Oh wow. *Where* did you get that?"

"Over there," she said pointing to the Poor but Proud rack against the wall. They started to giggle. All the racks in Judy's thrift shop were identified by name, and laughter was a common reaction to them. There was Lapse in Taste and Flight of Fancy for the adventurous and outlandish, Quality will Out and Poor but Proud for the more conservative, Ten Pounds Lighter for the wishful, and Third Hand Rose for the almost destitute. No one had thought the store would make much money since there was no way to mass market second-hand clothing, but thanks to Judy's wacky sales and marketing techniques, women bought her clothes for the little red rose, her label, instead of for its original label, which might be anything from Gucci to Gap. Second Hand Rose had been open for less than a year, but right from the start, it had attracted attention with a full-page black-and-white ad in Vogue. The ad featured a white Jaguar on a circular cobblestone driveway, a barefoot woman in a flowing white gown ascending the steps of a chateau, her long black hair windswept, her diamonds sparkling, her white gloves and black dress sandals dangling limply from her hand in the dreamy pre-dawn post-coital hours. In the tradition of the high-line, glossy black-and-white ad, prices were listed off to the side in tiny print, only in the case of Judy's ad, a dress that would ordinarily cost hundreds was selling for $29.99. Readers did a double-take.

"Were you really so surprised that your ratings dropped?" Judy seized the initiative. "How did you think people would react to your blah reports?" She had finished filing her nail and was holding her fingers out for inspection.

"I thought I had built up a certain amount of good will...appreciation for what I've done."

"I'm afraid," Judy said, refraining from adding the deprecating phrase *my dear child*, "that what you've built up is expectation for what you can deliver. Television makes spoiled brats of us all. It's gimme, gimme, gimme. If viewers don't like what you have to offer, they just go someplace else. Doesn't mean they won't be back. It just means they're putting you on notice."

Claire settled into the chair reserved for customers and waited for the girls to leave. The phrase "putting you on notice" was galling, but she decided to leave it alone. "My heart's not in it anymore," she resumed, after the teenagers left without buying anything. That was only partly true, but Claire wanted Judy to protest and tell her she couldn't possibly mean what she was saying.

"Teenagers," Judy said, as if that one word encompassed everything you needed to know on the subject. "What's your heart got to do with it? Do you think my heart is into sitting behind this cash register every day? Here," she said, changing the subject to avoid an argument, "try this on." She handed Claire a dress from the Quality will Out rack. "It will raise your spirits."

"You're at the wrong rack. Quality is irrelevant. Maybe if you gave me something from Lapse in Taste."

"That doesn't sound like you."

"It's who they've made me into."

"You are a huge success." Judy's response came back hard and fast, a pinball bouncing off the spring of unwavering opinion.

Claire did not want to be reminded of her indebtedness to JTF and slumped back in her chair again. "Yes, but my success is based on a complete misperception of what I've been doing for the past two years."

Judy put her arms up in the sentimental posture of someone playing the violin, the right arm extended in front of her, the left bent at the elbow and turned inward. "I hope you'll pardon me for saying this," she made the gesture of drawing a bow across a string, "but so what?"

"What do you mean *So what?*" Claire asked reproachfully. "You sound just like Goodwin."

"I am like Goodwin. I'm a business woman. I know that you have to sell your product, whatever it is and however you do it. Don't you know that we're a country obsessed with numbers? Ratings, polls, calories, stocks, cholesterol, blood pressure, you name it. Numbers. We are measured and controlled by them; we are bullied and inspired by them; those little digits reduce and motivate us; they define and ignore us; they whip us into submission, and we love them in return. Just look at how many people spend their days—their lives!—watching the numbers go up and down. Up and down, up and down, as if there were something fascinating about it. The height of the bar is numerical, honey, and the quality of your reports, well I hate to say it, but it's only as good as the number it produces."

What followed next was a long silence. What could you say after such a comprehensive statement about a society's defining characteristics? You could either engage in a major rebuttal, or you could lean back and ruminate.

"Yes, I suppose you're right," Claire said at last, "but I can't say that your exposition is exactly inspiring me to…"

"Stop right there," Judy jumped back in. "Excuse me for interrupting, but inspiration is not what this is about. Inspiration is asking too much from a job."

"Why?"

"Because it's too rare, too entitled."

"Too rare for whom? Too entitled for what?"

And now it was Judy's turn to pause and reflect. "For ordinary humanity. We're just slugging it out, the rest of us, and it's kind of…Darling, you know I love you, but you can be a little uncompromising."

Claire looked at Judy sharply, seriously, intently. She didn't say anything. Judy had gotten to the heart of the matter, and Claire knew it.

Compromise, the word alone made her spine stiffen. For Claire, the word might as well have had a "D" at the end of it, so strongly did she feel that to compromise was to be lessened. And yet, all kinds of people from parents to diplomats spoke of compromise as a good thing, an art. Was that true? If it was, then why did artful seem like a better way to describe compromise, and why did the word's application so often seem to involve chicanery and deceit?

"You have no competition out there," Judy was saying. "That Louis character is a joke, a flash in the pan—an absurd imitation of you. He was on to something with, what was it, water ballet, but he won't be able to keep it going and as soon as that becomes obvious, you'll go back to being the only game in town. You just have to stay the course. Forget all this other stuff. Think about your work."

Almost immediately, Claire started to feel better. Maybe Judy was right. She was usually right when it came to matters involving hard-headedness and the big picture. "Stay the course, huh?"

"Nose to the grindstone."

"But I'm all out of ideas. The well is running dry."

Judy stopped to think. She had already solved one problem that day and there was no reason she couldn't solve another. "It's a shitty time of year. Why don't you do something on the dog days of summer? These are the dog days, aren't they?"

"That's a great idea," said Claire, getting up and moving toward the door. "Judy, what would I do without you?"

Twinkle, twinkle, little star,
How I wonder what you are,
Up above the world so high,
Like a diamond in the sky,
Twinkle, twinkle, little star
How I wonder what you are!

When the blazing sun is gone,
When he nothing shines upon,
Then you show your little light,
Twinkle, twinkle, all the night,
Twinkle, twinkle, little star,
How I wonder what you are!

Then the traveler in the dark,
Thanks you for your tiny spark,
He could not see which way to go,
If you did not twinkle so.
Twinkle, twinkle, little star,
How I wonder what you are!

Author Unknown

CHAPTER TWENTY-FOUR

Claire followed Judy's suggestion, and three nights later, she was televised on an elevated platform at the base of a five hundred pound telescope. The telescope was housed in the Bridge Haven observatory, which was an annex of the Bridge Haven Planetarium and one of the few reasons to visit Bridge Haven. The observatory's white dome could be seen from the far side of the wall dividing the planetarium grounds from the road running parallel; once inside those walls, it came into full view like a jumbo egg inside its carton. One side of the egg was flattened and divided by a long rectangular slot, which housed its highly acclaimed telescope and into whose eye Claire was now looking.

After turning away from an image of the night sky, which was projected onto viewers' screens, Claire explained that the dog days of summer were named after the "dog" star, Sirius, the brightest star in the constellation Canis Major as well as the brightest star in the Northern Hemisphere. "In summer," she said, "Sirius rises and sets with the sun, and the ancients believed that its heat added to the heat of the sun and thereby created a stretch of hot and sultry weather which became known as the dog days. Now, of course," Claire continued, stepping away from the telescope and facing into the camera, which was no longer her prosecutor and had become her collaborator again, "we know this is not true and that the heat is a direct result of the earth's tilt. But as the only star in our Milky Way whose heliacal rising exactly matches the length of our solar year, Sirius has a unique relationship to our solar system. Somehow, the ancient Egyptians were aware of that relationship and, even today, our New Year's celebration is a continuation of an ancient ritual honoring Sirius's return to the mid-heaven position at midnight."

"Is that right?" Katie asked from the anchor's desk. She was annoyed that Claire had recovered from her slump and that her report was taking so long. A large clock facing the news team revealed that Claire was ten seconds into overtime.

"That's right," Claire answered with a beguiling smile. "It was believed that the midnight alignment of the star with the earth marked the moment when the energies of Sirius most directly affect us, and for thousands of years, we have celebrated that moment by jumping for joy at midnight." She was showing no sign of winding down.

"Fascinating," said Reed who had never been fascinated by anything in his life, but like Katie, was aware that Claire had gone over.

"In fact," Claire continued before Reed had a chance to cut in, "if you are interested in finding out more about this remarkable star," her heart started to pound, excited by the transgression she was about to commit, "please let us know. You can write in your questions by logging on to WJTF.com/sirius, or by calling 222-WJTF. Who knows, if there's enough interest, we might even dedicate a show to Sirius and the dog days," she added with reckless abandon, aware that her suggestion was unauthorized and might even be in violation of her contract.

Whatever had come over her? What diabolical impulse had possessed her to volunteer the station's resources without consulting anyone first? Only Goodwin and Russo had the authority to do that, and they only made that decision after lengthy deliberations and extensive consultation with marketing. And yet, here she was acting as if she answered to no one and could do whatever she wanted! That certainly wasn't what Judy had in mind when she suggested Claire focus on her work.

"Well, that would certainly be a treat," said Katie, who almost lost her composure. What the hell was going on, and why hadn't she heard anything about a show?

Russo was in the dark too and immediately assumed that Goodwin was pulling a fast one. It would have been unprecedented—the first time in all the years they had worked together—that Goodwin had made a major decision without consulting him, but there was no other explanation. The thought of Goodwin acting independently was infuriating and jettisoned Russo into action. He knew he had to nip this in the bud. There was no way he was going to let that son of a bitch take over. He started walking toward Goodwin's office when halfway down the corridor, his pace slowed. Then he stopped walking altogether. He'd completely forgotten that Goodwin had been called away on a family matter and was out of the office.

Russo stopped to think. Dan. Could Dan have suggested a special? It seemed highly unlikely. Dan was a team player and not the man to go it alone. That impression was confirmed when he saw Dan standing beside his desk looking as bewildered as Russo. "Beats me," he said with an exaggerated shrug, his raised shoulders pulling his shirt taut. The one person remaining, and the obvious person to ask, was Claire herself, but Russo hated confronting her. Claire seemed so superior, as if she herself were Sirius, the brightest star, that he felt uncomfortable telling her what to do. It was like telling a star how to shine. Claire had explained that Sirius was part of a binary system, and the second star, Sirius B, was invisible to the naked eye and completely overshadowed by the brilliant radiance of Sirius A. That was how Russo felt—obscure and insignificant compared to Claire—unworthy of being her boss. Nonetheless, just or unjust, he was management and it was simply out of the question that any member of the news team make independent and unauthorized decisions on the air.

The calls were already pouring in to the station when Russo half propped himself against the three-drawer file cabinet next to Claire's computer. The fact that Claire was reviewing the questions flooding her monitor did not make his job any easier for him. Tightening his belt as if it were the proverbial bootstrap, he cleared his throat. Claire waved hello without turning around. "Just a sec," she said as she finished typing something onto her screen. She knew that she had provoked a confrontation and that she would be strongly censured when she turned around, so to postpone the moment, she continued working at her computer a little longer than necessary. The truth was that she really had no explanation for what she had done. Something, as they say, had come over her, and like management's handling of hurricane Louis, it was capricious, self-serving, and entirely unjustifiable.

"Yes," she took the initiative, her full, but nonetheless fine features set to confront criticism, "I should have consulted you first." She wished it had been Goodwin who had come to reprimand her.

"You should have," he agreed.

"But I was given the clear and undeniable impression that ratings are all that matters. That," she said, pointing to the e-mails on her computer screen, "should translate into very high ratings, especially if we follow up with a special report on the dog days of summer."

"There's nothing wrong with the idea in and of itself. It's the way you went about it. Special reports are decided by management. Did you think we wouldn't have given it to you if you asked?"

Claire didn't know how to answer. Finally, in a voice lacking its usual determination, she said, "I didn't say there would be a special. I merely threw it out as a possibility." She was still looking at her computer, avoiding eye contact.

"I think you've been in this business long enough to realize, Claire, that we don't just throw things out unless we're prepared to follow up."

"I was thinking about ratings," she lied. "Goodwin made it very clear to me that they are all that matters."

Goddamned Goodwin, Russo thought, trying to figure out how to respond without criticizing his partner. Russo had gone on a management retreat once, and one of the exercises was in effective criticism. A cardinal rule was that you never complained about a colleague to an employee, even if the colleague was a total asshole.

"Ratings are obviously very important. But there are other considerations."

"Oh really," Claire's cheeks, neck, and collarbones reddened with anger. "Has there been a change in policy that I don't know about? No one ever said anything to me about other considerations." She wasn't lying anymore. Finally, she was saying exactly how she felt. "Why just the other day, Goodwin referred to my willingness to 'do anything' to get a rise out of people. My willingness to do anything was proof that I really understood how ratings define the business we're in. Take the hurricane for example. Was I rewarded for the accuracy of my prediction, or was I reprimanded for a lackluster performance that negatively impacted ratings?"

So that's what it was. Claire was still pissed about the hurricane, and she was getting back at them. He thought this was what his wife called passive aggression, but he couldn't remember how you were supposed to deal with it. He had never known how to deal with Claire anyway, and his discomfort unsettled his stomach. He stuck his thumbs under the rim of his pants, cowboy-style, to relieve the pressure, but he had to remove them immediately because a paper cut on his left thumb hurt when it got touched.

Most places would have fired Claire for what she had done, no questions asked. Maybe she was even trying to get fired. With Claire, there were unlimited possibilities for misunderstanding. But one thing Russo was sure of was that he didn't want her to leave, and if she was trying to get herself fired, he was not going to cooperate. Claire was the goose who had laid the golden egg, and her special might be the platinum. He'd be crazy to fire her. So what if she squawked from time to time; that's what geese did. Goodwin was a stickler for procedure and hierarchy and would probably have reacted differently if he'd been there; but Goodwin was not in the office, and Russo had no intention of disturbing him. Not only that, Goodwin was an asshole. No, this was Russo's moment and he wanted to handle it right. More than that, he wanted to rise to the occasion, to show a little class, which usually, in his experience, meant generosity.

"We'll make arrangements for the special," he said, loosening his belt a notch, "but in the future, I would appreciate it if you asked first." That was it, that was all, no reprimand, nothing more than a willingness to cooperate, and Russo went back to his office. Claire was rattled. That was not really what she'd had in mind. She had hoped to challenge Goodwin's authority, to make good on his assertion that she would do anything to get a rise out people, to make him regret ever having used those words; but, instead, she had brought out the best in Russo.

Russo thought so too, although he wasn't entirely sure since he'd had very little experience of largesse. After he went back to his office, he called his wife for confirmation that he had done the right thing. Barbara was pretty sharp, and he wanted to know what she thought of his handling of the situation. Basically, she thought he had wimped out. Claire should either have been fired or, at the very least, put on some kind of probation. Apart from the difficult position she had created for JTF, Claire was setting a very dangerous precedent for the rest of the news team. Suppose Fletcher wanted to host a special on the football draft, or Katie wanted an exclusive interview with the mayor. If Claire was free to do what she wanted, what was there to prevent the others from acting independently too? There had to be consequences, if only to keep everyone else in check. Russo picked up the picture of his wife and looked at her while they talked. She had looked so carefree at the time the photograph was taken. He had never imagined that she would become so tough.

"I don't know, Babs. We can't afford to lose her, and when you take steps like that, you know, probation, you have to be prepared for the person to leave. Do you remember what it was like before she came on?"

Stubbornly, Barbara denied any recollection, but her failure of memory was somewhat disingenuous, a refusal to acknowledge that another woman could make such a big difference in her husband's life. "How would it look," Russo persevered, trying to assuage his wife, "if after less than two years, our star performer left, maybe even to go to another station? A bigger and better station." Barbara didn't want to acknowledge Claire's importance, but she understood self-interest, and the more they talked, the more clear it became that Claire should stay on. By the end of the conversation, Barbara was telling her husband that her reaction had been impulsive, that he had handled the situation well, and that he should immediately set up the special, before Goodwin got back and messed things up.

Russo hung up the phone and kissed his wife's photograph.

CHAPTER TWENTY-FIVE

Russo had to act fast because it was August 23rd and the dog days of summer were over, strictly speaking. They were designated as beginning thirty-five days before the Fourth of July and ending thirty-five days after; and even though the public wasn't aware of those dates, people were waiting for a response to their calls and e-mails. To get maximum viewer response, JTF had to act before the subject got stale and before people lost interest in it.

The director of the Bridge Haven Planetarium, an urban astronomer named Gerhardt Harkin, who had once been involved in the design and implementation of planetariums worldwide, was only too happy to have the planetarium host the show. At 142 years old, Bridge Haven was older than Hayden, but for years it had lived in the shadow of the great institution in the great city to the south. That was especially true after the Hayden Planetarium was reconstructed and became a model for both science and architecture—a spectacular ninety-five-foot sphere inside a transparent cube with tubular trusses and structural steel cables visible from outside its clear glass walls. Even though Bridge Haven could not compete with Hayden architecturally, here was an opportunity for the planetarium and for its formerly well-known director to regain some prominence, and, with that in mind, Harkin did everything he could to set things up as quickly as possible.

The agreed upon format consisted of a tour hosted by Gerhardt followed by a star show moderated by Claire. A question-and-answer period from a live audience would wind things up. Claire's segment began in the observatory again, only this time there was a discussion of the technological advances represented by its telescope, which had a fancy lens, a state-of-the-art digital camera, spotting scopes attached to its side, and a clock drive that tracked the telescope to the rate of the earth's rotation. The room itself was a cave-like enclosure of gray concrete and metal reminiscent of the apocalyptic craters in James Bond movies; and at its center, looking dwarfed by all the technology, sat Claire.

Once the camera moved in and restored her to human predominance, she began her lecture, beginning with a description of how the heliacal rising of Sirius roughly coincided with the flooding of the Nile and marked the beginning of the Egyptian year. In the star's honor, Claire explained, the ancient Egyptians named it the "dog star," after their god Osirus, whose head in pictograms looked remarkably like a dog. The star, she went on to explain, had historical, religious, mythological, astrological, and astronomical significance; and every civilization, from the Sumerians to the Greeks, had something to say on the subject of the Sirian system.

• • •

Marie was delicately eating popcorn, one kernel at a time, her eyes riveted on the television screen, when Freddy joined her in the den. For a moment, the two of them were both staring at Claire. Marie was interested in the astronomy, but Freddy didn't care much about stars—they were too far away. He liked things you could touch, and that was what was fascinating about Claire because although she was flesh and blood, he didn't know if he could touch her. A) He didn't know if she would let him, and B) well, there was no B. Given the opportunity, he would have liked to touch her. She was sportily dressed in a loose-fitting blouse, open at the neck, and he would have liked to slip his hand inside to find out how much was there. She had a nice shape, tall and slender, although her loose-fitting clothing made it hard to tell how she fared in the breast department, and he had a special fondness for breasts. He kept staring at the screen, as if it would reveal what was beneath her shirt, but it exposed nothing, which pretty much confirmed his suspicion that she fell short. Tall, slender women were often on the flat side.

Even so, there was something almost transporting about Claire, as if she herself were some kind of celestial body—alive, sparkling, and distant; and he didn't know if he liked it. Maybe that was because he knew she was out of his reach and it made him angry.

"Marie, there's a baseball game on."

"Why don't you watch in the bedroom?" she suggested without looking up. She had just had her nails done, and even though she carefully removed the popcorn from the bowl, holding each kernel between the cushions of her thumb and forefinger, the popcorn was getting stuck underneath her nails.

"I just came downstairs. I don't want to go back up."

"This is almost over, and the game will be on for hours. Come on, watch with me." She patted the sofa next to her. He tossed the Ralph

Lauren throw onto the armchair and sat down next to Marie on the loveseat. Claire was talking about the relationship between Sirius A and its sidekick, Sirius B. The subject seemed to really excite her because her whole face was animated. Freddy listened for a minute and found out that Sirius B traced an elliptical orbit around Sirius A, which took fifty years to complete. The closest period of connection during their circling of each other was called the periastron, and during that period, their gravitational attraction for each other was so great that it almost defied human comprehension.

Freddy was about to make some comment about the periastron of Freddy and Marie when Marie turned the sound off. "What did you do that for? I was getting into this part about the way Sirius A re-unites fusion reactions in Sirius B. The stars are getting it on," he said, cocking his head and looking at Marie in a way that could lead to sex. He did it on purpose because he knew that it turned her off when he made oblique sexual reference, and he really had no interest in having sex with her. But he wasn't interested in talking to her either; and the decisive way she pressed the mute button with a dramatic flourish of the wand and then turned her small but ample body toward him, her slightly comical face serious, suggested that she wanted to talk…to *really* talk.

"Freddy, why did Boxer-Stanton accuse you of all those things? You know, the racketeering and nepotism and such."

The question was completely unexpected. First of all, they were in the middle of this show about the dog days of summer. Second, the scandal had gotten buried in the hurricane, and there hadn't been any talk about it for days. Why bring it up now? Why bring it up at all? Freddy was leading in the polls; Boxer-Stanton—who he had taken to calling

B.S—was political history; and for all intents and purposes, the matter had died at birth. He sometimes wondered about Marie, what world she lived in. As long as the issue had been red hot and all over the news, she hadn't said a word; but now, now that it had died down and he thought that he was home free, she wanted to talk about it.

"What do you mean?" he groped for response.

Silence.

"Alright, alright. It's true," he said, not quite sure what had come over him. "Did I give contracting jobs to your brothers when I might have given them to someone else? Sure I did, you know that. After all, they're family. Did they, in turn, hire their buddies, you know, their cronies?" he asked, not knowing whether Marie knew what cronyism was. "Yeah, I suppose they did. And as for the racketeering, well you know them better than I do—they're *your* brothers, after all. You tell me whether there was racketeering."

Masterful, he thought to himself. And true. Why had he been afraid of talking to her?

Marie's face began to disorganize and collapse. How had such a sweet, simple, and naive woman as Marie grown up in the same house as those two thugs?

But he had misread her expression. "Are you trying to lay this on my brothers?" she asked, her beady, DiMotta eyes narrowing. Maybe she wasn't so sweet and naive as he thought.

"Well, Marie, it wasn't as if they gave me much choice. To say they leaned on me would be putting it mildly."

"You couldn't lean back?" She asked, looking almost vicious now. Italians, he thought, with utter contempt, they always put blood first, no matter what. He looked at the television screen where Claire was sitting next to a man in a suit, and both were surrounded by an audience. Boy, did he wish he could have been sitting there instead of the hot seat he was in. "Thanks to them, you're mayor, and now you want to accuse them," she persevered, one hand clutching the cross around her neck.

"Whoa, whoa. For openers, I wasn't the one who made the accusation. It was my opponent. Second, I wasn't the one who brought it up just now. You did. I was sitting here happily watching the star show until you turned the sound off and started making noises of your own."

"So go back and watch then," Marie said, aggressively restoring the sound by hitting the mute button. She got up abruptly and dismissively, and with posture perfectly erect, as if she had taken the high ground and was justified in walking out on him, left the room.

Freddy watched her waddle away, head held high, and then returned his attention to the television. Members of the audience were standing up and asking questions. Were there other stars that shone as brightly as Sirius? Did the stars influence the seasons? Were the dog days the same as Indian summer and would Claire dedicate a show to it? Was it hard to become an astrologer? The questions held Freddy's interest for a minute, and he thought that he might even be a better person if he paid attention to the answers. But self-improvement had never been the kind of effort he engaged in, and after two or three more questions, he switched to the ball game.

CHAPTER TWENTY-SIX

The special went extremely well. Within hours Claire's ratings shot back up into the pre-Louis stratosphere, and when Claire got to the station the next day, she had the impression that people were toning down their conversations and cutting a swath before her. Once again, she was a media sensation, JTF's star reporter, the darling of the news team.

Most people would have been delighted, but Claire was unimpressed. Worse than unimpressed, she was disillusioned. How was it possible that the same viewers who had embraced her one day could dump her the next, and then champion her again the week following? How was she supposed to continue caring about such a one-sided relationship? The public she had romanced was proving an unworthy lover, and preparing for their nightly encounters, which only recently had been so rewarding, was becoming drudgery. Success and failure simply had too much in common with each other to engage her interest anymore. For two years Claire had shown that weather reporting could have greater depth and resonance than anyone ever imagined…but to what end? What change had she wrought? After all, the public had liked Norwood Fossil too.

If at least she had gotten through to Goodwin, that might have helped. But if her power play had made any impression on him, he certainly wasn't letting on. In fact, on the morning of the special, Goodwin, the stony, stalwart New Englander, had winked at her—Goodwin, winking! It was entirely possible that he didn't give a hoot—a favorite expression of his—about the reckless way she had suggested the special. After all, he had made it quite clear that ratings were all that mattered, and since her special was benefiting the station, what difference did her little act of insubordination make? Maybe there was no such thing as revenge. Certainly there was no such thing as loyalty. There was, however, such a thing as despair, and Claire was feeling it.

"You've got some vacation days coming to you," Russo volunteered when she broached the subject of taking a break. They were in his office, which had sprung several leaks during the heavy rain, and he had moved his desk into the middle of the room to keep water from dripping on it. Once the desk was there, he decided the room looked better that way and left it. "A few days on the beach will do you a world of good."

"I don't know whether that will be enough," Claire said skeptically.

"Tack on your sick days then. Strictly speaking, you're only supposed to use them when you're actually sick, but if you need a few extra days, I don't see why we can't give them to you."

"This is not exactly about rest and relaxation."

"Well what is it about then?" Russo asked, wondering if Claire had gotten an offer from another station. He felt the semi-circles of sweat in his armpits expand, even though the AC was on and the office was quite cool. Claire tried to explain herself, but by the time she had finished, he was not sure what she had said. Something about dazzling the public but not fulfilling herself.

After she left his office, he called Goodwin on the office intercom. "Phil, could you come in here? I think we've got a problem." Ordinarily, Russo would have tried to work things out without involving Goodwin, but this time, he had no idea what she'd been talking about and didn't know how to respond to her. He tried to repeat her words, but his vague generalities only made Goodwin impatient and irritable.

"It's incomprehensible hogwash," Goodwin said, the nostrils of his pinched nose flaring. "Incomprehensible hogwash," he repeated. "Distortion, hype, and authenticity...I've never heard such nonsense. The woman is weird. Her ratings go up and she's feeling—what was the word you used? Ennui—she's feeling ennui." The two of them sat in perplexed silence with Russo looking at the picture of his wife, and Goodwin staring down at the stained industrial carpeting. He had put a Persian carpet in his own office, which had improved it 100 percent.

"Maybe we should offer her a raise?" Russo suggested, still afraid that she was being courted by another station.

"Did she ask for a raise?" Goodwin sat up straight. The subject of money always made him stiffen.

"No, but if she's thinking about going somewhere else..."

Goodwin was having a hard time with Russo's suggestion. It was his job to keep costs down, and it went very much against the tight weave of his Lutheran grain to offer an increase before the expiration of a contract, especially when no increase had been requested. It took all Russo's powers of persuasion to convince Goodwin that diminishing Claire's malaise—another French word and another concept Goodwin hated—was worth a few extra dollars; but when he'd finally talked him into it and they went ahead with the offer, to their utter amazement, Claire refused. She was very polite, very gracious and appreciative, but, as she put it, in light of what had taken place, she simply could not accept.

Neither of them said anything, but privately they were both wondering what had taken place. The special was a success, and the hurricane was ancient history. What else could be bothering her? What could bother anyone so much that they *could not accept a raise?* They were dumbfounded. Claire had always been a mystery to them, but never more than at the present moment. Russo had assumed that his forgiving attitude toward the special had put them on a pretty sure footing; but now he didn't know what to think, and for the first time in his dealings with Claire, he found himself getting angry. She seemed to think that she was still an academic who could take time off whenever she needed to, and that her job would be waiting whenever she decided to return. Claire was undeniably a very smart lady, but she didn't seem to have any understanding of the world she had entered.

"You talk to her," he told Dan, when he realized that neither he nor Goodwin had any idea of what to do next. Dan was in his favorite position, his head facing the ceiling, his chair dangerously poised on its two back feet. "You're gonna fall down and crack your skull one of these days," Russo said to him. "Please sit up; you're making me nervous. Anyway, I can't talk to you with your head tilted back like that. Listen," he said once Dan was in an upright position, "you've always been able to talk to Claire. Better than the rest of us anyway. There's something going on with her, and we've got to help her work it out. Otherwise…I don't know," he scratched his head, refusing to say that he was afraid she might leave. "Talk to her, but be tactful. We don't want to alienate her," he added, as if asking for an unspecified amount of time off weren't alienation enough.

The staff lounge was noisy even though it was empty. The noise came from the street, where construction was blocking traffic and cars had to take turns using the open lane. The arrangement exceeded the patience of many drivers; and the intermittent blasting of horns and the intermittent drilling of pavement combined with the room's poor lighting and cheap furniture created such an uninviting atmosphere that no one went there and Dan usually had the place to himself.

On this particular occasion however, he asked Claire to keep him company. They sat down at the long linoleum table, which had burn marks left over from when people still smoked. After Dan lovingly opened the wax paper swaddling his sandwich and gave it an appreciative glance, he moved to the head of the table and stood up. "The reason I have invited you here today," he said, addressing an imaginary assembly, "is to ask you to join us in honoring Claire Day who, after two years of tireless service and dedication to weather broadcasting, will be taking a leave of absence." Was she being mocked? Claire squirmed slightly. "We hope her leave from us will be brief. In addition to her daily forecasts, she has brought integrity, boundless creativity, and a rare combination of scientific and literary depth to her subject, and I know that I speak for everyone here at the station as well as for the general public when I say that she will be missed. True," he held up his hand as if to stave off applause, "it will be difficult for us to find someone to fill in for *'an unspecified amount of time,'* but," he said, taking a bite of his sandwich and pausing to chew, "we wish her every success in finding the intellectual legitimacy and peace that she is searching for.

"Claire is someone special," he continued, speaking directly to her instead of to his audience, "because she brings the world to life. We need her to do that for us." Parody was succumbing to sincerity and Dan had to pause. He had not intended to make a personal appeal and had to regain his composure before he could go on. There was something about Claire that always made him feel slightly emotional. "But although we will miss her, we hope that her leave is fruitful and that she will pursue it with the same..." he held up his hands again as if to restrain an uncontrollable audience... "the same effort, commitment, and...*authenticity* that she has brought to JTF...Claire," he said, stepping aside and graciously offering her the podium.

But Claire did not move. Her hands were folded in her lap, and she did not lift her eyes from them. She was truly surprised by Dan's statement, with its strong under current of irony.

"You think I am being a brat."

"That is very harsh," he protested.

"But it's what you think?"

Dan didn't say anything.

Claire nodded. No one had ever called her a brat before. Even the people who thought that her decision to drop out of academe was perverse had not labeled her a brat. "What would you have me do? They wanted me lie, to distort, to rig the weather so that a two-bit politician could win an election and so that a disgruntled meteorologist could manipulate some stocks." Claire was not at all sure about this latter part, but it was a distinct possibility—Judy had suggested it—and she wanted to say as much as possible to bolster her position. She hated the idea that

Dan thought she was a brat.

Dan looked interested. He had heard something about erratic energy prices and stock sell-offs, but he hadn't made the connection. He'd have Fremd look into it. At the moment, however, that wasn't his objective.

"And did you do it?" he asked. Michelle came in to use the soda machine, and he waited for her to leave before he continued. "Did you lie? Did you distort? Or did you do what you thought was right?"

She didn't respond. "Exactly," he said. "And after you refused to cooperate, were you punished? Did you get fired for not playing ball?"

Claire looked a little sheepish since, far from being reprimanded, she had just been offered a raise. "That's not the point," she said, anchoring a curl behind her ear.

"It's not the *only* point, but it's a very important point. You can't ignore it."

"No, maybe not. But neither can I ignore the fact that these are the people I work for. I am part of an organization that engages in dishonest, disreputable practices that I don't want my name associated with," she contested.

Dan was getting annoyed. "Who do you want to work for? The heavenly hosts?" He scrunched up the brown paper bag his sandwich had come in and, aiming for the waste paper basket, threw it in a high circular arc. "They gave you the special, for God's sake. Anywhere else, you'd have gotten your walking papers for volunteering the station's resources like that. Specials cost money, you know." As if to emphasize his point, there was a loud blast of horns from the street. "Look Claire, you are the last person in the world I want to lecture, but you are way out of line here."

Claire was not used to being scolded, and she was eager to get up and leave. "What," she asked, "do *you* think I should do?"

"I think you should take your vacation time—no more, no less than is coming to you. You haven't had a break in two years, and you deserve it. Then, I think you should come back and get on with it."

Claire thought that might be good advice. She hadn't seen her parents in months, and it seemed like the perfect time for a visit. Nonetheless, she couldn't let anyone—not even Dan, whom she liked and trusted—tell her what to do, so instead of admitting that he was right, she simply said she would think about it.

> "O what unlucky streak
> Twisting inside me, made me break the line?
> What was the rock my gliding childhood struck,
> And what bright unreal path has led me here?"
>
> from "Nothing significant was really said"
> *Philip Larkin, before March 1940*

CHAPTER TWENTY-SEVEN

Claire liked visiting her parents, especially since they had moved to Maine. While they still lived in Connecticut, she had felt an obligation to see them regularly and sometimes more often than she wanted to. It was not that visits were unpleasant. It was just that they were something duty required more often than she was personally inclined toward; and their move provided welcome relief from the filial responsibility Claire, as an only child, shouldered alone. That was how she felt during the first few months after their move. Then, as time passed, she wished she could see them more easily and welcomed their time together.

Nonetheless, when she did see them, it always took a slight adjustment on her part. For more than thirty years, the three of them had sat at the same sofa in the same living room in the same house, and it had seemed like nothing would ever change. Twenty-one Concord Street, Richmond, Connecticut was the setting of all Claire's family associations, and the place where, like a coat removed at the entrance, she immediately shed the mental uniform required to function in the world. It was home. Once her parents moved, however, visits became more formal. The sentimental memorabilia of childhood had been packed away and closeted, and the informality that went along with knowing where to find everything was replaced by the need to ask and to have things shown to her.

And then there was her father's health. While they still lived in Connecticut, Claire would arrive at her parents unannounced and enjoy the regressive abandon of childhood. However, with the physical deterioration that began with his arthritis and followed a circuitous route to high blood pressure, everything changed, and abandon was replaced by caution. In keeping with his doctor's recommendation that he lead a stress-free life, efforts were made to shield him from unnecessary aggravation, and that, too, took some adjusting. In a way, it meant that the adult phase of their family life had begun, and the adult phase also felt like the final phase.

Mr. Day did not like being left out or treated like an invalid, and he frequently made the point that he wanted to be included in what was going on, especially when he heard hushed conversation in the background. Exclusion, he insisted, would be more stressful than information. But there was no getting around the fact that family life had become more subtle, and that it had come to involve frequent decisions about what to tell Dad and what to keep from him.

Clearly, Claire's dissatisfaction with her job was important, and at some point during her visit she was going to have to talk about it. Even so, she was in no hurry, and it was more than a week after she got to Maine before she could make herself bring it up. The subject was too raw, too tender, and needed to settle into its own shape before adjusting to the contours of another point of view. It was also possible that the matter of her job would lead to the larger question of her life as a whole. Claire's father had always said that there are moments whose importance is only clear in retrospect, and that the trick was to foresee hindsight. Claire couldn't help wondering if she had arrived at such a moment and whether hindsight would eventually reveal a single, childless, unemployed woman who'd had her chance and blown it.

For the first week of her visit, they engaged in their Maine rituals: dinner at the Boothbay Inn where Claire learned a new lobster-eating technique, homemade blueberry pie from the green market, and a concert of chamber music at Pine Hall. The town, Pine Hill, was known for its music. There was the year-round concert series, the summer festival, and the school, which was attached to the summer festival and attracted a fairly large number of Eastern European musicians, who gave the place an aura of greatness and possibility during the summer months. When the musicians left again at the end of August, the place returned to being fairly ordinary, with little to distinguish it from other towns along the Maine coast: nice views, great seafood, cold weather, and high unemployment. But, perhaps because of its contrast with winter, the summer hovered over the town's permanent residents the entire year, leaving them aware both of the exoticism they personally lacked, and of the special grace bestowed upon them annually when the town would once again be taken over by aspiring talents and accomplished performers.

Claire got to Pine Hill after the summer season was over. The last concert of the festival had already taken place—a student performance that represented the culmination of the summer's efforts—but there was another, a post-season faculty concert, and that was the one Claire and her parents went to. Seating was on a first-come, first-served basis, and Claire's father insisted they get there early enough to choose their seats. He was adamant on the subject of seating. He preferred to sit far enough back for the voices of individual instruments to project and come together in one unified sound, but he wanted to sit close enough to see the performers' fingers and facial expressions. The idea, in short, was to sit in the middle and hope that no one tall would block your view.

Claire was sandwiched between her parents. The distillation, as they saw her, of their combined best, she belonged in the middle. When people asked why they'd only had one child, they said they didn't need more—they'd had beginner's luck and done it right the first time. The program included two well known and one unfamiliar work. The first was a late Beethoven quartet, whose popularity gave the performers the freedom to follow it with a more contemporary piece. The Beethoven was sure fire, but the Czernoff trio was getting a tepid response from the audience. People were beginning to sneeze, cough, and rustle their programs. Claire usually made an honest effort to understand contemporary music, but this time her heart wasn't in it, and after one movement of harmonics and sudden pizzicato assaults, she found herself looking at the dark outline of trees outside the windows lining both sides of the room. Her mind was wandering. Suppose she was asking too much from her job? Suppose her dissatisfaction said more about her than it did about her employment conditions? Suppose Jesse never came back to the States? Suppose she waited for him because he was *her* ideal, but he had already found perfection abroad? Suppose her expectations of the world were those of someone who had never made any real concessions to it?

That reprehensible and totally unacceptable idea was beginning to make inroads into her thoughts, leaving her so distracted that she decided to avoid her parents after the concert because she knew that their unerring parental radar would detect something wrong. The concert concluded with Schubert's "Death and the Maiden," a guaranteed crowd-pleaser, which produced a standing ovation and two encores. As the audience filed out of the hall, Claire said she wanted to breathe in some of that pure Maine air and preferred to walk back to the house. There would be no need for anyone to accompany her. Her father was about to say something—he didn't like her walking alone—but her mother gave him a quick look, and he kept quiet. Her parents were well trained: in the small arena of family life, Claire had actually exerted the influence she had grandiosely imagined exercising over the larger environment, and she usually had her way. On the gravel road leading down from the hall, the evening air full of promise, she felt the momentary relief of a big, forgiving sky. She walked for a while and then, once the flow of cars from the concert had dwindled to a trickle and there seemed no one left to observe her, she began to run. The running could not last long because she was wearing heels and the road was unpaved, but for a distance that might have been the length of two or three city blocks, she felt the return of her old athleticism. In addition to her other accomplishments, Claire had been something of a jock in high school, the captain of the girls' lacrosse team in her senior year; and her physical prowess had been simply one more reason to think that the world was her oyster.

Claire's mother was particularly fond of the oyster metaphor and used it to describe Claire's upbringing. In the shell of their household, she would say, a pearl had been cultured, and that pearl was Claire. The process of cultivation included lessons, social advantages, and summers in Maine. Since her father was Jewish, they were not part of the tradition of boarding school and coming out parties; but thanks to her personal attributes, Claire had something of an honorary membership among the social elite who did those things and in whose company she had learned the value of a single strand of pearls that just skimmed the rim of a cashmere pullover. Through college and graduate school, the good fortune and benefits just continued to accrue until, at some point or other—she didn't know exactly when—the upward trajectory began to level off. It wasn't simply that her love life had frozen in time, but her relationships in general seemed to lack something. She didn't know what it was, and when, during an afternoon visit to Judy's store, Judy had commented that what they lacked was perfection, Claire had not understood what she was saying. Could it be that she was finding out now, and that her perfectionism was standing in her way?

In the vicinity of the concert hall, the houses were ample and rambling, set off from the road by correspondingly large and gracious lawns; but after the gas station at the intersection with Route 28, which was hardly more than a pump in front of a run-down shack, the houses became small and compact. They were relatively well-maintained, but undistinguished, and to Claire's continuing surprise, it was one of those houses that her parents had bought. Even now, several years after their move, she still couldn't get used to their little brick cape. Their house in Connecticut had been more like one of the desirable houses on the hill, and yet here in Maine, where you could still buy a large frame house relatively cheaply so long as you didn't need a view of the coast, they bought a modest home. Their logic made perfect sense: fuel bills in Maine could be exorbitant, and they didn't need much space. True, and yet Claire had expected something bigger and better from them.

Maine houses should have entrance halls, she thought, when, back from her walk, she practically stubbed her toes on the stairs that were only a few feet from the front door. They should also have entrance closets, she observed, hanging her coat on a hook. They should be old, suitable for Persian carpets and antique paintings, and, she thought, standing at the sink to brush her teeth, the bathrooms should have wooden walls and tubs with claw feet. These thoughts, one following upon the other, comprised a body of expectation and, as she stared at the ceiling of the bedroom/study, not even nine feet high, she began to realize that they translated into an attitude others might find off-putting. Maybe she did expect too much of the world.

The following morning Claire and her mother were alone in the kitchen. It had that unlived-in look her mother had come to prize. There was nothing on the counters but a set of canisters and a spice rack. Everything was shiny, the glasses and plates neatly aligned on spotless shelves. When had that come about? Was Claire's mother's neatness connected to her father's health and part of a need to control those few things within her grasp? Or did it go further back and had it laid the groundwork for Claire's perfectionism? Did Claire herself have those tendencies, she once again wondered, a perfectionism she imposed on the world in the form of utopianism? Had she judged Russo and Goodwin by utopian standards?

"Do you remember Jesse, my high school boyfriend?" Claire asked as she dried a dish and added it to the stack on the shelf.

Her mother suddenly became alert. "Yes, of course I remember him. You were quite smitten, as I recall."

"I got a postcard from him recently."

"Oh, that's nice." Her mother quickly retreated to a more casual tone. She knew better than to show too much interest in Claire's love life, which somehow, mysteriously, had become a charged subject during the past few years. "What is he doing with himself these days?"

"He didn't say. He lives abroad, that's all I really know."

Her mother waited for more.

"He'll be in town soon and suggested we get together."

"Oh, that's nice," she said again. She would have liked more information, but asking too many questions was risky. Long experience had taught her that if Claire had more to say on a subject, it wouldn't come from prodding. "Let's go on a little shopping spree," her mother suggested, changing the subject. "Mother, daughter. We haven't done that in a long time."

The short car ride downtown always seemed to elicit the same comments about the deplorable changes taking place in Pine Hill. Both of Claire's parents thought their little Maine town was getting more and more like some place in the Berkshires, with pricey boutiques selling vintage clothing, modern art, and antiques. They went into a store that smelled of incense and featured clothes whose flaws were part of their supposed authenticity. "Look at this," her mother laughed, pointing out the uneven coloring in a linen skirt. "You'll never believe what they're asking for it. It looks used."

"Ma, what do you think of these?" Claire asked, pointing to a pair of earrings inside a glass case by the counter. She liked the earrings, and she liked saying Ma, the word a warm blanket. She and her mother were often a little uneasy together, never fully sure how to be mother and daughter together, the mother too young and the daughter too old; so when they got it right, comfortably in mother/daughter mode, they were both happy and had a good time. The earrings were an inch long pendulum, a flat black stone dangling from a straight silver rod. Everything on the tray was made by a local artisan and quite tasteful, although, as Claire's mother was quick to point out, the words "local artisan" were like the phrase "imperfections in the weave" and just another justification for an unjustifiable price. Claire could probably do as well if not better in a major department store.

"But they're only twenty-eight dollars."

Her mother hadn't noticed the sticker and, as a result of the knee-jerk frugality she had developed from living on a fixed income, automatically assumed they would be expensive. Secretly relieved to discover that she could afford them, she offered to make Claire a present. Claire objected on the grounds she could easily pay herself. That wasn't the point, her mother insisted. It went back and forth until Claire finally gave in.

"Now that wasn't so hard, was it?" But, actually, it had been very hard, that little relinquishing of control like letting go of the steering wheel. The small white bag containing the small white box of earrings brought with it that old feeling that can only exist if it existed once before in childhood. It is the indescribable sense of having entered a world almost completely forgotten and yet entirely familiar; and in that world, Claire was protected and free to be herself, without performance or fear of condemnation.

Assured of support and understanding, Claire suddenly announced to her mother that she was having trouble at work. She had asked for a leave. They had just left the store and were heading toward the car when she dropped her little bombshell. Claire kept on walking, as if the information could literally be taken in stride, but her mother stopped in her tracks.

"I don't understand," she said, putting her hand on Claire's arm once she had caught up and they were seated in the car. "I thought everything was going so smoothly. You're so well liked by the public." Her expression was one of maternal solicitude, the liver spot on her cheek darkening as it always did when she was upset.

"I am popular, but the public is so…so fickle. My viewers are like children who want constant stimulation, and when they don't get it, they immediately look for it somewhere else. And it's not just the public I'm having trouble with either," she added quickly, recognizing that her complaint might not sound serious enough to justify a leave. "I'm having a problem with management, too. They want me to lie about the weather. To sensationalize it. I can't do that."

"You mean make it better or worse than it is?"

"Exactly." Claire's eyes were on the road. "They wanted me to say that a thunderstorm was going to be a hurricane, and that there was a chance it would threaten Bridge Haven."

"How odd."

"Have you heard of Hurricane Louis? It skirted the coast of Georgia without ever making landfall. *That's* the one they wanted me to talk up. They actually set up storm shelters in preparation for it. It's too absurd," Claire laughed.

"Maybe they were trying to be extra careful after Katrina." Concern was folded into her mother's brow as she tried to figure things out. "That would certainly be understandable." Claire was driving too fast for her liking, but she didn't say anything.

"It would be understandable if there had been a scientific reason to take special precautions, but there wasn't," Claire answered somewhat sharply, irritated that she wasn't getting immediate support. This, after all, was the woman who had just mocked the practice of justifying imperfections in fabric.

After a moment's deliberation, her mother inquired whether they had asked Claire to misrepresent information repeatedly, or whether it had happened only once.

The question disorganized Claire. "What difference does that make? How many times do you have to commit a crime for it to count?"

Her mother ignored Claire's testiness. "Was there any possible reason for thinking there *might* be a hurricane?" she persevered.

"*I'm* their weather reporter. The opinion of another meteorologist shouldn't make any difference."

"I'm just trying to understand," her mother settled back in the passenger seat. She had the distinct impression that JTF had gone over Claire's head and listened to someone else; but she decided to leave it alone for the time being, and the rest of the ride was heavy with silence as each of them tried to grapple with conflicting and disheartening emotions: Claire with the growing certainty that she'd over-reacted to Goodwin, who was merely a jerk and needn't have such an impact on her life, and her mother, with the on-going and enduring desire to get it just right with her beloved but rather entitled daughter.

CHAPTER TWENTY-EIGHT

As soon as Mrs. Day was alone with Claire's father she told him what Claire had said. She had a strong suspicion that Claire's problem was only partly work-related, and that Claire was also worried about still being single. Mr. Day was upset and went for a pill. When he came back he said that he wasn't interested in Claire's love life and that the only thing that mattered at the moment was her job. He would, of course, like nothing better than to see his daughter happily married, but Claire was self-supporting, and whatever else, she had to keep her job.

He went into the living room with its knotty pine paneling and waited for Claire to return from her walk. She was out with her dog, Mario, who she'd brought up from Connecticut with her, and had already been gone for half an hour. As soon as she came back and had flopped down on the sofa, he asked what was going on. "What's this I hear about your not liking your job anymore?" It was not exactly the best way to approach Claire, but if Mr. Day's high blood pressure had left him physically vulnerable, it had also left him combative and not the least bit reluctant to take advantage of the freedom that his uncertain health had given him, especially when it came to speaking up.

"Wow, that didn't take long."

"I'd say it took altogether too long, considering that you're leaving tomorrow," he responded. "How come you waited till now, the night before you're leaving, to tell us?" He looked grizzled and sallow, despite the Maine air, and spotted too, with liver spots and moles, a little like the wall paneling. Claire found it unsettling to look at his thin frame, which, more than thin, looked reduced to bare essentials, his neck and hands a gaggle of bungee cords.

The kitchen door was open so that Claire's mother, who was at the stove, could hear. She had aged differently, and instead of shrinking, she had puffed up and rounded, her torso a pillow whose stuffing was held in place by a narrow belt and supported by thin, stick legs. From the sofa, Claire could see her soft bulges, her stomach and breasts and neck, which was like a frog's gullet and so protuberant that in profile it was more pronounced than her chin.

Claire was lying sideways on the sofa, her head flat against her extended arm. Her father cocked his head to the side so that they were at the same angle and could see eye to eye. The loose flesh of his neck and jowls fell to the angle of his head. Claire accepted the prompting and sat up. "Do you remember telling me that my eyes would turn muddy if I lied? You told me that when I was little."

"I remember."

"My eyes are changing color. That's why I'm having trouble with my job."

"So, it's my fault."

Claire laughed. "Yes, actually. It's thanks to you that I have these ridiculously high standards."

Her mother stuck her head in. "It's thanks to these ridiculously high standards that you got the job in the first place." She was usually right, but very literal-minded. Having made her comment, she went back to braising leek for the vichyssoise, Claire's favorite.

"Claire, honey, don't do this." It was her father again. When it came to this kind of discussion, he was the one with the authority. There were several stacks of books by the side of his chair, all classics, so that, as he explained it, he would know something when he died. "This job is right for you. You have transformed weather reporting into something truly alive. You are making a real contribution. Do you know how rare that is? Hardly anyone makes a real contribution anymore. It's all just so many papers and so many voices. If you have problems with management, work them out."

Claire knew he was right and had begun to realize it days ago. In fact, it was mostly to give her parents the opportunity to "talk some sense into her," in other words, to be parental—something she knew they still missed—that she consulted their opinion. "They have no idea of who I am, or of what I've been trying to do. Goodwin—he's one of the producers—actually told me that he had no objection to my telling the truth so long as it didn't interfere with ratings. No objection!" she repeated, still slightly incredulous at the remark.

Claire's father laughed loudly. "That's marvelous," he commented, genuinely appreciative of the cynicism. "Look," he said, fixing his gaze on Claire and adopting a no-nonsense expression, "they don't have to understand you. That's not their job. They're not your parents, after all. All you have a right to expect from them is that they not interfere too much and that they pay your salary."

"Right." It was her mother's voice again, emphatic in her agreement.

"And so what if they elbow you a bit. There's not really that much they can do to you. After all, ratings are a double-edged sword. They *depend* on your ratings."

"That's just it," said Claire, feeling they'd finally gotten to the point. "I don't want them to depend on my ratings. I want them to look to me for quality." She was sitting up and looking at both parents earnestly.

The comment surprised Mr. Day, who had imagined his daughter more worldly and mature. It was hard to understand how she'd managed to be on her own so long without figuring out the basics. "You are being proud and childish," he said. It was years since he had criticized her, and Claire felt its impact like a call to attention. "Every job has its requirements. Theirs are ratings."

"I guess," said Claire, who was beginning to feel relieved of some terrible burden.

"You have a following, and they don't have anyone who can replace you," said her mother, anxiously interrupting a significant moment, her body halfway between the kitchen and the living room. She had a low tolerance for confrontation and was eager to soften its edge. "There's no one who does what you do," she was wiping her hands on her apron as she came into the living room, "and if anyone tried, they'd embarrass themselves. Remember the water ballet you told me about? The guy at the rival station?"

"Yes, Mom," Claire laughed, the image of Louis's wet head still bubbling up inside her like the water in the pool.

The conversation continued a while longer until her parents were satisfied that Claire's attitude had improved. At first, it seemed that she was agreeing too easily, which raised doubts about her sincerity. To reassure themselves, her parents made the same points over and over again—Claire had unusually wide-ranging talents, Claire had prestigious degrees, Claire had a large following, Claire was making a unique contribution. It was only after Claire went beyond cooperating and insisted that she would work things out that they began to relax again.

• • •

There were several good-byes before the definitive hug and kiss at the car. "I'll call you as soon as I get back," she promised. It was almost 11 a.m., late to be starting out, and the hour just added to Claire's sense of urgency. She had reached a decision about her job—it was a good job, a great job—and having reached it, the opposing arguments, which had been so persuasive only days earlier, became jejune and completely inconsequential. Before getting on the road, she called JTF and asked Dan to let Russo and Goodwin know she'd be back at work at the beginning of the week. It would make a total of two weeks that she had been gone—the exact amount of time she had coming to her. "If they ask about my leave," she said, "just tell them that's academic lingo for vacation."

All that mattered was getting back and making things right at the station. She could have taken Route 1, but she'd had enough of scenery and wanted to get home. It was all she could do to stay within ten miles of the speed limit. She picked up I-95 in Augusta and stuck with it all the way, watching the speedometer climb up and down the seventy to eighty mph ladder as she made her way from Maine to New Hampshire to Massachusetts, constantly heading south. Objectively, there was no real reason to rush. It was not as if she was going straight to the office. But she wanted to be one step closer to re-instatement, and that kept her foot on the gas. A mistake in her professional life and a stagnant private life would leave her with nothing but her scruples, and scruples did not pay the rent. Not only that, a week of self-righteousness, self-justification, self-doubt, and self-recrimination—all spawned by scruples—made it clear they did not make good company either.

During the entire trip, her mind was on her own short-comings. She was gradually becoming aware that she was too convinced of her own superiority, too persuaded that, more than others, she knew what was right and important, and that, at the same time, she was unwilling to accept or even consider the possibility she might be arrogant. Judy had been right when she said that it was Claire's own perfection that would get her in the end.

Another internal debate holding her in its grip had to do with corruption. She was quite sure that she was not corrupt and did not have to include it among her newly discovered weaknesses, but she was not sure how strongly to react to it in others. Freddy was corrupt—no surprise there—and it looked like Emmett might be corrupt too, which she would never have expected. But did that mean she should refuse to have anything more to do with him? The rest of them, people like Katie, Reed, and Louis, they were just practical, which might mean they were corrupt too—Claire wasn't sure. Practical, corrupt, or just plain human, the lines were getting blurry. The problem was that she had tried to draw them with a thick black marker, and like the cars now passing on her left, it seemed as if everyone was going the opposite direction. She, self-appointed arbiter of human perfection that she was, had deemed it the wrong direction; and now, in a profound and wrenching change of heart, she wanted to join the traffic, be part of the imperfect human flow. It was becoming dusk and, with the sense that she was facing her destiny, she spent the next couple of hours driving south in the harsh, uncompromising glare of oncoming headlights.

CHAPTER TWENTY-NINE

When Claire got home, she found a large bundle of mail between the inner and outer doors of her front entrance. A glossy black-and-white photograph of Paris was stuck in the pile of catalogues and credit card promotions that had accumulated during her absence. Mansard roofs with tiles like fish scales and flower pots chimneys filled a misty Gallic sky. The word Inenubilable was scrawled across it like skywriting. On the flip side, a sketch of two stick figures stood holding hands in front of the Eiffel Tower.

Judy and Murray had been home for several days by the time Claire read the card, and Judy was very eager for Claire's return. Her mother-in-law was coming to dinner and Judy wanted Claire to join them. "I'm begging," she wailed into the telephone. "I know you just got back last night and are probably tired out from the drive, but I need you. Murray's mother is going to spend the entire afternoon and evening with us, and I don't think I'll be able to take it alone. Not now. Not so soon after Paris. I need a buffer. Puh-leez…"

"Oh come on."

"Really. You have no idea."

• • •

Judy greeted Claire at the elevator. It opened directly into a foyer elongated by a twenty-foot Aubusson runner. "They're in the den," she said, mouthing the words inaudibly as they walked from one end of the foyer to the other. Claire did not know why they were avoiding detection since Judy was opening the door to the den anyway. With the door open, the apartment suddenly became noisy, the volume on the television turned high to accommodate Murray's mother.

"What did she say, Murray? I couldn't make it out?" The voice, a caw as harsh as a crow's, was hidden by the high back of a Queen Anne armchair. Claire, who was still standing in the doorway, jumped, startled by the unseen voice.

"How could you not make that out?" Murray raised the sound. "The volume's practically all the way up as it is."

"I couldn't make it out because you're talking."

"Now. Only now I'm talking. Before, when you were complaining, I wasn't talking."

"Oh, pipe down, Murray," the voice too large for its diminutive, birdlike frame, all beak and bone, croaked. "How do you expect me to hear anything with you carrying on? First you turn up the sound and then you yell."

The television was tuned to a cooking show where a full-bodied Italian woman was pushing diced onions from a carving board into a frying pan. "This," she said, "goes in before the tomatoes. The onion takes longer to soften, so it has to go in first. Mmm," she lowered her head to the stove, "it already smells good. Now, as soon as the onions are a nice translucent color, we add the tomatoes," she dumped a bowl of prepared tomatoes into the mix. "Next we add the fresh basil, basilica as we say in Italy, from my garden." She held up a few basil leaves for viewing. "Dry basil is never as good as when it's just picked. Most markets carry it fresh year round, so if you don't have your own garden, you can still get it fresh." She put the basil down and chopped it up with rapid, sure-fire wrist motions. "It gives a nice color to the dish, too. It's a little like a painting, isn't it? Red, green, and when we add the pasta," she laughed, "it will be the colors of the Italian flag." A frying pan sizzling with hot oil and dotted with onion, tomato, and basil filled the screen. "And now we are ready for the ziti, which we will cook until it is al dente, which means that it is cooked through but still a little firm."

"There are a lot of cooking shows on television now," the voice from the chair spoke up, "but I like this one best. There's this one guy with a big chef's hat who's on all the time, but I don't like him. There's something rough about him. And then there was Jeff Smith, The Frugal Gourmet, but he died. He was good for people on a fixed income, but he was a cheapskate, and I can't stand a cheapskate."

"He wasn't cheap. He was frugal. There's a difference."

"There's no difference between tuna fish and tuna fish. Anyway, I didn't like him. I wonder why there aren't any kosher cooking shows."

"Because kosher food stinks. It's tasteless and stupid." Murray was doing the Times crossword puzzle on his knee.

"How can food be stupid?"

"It's stupid to bless food. I'm not talking about giving thanks—I'm talking about actually blessing the food. What's a three letter word that means 'beginning of colonialism?' The first letter is N."

"Neo," Judy answered, "and it's a prefix."

Both Murray and his mother turned toward the door.

"I don't think you've ever met my friend Claire," Judy said as she and Claire walked around to the front of the chair where Claire leaned over to shake hands. Pearl Strongman was little—barely five feet even before she'd developed osteoporosis—with a large round globe of white hair.

"Nice to meet you, dear. I just want to see how the dish turns out. Then I'll talk to you." Judy rolled her eyes and Claire smiled. As soon as the Italian woman had tasted her creation and emitted a sigh of pleasure, Pearl turned back to them. "The show always ends that way, with her taking a bite while you sit there starving."

"We'll be eating soon, Pearl."

"I hope so. My stomach's beginning to growl. I think I've heard something about you," she turned back to Claire. "You're the one that's on television." It was not clear whether she was asking a question or making a statement.

"Yes, I'm a weather reporter."

"Well, I hate to say this, but you people never get it right. I don't mean you in particular. I've never seen you on television actually, but that Mr. G, with his turtlenecks, he's wrong half the time. And when he reports the weather he always says, 'Alright, let's do the numbers,' which I find stupid and annoying. And then there's the fat one, he's another putz. I can't remember his name, but you know the one I mean. The…"

"Don't say it, Ma," Murray jumped in.

"I'm not allowed to say *schwarze,*" Pearl rejoined. "I don't see what's wrong with it. It's Yiddish. It's Yiddish and I'm Jewish; they go together.

It's like 'people of color.' They used to be the coloreds, but now that's bad and they're people of color. Frankly, I don't see the difference. And then there's Sam Champion, the pretty one. I don't like him either. A real phony, that one. Janice Huff is the only one who's any good. Her and Lee Goldberg."

"Well, that's only because you've never seen Claire," Judy told her mother-in-law. "But let's continue this conversation over dinner. I don't want my potatoes to get cold."

Murray went to help Pearl out of the chair. Her small crumpled body belied a strong grip hardened by the rings on her arthritically knotted fingers. They, in turn, contrasted with the loose combination of flesh and bone she linked inside his arm. After she had gone through the several stages of standing up, Murray escorted her across the room. They had left her walker by the door of the den because it was too hard to use on the thick pile carpeting, but as soon as she was about to transfer her weight to it, he said. "You don't need that. I'll walk you."

"Don't think he's really that helpful," Pearl said, turning to Claire. "They just don't want me to get scuff marks on their fancy floors."

"And you weren't particular when I was growing up?" Murray asked in rebuttal.

"And you weren't messy, Mr. Weisenheimmer?"

"Don't start with me, Ma."

Claire laughed and went to help Judy in the kitchen while Murray and his mother inched their way to the dining room.

"It will be breakfast time before we're all seated," Judy said as she pushed the dining room door open with her back.

"What channel are you on, dear?" Pearl asked once Murray had pushed her chair in. The table was set with tall, silver candelabras at either end. Each place setting had two glasses, one for water and one for wine, two forks, two knives, and three spoons. Several serving utensils lying parallel to each other were next to the trivets flanking the bowl of decorative, stainless steel fruit in the middle of the table.

"Fancy-schmancy," Pearl observed.

"No one says fancy-schmancy anymore, Grandma." It was Rachel.

"No one but me, sweetheart. You were telling me the channel, dear," she turned back to Claire.

"It's a local channel that broadcasts out of Bridge Haven."

"Well, no wonder I've never seen you. I'm a city girl. West End Avenue. Not that I've got anything against the country. I'm just trying to explain why…"

"She understands, Ma."

"Listen dear, I want to know about global warming. Global warming and, what do they call them, green house emissions. I want to know whether they're the reason for all these hurricanes we're having."

"They are certainly a contributing factor. Hurricanes are sustained by warm water and both water temperatures and water levels have been rising for years."

"Is that why Louisiana flooded?"

"Well, I think that had more to do with the levees. They should have been better fortified. But, if you don't mind, I'd like to ask you a question."

"Shoot," the little woman said.

"Do you really think the weather reports are usually wrong?" Claire asked, genuinely curious.

"Well, take Saturday, for example. I know it was Saturday because I had a lunch date, and they said it was going to rain. I took my umbrella with me and was carrying it around all day like a fool. Since I had it, I was thinking of using it to keep out the sun, you know, like the Japanese women do, but I can't hold the umbrella and my walker at the same time. I think it was Mr. G's forecast—Sam Champion never forecasts rain—he hates rain—but Mr. G said it was going to rain so, like a good girl, I took the umbrella. Needless to say, it was gorgeous, the sunniest day of the week. They don't really think about what it's like to hold a walker and an umbrella at the same time or they would be more careful. Anyway, I've made up my mind. From now on I'm going to ignore them and trust my bones. My bones don't lie."

"Arthritis?" Claire asked.

Pearl put two hands with bulging joints out in front of her. "What do you think? Do I have arthritis?"

"And you really believe that joint pain is an accurate predictor of rain?"

"Listen to me, dear. The other day I had a pain in my left hip. Unfortunately, the arthritis is not just in my hands. I knew it was going to rain, and let me tell you, it poured cats and dogs. By the way, where does that come from, it rained cats and dogs?"

"The origin of the expression is unclear, although some say the most probable source of the idiom goes back to seventeenth century England when dead dogs and cats would float down the streets during a heavy rain. The first documented use of the expression is in a seventeenth-century play called *The City Wit or The Woman Wears the Breeches* by somebody named Brome."

"Wow," said Pearl, really impressed.

"I looked it up for a broadcast I gave a while back," Claire said in explanation.

"You have a smart friend," Pearl nodded to Judy. "Smarter than the Misters Champion, Roker, and G combined. I am sure that there's not a single one of them who could tell you the origin of that expression. Now, if you don't mind, I want to change the subject for a minute. I want to ask you something else," she said, "not about the weather. You can tell me if I'm getting too personal, but…"

"You're getting too personal," Judy and Murray said in unison before Pearl uttered another word.

"…but I see that you're not wearing a wedding band," Pearl continued, "and I'm wondering how it is that a young woman like you, smart, beautiful, successful, isn't married. I'm a *Menschenkenner,* and I know people. I can see that you're a lovely young woman, and I don't understand why somebody like you is alone. You can tell me to mind my own business if you don't want to answer."

Again, in a chorus of two, Judy and Murray told Pearl to mind her own business.

"No, it's okay," Claire responded. "I've only known one man who I thought I would want to marry, and he's been living outside the country."

"Tell him to come back," was Pearl's instant and unabashed advice. "He should thank his lucky stars that you're waiting for him. If he doesn't know that, he's not good enough for you."

"Amen," said Judy.

• • •

A dozen long-stemmed roses were on Claire's desk when she got back to work the next day. A small card poked out of the delicate spray of white baby's breath surrounding the flowers. Everything Claire had been feeling before her trip—anger, frustration, dissatisfaction, and ennui—was immediately forgotten, completely eradicated by the card's simple message of good will: *Welcome Back, Phil Goodwin and Don Russo.* The roses, pale yellow with a pinkish tinge at the tips, came as a complete surprise to Claire, who had been dreading the reception she would get when she walked in the door. She had been afraid management would still be angry that she had left without a definite return date, and the last thing she expected was a show of support.

She had no way of knowing that while she was away things had gone very badly for JTF, and that Goodwin and Russo were desperate for her return. She'd been replaced by a temp whose only previous experience was in radio, and he was a total disaster. If he had been a disembodied voice, that would have been fine, but Spiro Theophanidis's appearance was so distracting that it was hard to listen to what he said, and judging by his daily ratings, people were deciding not to. Mostly, the problem was that he looked Cro-Magnon, with a broad face and an unnatural amount of hair. He had one thick, black eyebrow hyphenated by a few hairs at the bridge of his nose and reinstated by a thick, black mustache hyphenated by a few hairs on his philtrum, and all beneath a head of black hair combed straight and slick and above a neck with hair crawling out from under his collar. He looked animalistic, out of control, fierce, and mean. Actually, he was only Greek, and when he started to talk it became immediately obvious that, far from being threatening or sinister, he was a rather jovial fellow with a highly theatrical sense of reporting. That would not have been a problem if he'd given the performance of a weather reporter, but once he was on camera, he moved backward and forward like a crooner and ended every statement with his arms open wide. Dan thought the guy was hilarious and couldn't resist making the identical gesture every time he saw Goodwin, who hardly needed reminding because Russo was on his case about Spiro—who he'd taken to calling Zorba—and never stopped complaining about him.

"Well what do you want to do about him?" Goodwin asked Russo. It was 8 a.m., Monday, and he and Russo were still in the dark about Claire's intentions, unaware that Dan had spoken to Claire before the weekend and that she would be back that morning. "There's no point to looking for someone else until we know what Claire's plans are."

Russo knew that it was senseless to replace Spiro, but he wanted to drive home the point that Spiro, or someone just as bad, was the alternative to Claire, and that the whole thing was Goodwin's fault. "It's clear as day," he said, thinking that would make a much better title for Claire's segment of the news than The FabuWeather Forecast, "that none of this would have happened if you hadn't made such a fuss about the hurricane. We were blessed with Claire and all we had to do—*all* we had to do—was show our gratitude. Our only job was to thank our lucky stars—Sirius in particular—that she came to work for us. But *nooo*, you had to be the big man and throw your weight around."

They were in Goodwin's office seated at a glass coffee table that Goodwin had installed at his own expense to make the place more gracious, more executive-looking. Both of them had been thinking about Claire all weekend, and they were starting the week the same way they had ended the last, with a conversation about her. All they could think about was Claire.

Goodwin saw things differently. "Don," he said—he never called Russo by his first name, and it was a clear indication Russo had the upper hand and that Goodwin was trying to placate him—"I know you're pissed off"—he never spoke that way either—"and think this is all my fault, but I can't agree with you. Claire has her job to do, and we have ours. Just because she's good doesn't mean we should hand over the reins. True," he acknowledged, "if her leave becomes permanent, we probably won't be able to replace her with star power, but that doesn't mean we'll end up with a dud like Spiro either."

"No, we might end up with another Norwood Fossil," Russo countered bitterly. "After all, every cloud has a silver lining."

"CBS or NBC would never have agreed to an arrangement like this one..." Goodwin went on, developing his argument. But the observation only made Russo more irritated because JTF had nothing in common with CBS or NBC, and the comment was simply another example of Goodwin's self-importance. "None of those stations would have let one of their principals take an *indeterminate* amount of time off," Goodwin continued. "It's unheard of, crazy. We should have insisted that she be clear about her intentions. Alright, I admit that I may have been a little heavy-handed about the hurricane, but we made it up to her. We were more than generous in giving her the special considering the underhanded way she went about getting it, and..."

"*I* was more than generous. *You* weren't even here."

"...on top of that, we offered her a raise."

"*We?* That was my idea too. I had to talk you into it."

"What more are we supposed to do? Beg?"

"Now you're talking," Russo said, just to get Goodwin's goat. "That sounds like a great idea. Begging is a time-honored profession. It's disparaged by Western society but it's a legitimate fallback position in the rest of the world, and nothing to be ashamed of. In fact, it's something to embrace. I would bring a tin cup to work if that was what it took."

Everything Russo said was designed to drive Goodwin nuts. Talk of begging made Goodwin feel like he was choking, like he had swallowed an indigestible curry from some dirty place on the Ganges, and loosening his tie a bit, he poured himself some water. The swan-shaped stainless steel water pitcher, his favorite touch in his new office décor, helped to restore his equanimity. The pitcher made him feel elegant, pure, civilized, like the men on Charlie Rose who had to lubricate throats talked dry by the length of their learned remarks. He was very attracted to the well-tailored gravitas of those men, and he was correspondingly repelled by coarse men like Russo who seemed to lack any sense of what was proper and correct. The difference was in their backgrounds—Goodwin's was Lutheran, Russo's was Catholic—and, as if he was reliving the Protestant Reformation in the modest context of JTF, Goodwin repeatedly tried to purify and reform his colleague. But true to the history he was totally ignorant of, Russo had mounted his own Counter-Reformation and rejected any attempt by Goodwin to scold or to chasten. After all, who was Goodwin to represent himself as an example of purity or to hold Russo up as an example of debased virtue? Especially in their current situation. It was Goodwin, after all, who had given in to the mayor's need for a hurricane.

Claire's leave coupled with Spiro's presence had created a deep rift between the two of them, and after several meetings, Goodwin and Russo still couldn't agree on how to deal with it. They needed a third opinion, and according to their employment manual, that opinion had to come from Dan, their news director, who fell directly under producer in status and authority. Dan had been about to talk to them anyway when Russo asked him to join them. Dan still hadn't let on that Claire would be back that morning and was enjoying the little bit of power that his exclusive piece of information gave him when, pale and watery from an autumn attack of allergies, he walked into Goodwin's office. In the interest of professionalism, he resisted the temptation to do his Spiro imitation and tried to look as serious as a red, runny nose would allow. He sneezed and pushed a small, wet ball of Kleenex against his nostrils. Goodwin walked over to his newly installed wall unit and brought back a box of tissues neatly housed inside a stainless steel box, another gracious touch.

"Here," he said, offering the box to Dan. "We have been talking about Claire and are trying to figure out how to improve her relationship with the station. This whole leave thing…" Goodwin scratched his head. "There is no such thing as a leave from television."

Dan feigned confusion. "Leave? She must have meant vacation. In the university, leaves and vacations are practically the same thing since they get so much time off. In fact, she called Friday to say that she'd had a great vacation and would be back today."

Russo and Goodwin were both amazed, especially Russo. Was it possible that he had totally misunderstood her? It was true that he hadn't known what she was talking about when she asked for a "leave," but he could have sworn that she had referred to an indeterminate amount of time off. While he was trying to remember her exact words, Goodwin was feeling the return of his usual irritation with Russo. Couldn't the man ever get anything straight?

"As for improving Claire's relationship with the station," Dan continued, pretending that the information he had just imparted was not the improvement they needed and that, despite her return, they still had a problem, "there's only one way to go about it." The two other men waited while Dan blew his nose. "You have to apologize for asking her to doctor the weather. She was profoundly insulted when you did that. You have to tell her it won't happen again."

Russo nodded in self-vindication. He might have been wrong about the time off, but he was right in thinking that Claire was not happy. Goodwin averted his gaze. Nobody said anything, and Dan was very pleased at having been able to create a situation that left them both speechless, especially Goodwin, who liked to have the last word about everything. Looking from one to the other, he said, "Well, if there isn't anything else, then I think Ill go back to my desk while I can still get some work done. These anti-histamines I'm taking are making me awfully drowsy."

• • •

That was how Claire ended up with the roses. As soon as Dan left, Russo rushed out of the office to buy her flowers, overjoyed that she was coming back *that same morning!* and eager to do everything in his power to make her return as pleasant as possible. He even bought the roses from the flower shop instead of from the stand on the corner, whose flowers were cheaper but not as good as the florist's. The idea that flowers could vary in quality seemed kind of strange to him, but after he'd gotten flowers at the stand a couple of times and the first bunch died in two days and the second bunch never opened, he could only conclude that there were good flowers and bad flowers, or—not to be too judgmental—that not all flowers were equal. Also, the flowers from the stand developed a putrid smell—what was that all about?—and when you removed them from their vase to throw them out, the stench was overwhelming.

At first, Goodwin had to be talked into the roses, but once he realized they might spare him the humiliation of apology, he was all in favor of them. "It's a small enough price to pay," Russo had insisted, and Goodwin, appearing to be generous but secretly hoping the flowers might obscure or substitute for their impulsive offer of a salary increase, agreed. Maybe, he said, never wanting to be outdone by Russo and continuing to hope for a way out of the raise, they should give her two dozen.

CHAPTER THIRTY

What followed was peace and tranquility. The station had lived through two weeks of Spiro, Claire had lived through her own personal coming to terms, and like cars observing the obvious but useful roadside reminder "slippery when wet," everyone was careful, cautious, on best behavior. Even Katie, who still thought of Claire as a snob and a rival, had begun to think there might be some advantage to having her around. With the two of them on the desk, JTF could almost be considered a feminist station, and that idea really appealed to Katie, especially since her days as a slut were numbered.

It was Katie's visit to City Hall that made her position clear to her. Freddy had all but won re-election; and in the spirit of re-awakened ambition, he decided to treat the event as if its significance justified a full day's media attention. That was what he wanted to talk to Katie about. He wanted her opinion about whether press coverage should begin the moment he left his house or the moment he walked out of the polling booth, and Katie, acting on the assumption that his victory was her victory too and that, like Ronald Reagan and Peggy Noonan, they were a team, went to his office in the expectation they would celebrate together.

She hadn't seen Freddy since his well-publicized visit to the Flats, and in anticipation of their private victory party, she dressed in a boucle suit that all but screamed power, professionalism, and politics. The suit was also charged with passion, its deep red the color of blood; and in choosing to wear it, Katie was letting Freddy know that although she would still be his mistress, she was also his associate now.

She was right about everything but the mistress part. Waiting in the outer office reception area, same as usual, and leafing through the latest *Economist,* which seemed like the right reading for a news anchor, she was biding her time, putting in her pre-designated ten minutes, when a young woman with very high heels and a very short skirt walked past her. The young woman, who had to be in her early twenties, walked out of the supply room adjacent to the waiting room and straight in to Freddy's office, a bunch of files in her arms. Without even bothering to knock or to ask Francine's permission, the new hire clattered past the two of them on her administrative mission. Katie had never seen her before, and Francine, who was well aware of that fact, couldn't resist glancing up to see how Katie was taking it.

Right then and there, Katie knew everything there was to know about the situation, and, proudly refusing to show her discomfort, she kept her eyes glued to her magazine. She only looked up after Francine announced that the mayor would see her, and then she defiantly walked into Freddy's office without so much as a glance in Francine's direction. Freddy was seated at his desk, and the new office assistant was leaning over a cabinet on the other side of the room. She was filing something in its bottom drawer, and although she could have reached the drawer more easily if she had crouched, she preferred to bend at the waist instead, and, in the process, to reveal so much of herself that a bullhorn could not have announced her intentions more loudly.

In that split second, Katie's anxiety radar really kicked in, and it would not be an exaggeration to say that her entire life changed in that moment. Immediately, before Freddy even had a chance to deal with the situation, Katie distanced herself from him by adopting a highly professional and business-like manner. As soon as Katie saw Freddy's eyes flicker, darting back and forth between her and the ass, Katie began to craft a new identity for herself that emphasized her role as counsel and repudiated his role as protector. *No way that he was going to dump her.* Leaning across Freddy's desk with her hand outstretched, her hair swinging, and her smile the public smile of the nightly news anchor, she said, "Let me be the first to shake your hand, Mr. Mayor. With a 9 percent lead in the polls, I think it is fairly safe to say that you can expect to win the election, and I would like to take this opportunity to personally extend my congratulations to you and your family."

Freddy was amused and relieved. Katie's handling of the situation was impeccable, nothing short of a deliverance—a blessing, as his mother would have said, or a mitzvah, as Hirshenbaum would have described it—and Freddy had never liked her better. He had been worried that she might create a scene, throw a fit, but to the contrary, Katie was so classy and self-composed that she made Freddy wish he had been more tactful himself.

He had hired the girl as soon as she walked into his office, her large breasts preceding, her firm buttocks following, and only after she had walked out the door did he realize that he should have waited until after the election to give her the job. When it came to women, he never seemed to learn. His impatience always got him into trouble, usually with other women, and that was what he was afraid would happen with Katie, whose visit he had anticipated with a certain amount of dread. This time, however, and for reasons he couldn't begin to fathom, it looked like he would escape unscathed and for that he was deeply grateful. He cocked his head quizzically, wondering if Katie would give him some indication of what was going on with her, but her act had become her armor, and she wouldn't take it off. Even after the new assistant left his office and they were alone together, Katie remained resolutely on-message, a professional to the end. From that moment forward and from there on in, their affair was a taboo subject between them, and it was as if they had never known each other intimately.

"Well, thank you," Freddy said, thinking that everything seemed to be working out perfectly and that he was truly a lucky man. "Things do look very promising. I don't want to be over-confident though. There can always be a surprise, an upset," he said, leaving Katie to wonder whether he was talking about the two of them or about the election.

• • •

Their new relationship marked the beginning of Katie's new self-image, and the new image was so much better than the old one that Katie wondered why it had taken her so long to recognize and adopt it. The new image was of a woman who could take care of herself and make her own way. The new image was not of a woman who granted sexual favors for personal advancement or depended on men for protection, but of a woman whose past was very different from her present and who, in the wake of her transgressions and in the light of her transformation, had achieved Greater Understanding and Awareness. She was a woman who had Learned from her Experience; a woman who had seen the Error of her Ways; a woman who had undergone a Spiritual Awakening; a woman who had seen the Light.

In other words, Katie had decided to become a reformed sinner—someone the public could really relate to. It was magnificent; it was brilliant, and it was amazingly easy to implement. There was nothing the American public liked better than people who re-invented themselves, and there was no re-invention it preferred to the penitent. She would become a reformed sinner, a penitent, and she would transform the anchor's desk, which had previously been her throne, into her bully pulpit. Katie had always thought that she had been visited by outside forces, and now she knew it was true.

CHAPTER THIRTY-ONE

It was mid-September and a weekday. Claire was in her bathrobe, a pot of coffee on the stove, a pile of books in front of her. In the continuing spirit of cooperation, Goodwin and Russo had agreed to let her work from home mornings, and she was leafing through a volume of Roethke's poetry when the telephone rang. Mario thumped his tail, the only part of his body that appeared alive, as Claire shuffled to the phone in loose flip-flops. She was thinking about the poem she had just read and not in any hurry. A male voice, unfamiliar yet somehow recognizable, asked to speak to her. Even before he identified himself, in that brief moment when anticipation precedes reality, Claire knew who it was.

Jesse's voice was muffled and far away. The poor quality of the connection, the static and echo like an acknowledgement of the time and distance between them, actually made conversation easier because it spared them from trying to catch up on lost time and pole-vaulted them into the present: yes, it would be wonderful to get together; yes, she would be in town next weekend; yes, she would be looking forward to seeing him. After she got off the phone, Claire paced the floor. Round and round the kitchen table she went, heartbeat and footstep at long last in unison.

It was not long before Claire told Judy about the phone call. The subject came up after they left the Rite Aid on Lexington where Judy had picked up her Paris photographs. "It's so much prettier over there," she commented, as they waited for the light to change. "You should go. It would help you get over what's his name."

"I spoke to what's his name," Claire retorted, proud, defensive.

"What?" Judy stared at her, suddenly alert. "You're kidding. Tell me."

"There's nothing to tell. He'll be in the States soon, and we're going to see each other." They were on the median strip dividing Park, and a black Honda, it must have been a stick shift, was rocking back and forth, ready to peel out.

Claire's answer wasn't nearly informative enough. "Tell me, *tell me*. When did he call? Where are you going? And most importantly, what are you going to wear?"

"I don't know. We don't even have a date yet. Listen Judy, I'm a little superstitious about things that haven't actually happened. I only mentioned it because you brought him up."

Judy nodded. She respected superstition and changed the subject. "Boy, they make these things hard to open," she said, tugging on the envelope containing the pictures of her trip. "This," she explained, holding a picture out for Claire, "is the Place Vendôme—that's me in the red—and this is the Palais Royale with Murray in the background. There," she put her pinky on a corner of the photo. "Here's one of the Seine taken from the Isle de la Cite. We ate in this wonderful little restaurant near Notre Dame. I had a steak with a slab of melted herb butter on top of it...simple, straightforward, yet somehow special. And you should have seen our hotel room. It was in a seventeenth century stone house. Seventeenth century! Wood beams everywhere, even in the bathroom. What can I tell you? I was enthralled."

The photos brought back memories for Claire too. She had spent the first semester of her junior year in Paris, and she particularly remembered the streets and the casual romance of the couples who strolled down them: linked pinkies, hands cupping buttocks, arms loosely draped over shoulders; everywhere, an acknowledgement of the human connection.

The last photo—a radical departure from the pretty Paris photographs—was of two gnarled hands. The hands were held up for viewing. It took Claire a moment, but then she remembered. Murray had been about to photograph Claire, Judy, his mother, and Rachel all huddled over desert when Pearl held up her hands. "Take these," she said, "they're my best feature. They can predict the weather."

"I liked your mother-in-law," Claire said, thinking back to their conversation.

"That's only because she doesn't wake you up at six every morning."

"I thought what she had to say about the weather and arthritis was interesting. I've never really taken the claims of arthritics seriously, but maybe there's something to them."

"Who knows?" Judy was looking at her pictures again, hardly paying attention.

"Judy, do you remember that day when you called to find out if it was going to rain? You were getting your hair done, and you'd had a dream about heavy rain." She anchored a curl behind her ear.

"Yeah, kind of. Your colleague, the vixen, answered the phone."

Claire smiled. "When you called you said that your mother-in-law was predicting bad weather because her arthritis was acting up."

"Yeah, so?"

"Well, I was thinking that maybe...how do you think Pearl would like to go on television with me?" she asked. The traffic light had just changed and as the traffic slowed, so did Judy.

"You're kidding. Tell me you're kidding," she said.

"Why?"

"For one thing, I doubt that JTF would share your enthusiasm for the idea."

"They wouldn't mind if people loved her. Anyway, I'm not talking about every day. I was thinking of once or twice a week. I would do the science and she could argue with me. The odds of one of us being right would be very high, and it would be funny."

"I think people are more interested in a prediction than a choice," Judy said, looking skeptical. She wondered what Murray would think of the idea. She had no doubt that Pearl, herself, would love it, but there would be no end to her crowing and complaining. "Claire, you don't know what a kvetch is until you've spoken to Pearl. I mean, she'll get on television and complain." Judy started to laugh. "You could call her segment the doom and gloom forecast. She'd be in her glory, the whole world listening to her complaints."

CHAPTER THIRTY-TWO

It came as something of a surprise when Claire requested a meeting with Goodwin and Russo. Things were going so well. What could be on her mind? She had never asked to meet with the two of them before, and the request set off alarm bells in Russo. Suppose she had been approached by one of the networks? Suppose she was going to announce her resignation? When that happened—and he was convinced it was only a matter of time—he would be relegated to obscurity again, the place he secretly believed he belonged and the place he dreaded going.

Barbara said the fear of obscurity was really a fear of mortality and common to people his age. He had just turned fifty, and there was no denying that he had become very conscious of the ways that things could suddenly and unexpectedly go wrong. Just that morning a kid had been shot dead through the window of his apartment building, and the fact that the kid lived in the Crown Heights section of Brooklyn and that he, Russo, lived in Westport, Connecticut was no guarantee that something equally bad wouldn't happen to him too. Even if he was unlikely to be the victim of a drive-by shooting or a train crash in India, that didn't mean he couldn't get some fatal form of cancer. He had smoked in his youth, and lung cancer was a distinct possibility for someone like him. Presentiments of mortality or anticipatory mourning were the way Barbara described his anxiety. She was taking an adult education course in psychology, and she was convinced that her husband's feelings of dread were part of the aging process and nothing to worry about. The fear of obscurity and the fear of mortality were the same thing, she said, and both could be dealt with by acknowledging the inevitability of death.

But Russo did not want to think about dying and was very reassured when Claire told him not to worry, the meeting was about nothing more serious than the format of her reports. His relief, however, was short-lived; it lasted only until Claire explained that the new format she had in mind involved teaming up with an old lady of her acquaintance. They were seated around Goodwin's coffee table, Claire on the sofa and Goodwin and Russo in the two armchairs opposite, when she made her proposal. They were both stunned into silence and simply stared at her in disbelief. Taking that as a good sign, especially since she expected Goodwin to reject the idea out of hand, Claire acknowledged that her idea might be a little unusual, a little unorthodox, but she had not become successful by following convention.

Russo and Goodwin had been quite prepared to go along with almost anything she asked for, but a septuagenarian weather reporter was the last thing they expected. The idea had catastrophe written all over it. Luckily, words failed them. Had they responded immediately and spontaneously, it would have been with something like horror; but Goodwin and Russo were conventional men, and Claire's proposal was so far outside the parameters of brains lined with nothing more exciting than wall units that her suggestion could not find a single neuron to receive it. An old lady predicting the weather? Who had ever heard of such a thing? Claire made it sound charming, engaging, surefire, but

Russo wasn't at all convinced, and Goodwin, well Goodwin looked like he was about to pull out all the hair he'd had implanted.

Once Claire had left Goodwin's office, which was where most JTF meetings now took place, it being the most gracious room at JTF, the two men looked at each other blankly, mystified by Claire and her sex. What was it, Goodwin asked Russo, that prompted women to make changes? They could never leave well enough alone; they always had to improve things. As soon as your guard was down and you started to relax, whammo! It never failed. Scratching his head in confusion, he went over to his new wall unit and opened a smoky glass door. "I think I need a drink. Maybe a little scotch will help." Russo was impressed. Russo had a flask of his own in his desk drawer—he even had an old, stale joint—but he'd never shared either with anyone...except for that one time when he and Barbara were having a rough patch, and there was this cute little receptionist working for the station. But that was different because it was private, sneaky, and part of something even more illicit. This, by contrast, was so open and adult, so acknowledging.

Goodwin treated the wall unit carefully. It was from Ikea, and even though it looked pretty good, it was too cheap to be solid. It cost only slightly more than his sterling silver water pitcher actually, but it completed his corporate image, which was the main reason he bought it. Goodwin was irritated by Claire's proposal, but not really as irritated as he appeared because he was in an uncharacteristically good mood, and even Claire's off-the-wall suggestion couldn't ruin it. His hair treatments were completed; he now had a thick head of hair; and the station's ratings were exceptionally high. Life was good.

Standing beside the wall unit, he removed two Waterford glasses.

He loved taking the bottle and glasses out of the cabinet, and after he'd poured a scotch for each of them—slightly more for himself than for Russo—he proposed a toast.

"To little old ladies," he said.

"You're kidding," Russo responded, as impressed by the toast as by the scotch. "I thought you were about to lose it when Claire suggested the old lady."

"I was, but you know something? I've decided not to sweat it anymore." A slight film of perspiration on his upper lip and brow contradicted him. "I've begun to realize that there's no point to an iron grip. Anyway, everything Claire has done so far has worked. Even using vocabulary," he laughed, as if nothing could be less likely. "Maybe she knows something we don't know. I say, let's give her idea a try. If it doesn't work, we'll tell her she's got to stop, that's all." He smiled complacently, unconcerned, as if he were the most reasonable man in the world.

Russo looked at Goodwin, whose long, Lutheran legs were stretched out and crossed, one heel resting on the toe of the other, his tie hanging in a loose knot several inches below his open collar. Could it be that his partner was finally catching on? Maybe. Or maybe he was simply in one of those enlightened moods that usually don't last too long. That, Russo decided, was probably what it was. Deciding to take advantage of Goodwin's mood while it lasted, he got up, walked over to the wall unit and came back holding the bottle of scotch over his head. "To little old ladies," he said, his arm locked at the elbow and stretched straight in the air. Goodwin wasn't sure he liked what had just happened, but he was stuck, having tacitly declared himself generous and easy-going: "To little old ladies," he reiterated.

Is it for now or for always,
The world hangs on a stalk?
Is it a trick or a trysting-place,
The woods we have found to walk?

Is it a mirage or miracle,
Your lips that lift at mine:
And the suns like a juggler's juggling-balls,
Are they a sham or a sign?

Shine out, my sudden angel,
Break fear with breast and brow,
I take you now and for always,
For always is always now.

"Is It For Now Or For Always"
Philip Larkin, 1943-4

CHAPTER THIRTY-THREE

Leaves fluttered to the ground around Claire. A powerful industrial fan with a long extension cord ran from the house to the garden where the fan was tilted toward the top of a tree. The idea was to make the leaves fall at a slightly faster rate than usual, just enough to reinforce the image of autumn. It took a bit of adjusting because at first the fan didn't have any effect, and then it had too much and leaves were blowing all over the place. When the production crew finally got it right and could count on a light, steady flow, Claire stood next to the tree with an upright rake in one hand and the reconstructed pile of leaves at her feet.

The tree was chosen for the rich color of its leaves and for the late season flowers at its base. The combination of flower and leaf was the perfect image of a season in transition, which Claire respectfully acknowledged by carefully separating the leaves from the flowers with the corner prongs of her rake. "This is the hard part," she said, teasing a leaf from the base of a showy, rayed dahlia. "I'm very careful because, much as I love the fall, I hate to say good-bye to any of my flowers. I guess that's pretty obvious from the state of my garden. I'm very eager to hold on to what I have, which is why I don't trim the lavender, which are still flowering, and why the perennials need dividing and cutting back. I've stopped deadheading my roses too, but I expect them to keep on blooming for a while yet. Some flowers get a second wind and bloom more than once, and other flowers, like this beautiful Othello rose," the camera focused on a cupped bloom with full, rumpled crimson petals, "emit their fragrance twice during the season. The Othello can misbehave and send up huge shoots that won't bloom until the following year, but once you've inhaled its extraordinary fragrance," she said, leaning in to smell the rose, "you can forgive all its faults."

The camera moved in for a close-up, and at the same time, the man at the bar leaned forward. He wanted to get a good look at Claire.

"There is a tension in October," she continued, "because it is so clearly transitional. I've tried to minimize the tension by setting up my garden so that it winds down fairly slowly and continues to offer up well into the fall, like these dahlias for example, which are still courageously flowering at ground level, even as the leaves on the trees above them progress through the color chart." A profusion of yellow, russet, and red tones filled the screen before the camera cut to an ad for Metamucil.

"She comes in here from time to time," the bartender said, proudly referring to Claire. "We got two local stations in Bridge Haven—well, one and one-half actually—and two watering holes. FYI drinks at my competition—that's Tattler's—and JTF comes here." He punctuated his sentence by belching softly, his cheeks inflating frog-like.

The man already knew that. He had spoken to Claire earlier in the week, and she had suggested that he meet her at Hooligans after her broadcast was over. That was fine with him. It was the same in Italy where people had a regular bar they went to after work. The difference was that in Italy, the bar was also a café and the place where people had their morning and afternoon coffee. In that respect, his Italian bar was nothing like Hooligans, which, despite loyal patronage, seemed like an aimless, irrelevant place for people with nowhere else to go. Its location next to a shoemaker, with shoes randomly piled against its display window, and, on its other side, a laundry with a large zigzag of masking tape running diagonally across the crack in its glass façade, did little to alter that impression.

When he was at home, Jesse would stop at the Bar Opera on the Corso every morning and evening, and along with a crowd of familiar faces, he would wait for his espresso to come skidding across the counter. The Opera, as its patrons affectionately called it, shimmered with the optimism of its marble elegance and mirrored walls and formed a stark contrast to Hooligans, whose dark interior gave the defeated impression that nothing was really worth seeing. The only vitality came from the neon Coors sign above the restrooms and from the flickering television screen above its rough-hewn wooden bar.

No one was watching the television. The handful of people scattered around the bar were intent upon their drinks, and the only person who seemed interested in the news was Jesse. Jesse was looking up at the screen, and Mike, the bartender, was looking at him. He had never seen Jesse before, of that he was quite certain. He would have remembered if anyone like Jesse had been in his bar. Even in the darkness, Jesse made an impression, and the impression was one that required continuing scrutiny; you wanted to look at him more closely. Everything about him, from his tailored shirt to his tousled hair, attracted attention, and yet he wasn't the least bit showy or ostentatious. Mike couldn't figure out what made the stranger different from his other customers, but the more he looked at him, the more he thought it was hidden in the wrinkles around his eyes. There was something about the man's expression, worldly and arrived at, each wrinkle an experience, which made him seem like a product of his history and unlike everyone else at the bar, who looked like mere products, cheaply manufactured and mass produced.

The ad for Metamucil was over, and the news resumed. Claire had removed her gardening gloves and plaid flannel shirt and was back at the station standing beside a weather map. She looked more at home in her gardening clothes than in her suit, and larger, too, the flannel shirt giving her an outdoorsy bulk, which contrasted with the streamlined tailoring of her pants and fitted jacket. "Brisk, breezy weather from the northwest will push the low pressure system out into the Atlantic and bring much drier air into our area…"

As in the past, Jesse found himself looking at her eyes. They were calm and clear and seemed to illuminate the somber bar. When they were children, Claire had told him that her father said her eyes would stay clear if she never told lies, and he wondered if that explained their clarity. Were they transparent because she had nothing to hide? Were they glittering translucent pools resting on a bedrock of family affection? It had been a long time since he had seen her, and he had looked into many other women's eyes in the interim. He had looked into them with intentions so unmistakable that when they looked back—and they usually did—the eye contact was just the first step in what had once been called pursuit. Pursuit, however, no longer seemed like the right word to describe what followed. Something more direct and far less nuanced took place, and it required little more than a bit of conversation and one or two glasses of wine. The prelude was short, and the relationships were short too, but the aftermaths were long and contentious, and that was the problem. The same women who toppled into bed as easily as ash falls from a cigarette became unhappy and indignant when Jesse didn't call the next day, as if the notion of virtue had been replaced by the concept of self-esteem; except that self-esteem simply meant fewer restrictions and more obligations than ever.

Another commercial was advertising Tylenol for the treatment of arthritis. A man running after a little boy had to stop himself because of back pain. He was shown leaning over, panting, one hand on his lower spine. Seconds later, the same man was smiling, his posture erect. Thanks to Tylenol, he could now enjoy his grandson, pain free. Clearly the news was appealing to an older crowd. Jesse didn't have aches and pains, but he had obviously aged since he had last seen Claire. Hair that had once been silky and smooth had grown wavy and course with gray, and a fine web of wrinkles encased his eyes. The transitional appearance of adolescence had matured into the well defined features of adulthood, and although he was still good-looking, or so they said, he was no longer the youth she had known. Would that matter to her? Claire had sounded friendly on the phone, genuinely happy to hear from him; but until he saw her, he wouldn't know for sure.

The commercial was over, and Jesse expected Claire to come back on. Instead, the face of a much older woman filled the screen. She introduced herself as Pearl Strongman, "coming to you live from West End Avenue."

Jesse looked at the bartender inquiringly. "Isn't Claire Day their only weather reporter?"

"New format," Mike explained. "They're doing it differently now."

Jesse returned his gaze to the television. The woman sat with her hands folded in her lap. A curtain of embroidered fabric hung lugubriously behind her in a room crowded with furniture. She appeared sharp-eyed and unsentimental, grounded in reality although no one would have called her salt of the earth. To the contrary, she looked formal and fancy, as if she'd been invited to a cocktail party but did not drink. Her ears, neck, wrists, and fingers were heavy with jewelry, and her face was framed by an immobile helmet of hair from which, like a bird in its nest, she peered with darting glances. Jesse was still confused. When was Claire coming back? Had the new format diminished her role?

The old lady was leaning into the camera. "For once my esteemed colleague got it right," she was saying. The picture was divided into a split screen, and from her living room, she gave Claire, who was standing by the chroma-key, an approving nod. The camera quickly panned the news desk. Everyone was smiling, Reed, Fletcher, and a new anchor named Wanda. "I can tell," Pearl continued, "because I don't have any aches or pains, which for me is a sure sign of dry weather. No pain, no rain. Don't quote me, but I have a feeling the guy on the other station—I'm not going to embarrass him and mention his name—I have a feeling he's way off base with his forecast of light showers. No way it's going to rain tomorrow. My bones don't lie." Pearl was really feeling confident now. "Between you and me, the guy over at FYI doesn't know what he's talking about." Too confident. There was background noise, and the camera switched to Claire, who diplomatically interjected that it was not unusual for forecasters to disagree, and that she and her colleagues frequently reached different conclusions about what to expect.

"Whoops," Pearl tittered, putting a bejeweled, arthritically twisted hand to her mouth. "I'm not allowed to say what I just said. I take it back, I take it back. And don't get me wrong," she continued, beginning to overcompensate, "I met him once and he's very nice, good-looking too. They say he's coming out with a line of swimwear. But what can I tell you, it's not going to rain tomorrow. Hey, we all make mistakes."

Jesse understood: Claire had not been demoted, she'd been inspired. There was another commercial break. "People love the two of them," the bartender commented, shaking his head in amused disbelief. He was right. Claire and Pearl were a media sensation, and everyone from the newly elected mayor on down watched them. They appealed to the skeptics, who thought the weather forecast was always wrong; they appealed to older adults, who saw Pearl as a champion for the elderly; they appealed to children, who reacted to Pearl as if she were their grandmother; they appealed to management, who witnessed a sharp rise in ratings; and they appealed to Jesse, who was in love.

Perhaps he had always been in love with Claire, he wasn't sure. As a younger man, he had needed to travel, to carouse all night, to study voice. It was possible that in the pursuit of those objectives, he had gone seriously astray. Not that he had regrets. He had, after all, become a major set designer for the opera with an international reputation and assignments all over the world. If he had it to do all over, he would do it the same way again. Nevertheless, while he had pursued his career abroad, something precious had been forfeited at home, and looking up at the screen and feeling an undeniable pang in his heart, he knew exactly what it was.

The commercial was over, and the news was back on. A throng of reporters was crammed into a reception room, and like Wall Street traders, they were all bidding for recognition. The man whose mouth was the object of the competing microphones had just been re-elected mayor, and a victory party was in progress. He was talking, laughing, gesticulating, getting patted on the back, patting others on the arm, ecstatic. Balloons and streamers filled the air, champagne filled plastic glasses. A short, pudgy woman and a teenaged boy were standing by the mayor's side. The woman, who was somewhat inconsistently dressed in a sari, could be heard telling reporters that she had never questioned her husband's integrity or had any doubts about the election's outcome. The boy was diverting his gaze in an effort to avoid attracting attention to himself. Freddy only wished his mother could have been there to witness his victory celebration, how proud she would have been. Maybe she was there, he thought, glancing up at the ceiling; maybe she was peering down through the streamers, seated on a front row bleacher in heaven, bragging to the other spirits. They would have to be female spirits. His mother never interacted with men, unless they were relatives, and even then there had to be other people in the room. Freddy had no trouble visualizing heaven. The part he couldn't imagine was his mother dressed in white. All her life, like someone in perpetual mourning, she had worn black; and white, the dress code for heaven, had come to seem like sacrilege. Maybe white would be her reward for a lifetime of black, or maybe, if she couldn't stand the idea, she would be allowed to wear whatever color she wanted; after all, it was heaven. If Marie could wear a sari to his victory party, then certainly his mother should be able to wear black in heaven.

A reporter, an African-American woman, was trying to get Freddy's attention. She had a pretty face, a cute figure, and he decided to bestow his favor upon her.

"They had someone else covering the news before," the bartender volunteered. "A redhead. She's got her own show now. She only left JTF a week ago. It'll be on right after this is over. You'll see."

Jesse was curious. He wondered what kind of job mobility local news—and, particularly, local weather reporters—had. "How did she get her own show?" he asked.

"If you ask me, it all comes down to who you know," the bartender explained.

"And did she have friends in high places?"

"Rumor has it she knew the mayor pretty well, if you take my meaning."

Jesse turned his attention back to the television. The image on the screen had switched from the re-election party to a sunny pier with a boatyard in the background. A man wearing wrap sunglasses, a sun visor, shorts, and Docksiders was standing next to a large sailboat gently rocking in its berth. Jason Fremd, JTF's reporter on the beat, was interviewing the man.

"That's new too," the bartender explained. "They've changed everything around. What you're watching now is JTF's weekly profile. They interview a different person every week—not necessarily somebody famous, just somebody who's doing something interesting or different."

"I wonder how they make their selection."

"Like I said before, connections."

In a way, the bartender was right. It was thanks to Dan's strong recommendation that Emmett Nelson had become JTF's personality of the week. Ostensibly, Nelson was chosen for his contributions to meteorology, but actually, he was picked for his role in predicting Hurricane

Louis. The press conference in the high school shelter had made it painfully obvious that the prediction was benefiting certain individuals, and the more Dan thought about it, the more he wanted to know who they were. Claire had intimated that stock manipulation might have been involved, and after the weather derivatives market shot up and down, its rise and fall exactly coinciding with the hurricane prediction, Dan told Fremd to poke around a bit and see what he could find out. When he did, the name he came up with was Emmett Nelson. Fremd tried to contact Nelson, but Nelson had taken early retirement and was no longer with the National Weather Service. That clinched it. Both Dan and Fremd were convinced that Nelson had a role in perpetrating a fraud, and that money was a big part of it. They also knew they couldn't prove anything—muckraking in Florida was not JTF's job—but at the very least they could make Nelson squirm a bit.

Water was lapping vigorously against a pier covered with boxes. Nelson and his wife were preparing to set sail and the boxes were full of provisions. The trip, Emmett explained to Fremd, who had flown down to Florida to interview him, was the fulfillment of a lifelong dream. He and his wife, Renee, would follow the route taken by several particularly destructive hurricanes of the past in the hope of discovering water temperature patterns that might be applied to hurricane prediction. More than a pleasure voyage, the trip would combine Emmett's knowledge of meteorology with his love of fishing, and maybe even, he added with genuine modesty, do the world some good in the process.

Emmett had rehearsed everything he was going to say. He would have liked to get out of the interview altogether, but Renee had persuaded him that he had no choice in the matter. "Look," she had argued, "it's an honor, not an accusation. Accusations usually come in the form of knocks on the door or subpoenas in the mail. This interview is in recognition of your work—how can you refuse?"

She had been right about everything else, so he supposed she was right about this too. Even so, Emmett couldn't wait for the thing to be over with. He stood on the pier with Fremd for a few minutes, patiently answering his questions, and then, as soon as he thought he could politely extricate himself, he began turning away and moving toward the boxes. That was his exit strategy. But Fremd was the aggressive type and not easily discouraged. Instead of taking the hint, Fremd followed him, even to the point of leaning over at the same time that Emmett leaned over to pick up a box. With his head lowered and his slack jowls hanging down, Fremd expressed his admiration for the project that Nelson was undertaking. How wonderful it would be, he said, if people could really prepare for hurricanes—the lives that would be spared, the money that would be saved. Emmett nodded, yes, yes, that was the idea. But then, as they straightened up, Fremd looked directly into Emmett's polarized lenses and asked whether it couldn't work the other way too, and whether technology didn't sometimes *create* problems. "Take, for example, that Hurricane Louis." Emmett's heart pounded. "All that unnecessary hysteria might have been prevented if our research were more accurate, don't you think? Some people were preparing for electricity failures, others were leaving the area, and all for nothing."

Emmett foundered. His moment of degradation had come, and he felt the horror of exposure. "Accurate information is always important," he mumbled noncommittally. "But Mr. Fremd," he managed to add, "although I really appreciate your coming down here, maybe we could continue this discussion some other time? I really have to go now," he said, backing away and then turning toward his boat and walking hurriedly up the gangplank.

"Bon voyage," Fremd yelled out after him.

The report was picked up by the desk in New York, where the anchors agreed it was a wonderful thing the Nelsons were doing. "There are so many ways that our older, retired citizens, with all their expertise and experience, can give back to this country," the pretty, new anchor was saying.

That statement provided a perfect segue to Pearl, who was back on camera, this time on the set of JTF. Although she was usually in her living room, every now and then they brought her up to Bridge Haven so that she and Claire could end the broadcast side by side. Before JTF had changed its format, the weather had preceded sports and followed the news, but the Day-Strongman team was such a success that management decided to break with tradition and to end the show with a closing message from them.

"I'm too old to be retired," the diminutive old lady said from her end of the desk, her head several inches lower than everyone else's. "That's how you know when you're really old," she added, engaging in the meaningless banter the news team seemed to like so much, "when you don't have the energy to do nothing." What did that mean? Pearl had no idea, but everyone laughed. Pearl couldn't get over it. Being on television was like bridge night with her friends: first a little conversation and then the game, the two interwoven, neither truly serious. After the exchange was over, she gave Claire a nod and then focused her sharp eyes directly on the television camera and delivered the motto that was now echoing in households throughout Bridge Haven. "This is Pearl Strongman, coming to you live—thank God—from JTF, and remember, rain or shine, tomorrow is another day."

Jesse laughed and turned his attention back to the bartender. "Is it far from here to JTF?" he asked, wondering how long it would be before Claire would join him.

"No, it's real close. Just a few blocks."

Jesse was starting to get slightly nervous. If JTF was only a few blocks away, then it wouldn't be long before Claire would be there. He looked up at the television screen again trying to distract himself while he waited. A redhead—she must have been the reporter the bartender had been talking about before—was seated at the center of a news desk similar to JTF's. There was a woman seated to her right, and a man seated to her left, and the three were holding hands. Their heads were bowed above their clasped hands in an attitude of prayer or meditation, and they were totally silent. They stayed that way for a moment before the redhead looked up. She was conservatively dressed, the top button of her blouse secured with a brooch, and her manner could almost be called demure. Looking directly into the camera, she said, "We are praying for peace in Darfur." Her expression was caring and earnest. "Hundreds are dying every day. Little children…"

"Praying for peace?" Jesse asked the bartender, not sure what he was seeing.

"It's a new thing," Mike shrugged. "Faith-based news. I don't think it's going to make any difference over there in Africa, but the public here really seems to like it. Anyway, I don't suppose it can do any harm."

Jesse wasn't so sure about that, but he didn't say anything because the door to the bar had just opened. It was, as predicted, a gusty night and, as if the wind were her butler and holding the door for her, it stayed open an extra second as Claire walked in.

Made in the USA
Charleston, SC
12 September 2011